# DANIELA

## Behira Graham

First Published in Great Britain in 2022

Copyright © 2022 Behira Graham

A CIP catalogue record for this book is available from the British Library

ISBN 978-1-3999-2333-0 (print)

Cover Design by Creative Covers
Typesetting by Book Polishers

With thanks to Susanna Jones
for her guidance and encouragement

# Contents

To Day Murch
with thanks for all his work, dedication and support

"Pearls don't lie on the seashore.
If you want one, you must dive for it."

Chinese proverb

# LONDON 1975

The razor blade on the mirror is shiny, enticing me. Two slashes, both wrists, and it will all be over. But I know I can't do it. The pain scares me. And then there is all that red blood spewing everywhere. Undignified. Pills then.

It starts to rain. I watch the drops rolling down the dirty glass, merging as they make their way downwards.

I put The Doors '*This is the end*' on the record player. In the kitchen I fill a glass with water.

'Why?' I ask loudly. 'Why?' I scream. I clutch my stomach and fold over. I go on screaming until I am hoarse.

In the living room, I fall into the armchair. I pick up the box of pills from the low table and start swallowing. The rain is coming in torrents, lashing loudly on the window pane, running down in sheets.

I lean back. I remember arriving in London full of hope. How did I get here? I swallow more pills. Memories roll like scenes from a movie…

# CHAPTER 1 1970

It was a summer's day, heat rose from the pavement and the white buildings of the city shimmered, my skin tingled and beads of sweat covered my bare-arms. People hurrying home for an afternoon nap stole glances at me. I was used to it. They saw a beautiful young woman; tall and slim, wearing blue velvet hot pants, raven black hair flowing from under her wide-brimmed hat. A car stopped at the traffic lights, the driver whistled and smiled at me. Another day I might have smiled back. My mind was elsewhere, I had to think, to make up my mind.

I walked down the meandering path. Below me was a calm sea with patches of emerald green and deep blue stretching towards the horizon. I took off my heeled sandals and skipped along the burning sand, gold trickling through my toes. I let the cool, gentle waves that rolled towards me lick my feet. When they retreated my heels sunk into the wet sand. I looked longingly at the distance where blue met blue. A white bird flew overhead. I wished I could fly. If I were to go, it would be the first time that I would be leaving my country.

Far away and across the sea was the vibrant city of London. It wasn't Big Ben nor St Pauls Cathedral that drew me there, it was the youth revolution. Here, we were behind the times. All I had to go by was what I heard from people who had been to London. They told me about freedom, about new ways of thinking, about questioning and breaking the conventions. It sounded good to me. When our newspapers wrote about it, they depicted the youth there as unruly and wrote that they had unrealistic notions driven by drugs. I wanted to be one of them.

I dreamt of the city where I could buy the latest fashion, go to venues where rock bands would be playing live, spend time in museums and art galleries filled to the brim with all that I had only seen in art books.

\*

I ran back and sat at the foot of a rock that offered some shade. I could leave my life behind and start anew, I had nothing to stay for, but if I did, I'd be going on my own. Benyamin had made no promises when he left the country and left me behind. We had lived together in his house, an act that was unacceptable to the so-called respectable society. I dropped out of university after a year. Father was furious and blamed Benyamin.

*You are letting yourself down. You are throwing away your life, your future, all that I hoped for you. And what for? For this man? I expected better of you. I promise you; you will regret it.*

My grandparents summoned me. I stood in front of them in their living room. They didn't even offer me a seat. I used to be their favourite granddaughter, but now there was no love in their eyes, only accusation and disappointment. I had brought shame on the family they had said. Apparently, there were conditions attached to their love for me. I had broken their rules, they withdrew their love. They let me go without a hug, without a kiss. Love was not to be trusted.

After Benyamin left, I went to live with my mother in her top floor flat in the centre of town. She held me in her arms when I cried, spoke soothing words, stroked my hair, and rocked me back and forth as if I were a baby, not a grown woman of twenty-two years. She too had had to face the family's wrath. My parents' marriage was not a happy one, she wanted a divorce. From behind closed doors, I heard the family arguing with her, telling her not to do it. One day, she just left. To my mind, she was right to do so. I thought she was brave.

A loud scream jolted me. A black and white cat was stretching on a nearby rock. Her mouth was open, emitting eerie sounds in a shrill screechy voice. A cat on heat, summoning, demanding. She wanted sex and called for it, any tom would do. How simple it was for a cat.

*

Back home, I found my mother in the kitchen. She was watching the Turkish coffee bubbling in the Finjan. It had to be taken off as soon as it started to froth. I looked at her long, shaped, red finger nails holding the handle.

'Daniela, are you all right? Where did you go to in this heat?'

'To the sea. Don't worry mother.'

It was what she wanted to hear. She took the Finjan of off the hob and turned to me. Her auburn hair, stiff with hairspray didn't move. Her lively brown eyes smiled.

'Come and join us.'

I took the small cups and saucers to the table. Her friend, the gypsy, or as she called herself, Tzigane, was sitting there. Her hair was dyed black, her face caked with makeup, her pencil skirt so tight that she had to climb stairs turning from side to side. She claimed that she could read the future in coffee grounds.

Mother poured the coffee making sure that each cup had a little of the froth. They chatted as we sipped. Once the liquid was almost gone, we sloshed the wet coffee grounds around the inside of the cup, turned it upside down onto the saucer, pressed a forefinger to our lips, kissed it and then touched the bottom of the cup for luck. They had a cigarette break and then the gypsy read us our future from the patterns that had formed inside the cup.

There was a long and thin coffee line on the outside of mine. 'It's a sign of a long journey,' the gypsy told me. She looked at the big lump of coffee grounds at the bottom. 'You have a heavy heart, a black heart.' She put the cup down and looked at me with her dark, almost black eyes. 'You'll get over it. You are beautiful. Your big green eyes can get you any man you want.'

I didn't need her advice or her opinions. I wished that mother hadn't told her. But my mother was a gossip, she couldn't keep a secret.

Nothing the gypsy could say to me would be of any help. It would only annoy me. I left the table. Their voices followed me.

'Go after her,' the gypsy said.

'No. Best leave her alone.'

Mother knew how to deal with my moods and my tantrums. She knew when to leave me alone and when to talk and soothe me.

*

In my room I put Cat Stevens 'Mona Bone Jakon' on my mono record player and lay on the bed. The coffee cup had foretold a journey. Was that the answer? I didn't believe in it anyway; I might as well throw a dice. I lay still and listened to the music.

*Trouble oh trouble can't you see,*
*You're eating my heart away*
*And there's nothing much left of me.*

I remembered my literature teacher from high school. She was passionate and had inspired and influenced me. When I went to university, I found her teaching there. Before I dropped out, I went to see her. I told her that I would be going traveling. That was when I thought I'd be going with Benyamin. She surprised me. She didn't try to dissuade me. What she had said was: 'Do travel, but not just with your body, also with your mind. Seek knowledge, look, listen, learn, live. You can always come back to university.'

I recalled her reading the class a Chinese proverb that was not in the curriculum. "Pearls don't lie on the seashore. If you want one, you must dive for it."

Words, I thought, they are pearls to be strung. It was a folly to make such a big decision based on a proverb, but it was as if it was a concluding footnote after what seemed to be a long and tortuous time of confusion and uncertainty. My mind had sent me a message, more reliable than a dice or coffee grounds. I took heed. I would be going to London.

*There's an empty space inside me now*
*A wasteland deep beneath the snow,*
*So cold – nothing will grow.*

I got up, put on my sandals, took the needle off of the record, grabbed my handbag, and went out.

*

The heart of Tel Aviv was a block away. The fashionable road was lined with boutiques, restaurants and cafes and was always busy. I didn't want to bump into anyone I knew, so I crossed to the less popular side of the street. At the luggage shop I chose a big red leather suitcase. I then stopped at a shoe shop and bought red shoes to match.

Walking back home I felt lighter, even a little happier. When I arrived, the gypsy was gone and Mother was having a nap. She heard me and came out of her bedroom looking sleepy. Her eyes lost their sleepiness and she became alert. She saw the red suitcase.

'Daniela? Are you going somewhere?'

'Yes Mother,' I said calmly. 'I am going abroad.'

She looked at me confused. 'You are?' she blurted. 'Where to? For how long?'

'To Switzerland to see Mina.'

The idea had just occurred to me. Mina, my friend from childhood, had moved to live in the Alps, where she and her husband ran a small hotel. She always signed her letters with 'Come visit. I miss you'. I knew that I would be welcome. A place to stop for a while, a starting point.

Mother's face relaxed. 'That's good. You need a break and you haven't seen her for a long time.'

I didn't want to upset her. She would find out in time.

*

At the airport, I worked the few months that were left on my contract as a ground stewardess. It entitled me to a free plane ticket. Meanwhile, I applied for a passport and went to get an army permit to leave. Nearer the time, I cashed in my savings. A painter had given me one of the paintings

I had posed for. I sold it. I paid the hefty traveling tax and collected my ticket.

On the day, Mother and I stood by the front door of the flat. Mother had tears in her eyes. We kissed and she pulled me to her.

'You're not intending to come back. Are you?'

How had she guessed? Maybe it was the size of the red suitcase, more likely it was her knowing me and her intuition that had surprised me many times before. She looked sad.

'Not if I can help it.'

'I'll miss you.'

Her eyes were moist. So were mine.

I carried the heavy red suitcase downstairs. Leaving was not a dream any more. For a moment, my legs wobbled. I felt a little apprehensive. I stopped on the landing and leant on the wall.

I thought of Benyamin, of a moment of happiness when we had swum in the Red Sea. I was not a confident swimmer but he had insisted that we go in. He gave me a snorkel and flippers and I followed him. Away from the shore, the water was clear and on the sea bed I saw a garden; corals, sea anemones waving their tentacles, and strange plants that looked like creatures, fish in extraordinary bright coloured patterns, swam alone or in shoals, changing direction for no apparent reason. I imagined myself a mermaid in a silent and beautiful underworld. We smiled at each other through our snorkels. We reached out and held hands.

I shook off the memory, picked up the red suitcase and went downstairs where my taxi to the airport was waiting. We soon left the city behind us and drove through citrus groves. The trees were full of buds. I would not be there to see and smell their delicious scent when they bloomed.

The thought made me feel a little sad. At the same time, I felt excited and full of hope.

# Chapter 2

Tenebrous mountains loomed in the moonshine. The train from Zurich ploughed through the night huffing and groaning as it climbed. I dozed off to the soothing rumble of the train. When we arrived at the station, I tumbled into the waiting minibus that took me to the small hotel near the ski slopes. Mina gathered me in her arms. she was a big girl, wide faced, blue eyes, blond and looking like a German frau. She promptly took me to a cosy bedroom in their private apartment.

'Sleep well,' she said. 'We'll talk in the morning.'

Morning came. Light filtered through the curtains. There was a small fireplace and the furniture was painted white and decorated with pictures in pastel colours. I ran to the window and flung open the curtains. I had never seen snow before. I had to feel it. I put on my boots without socks, and ran out in my long flannel nightie. My boots sunk and the deep snow crunched beneath my feet. Fluffy flakes, like a million butterflies fluttered and danced in the air, weightless and soft they kissed my long, black eyelashes. I put my hand out to catch them, but as soon as they touched my hand they disappeared. I gathered handfuls of snow and rubbed them on my face. I jumped up and down, I ran and sunk and fell and laughed with joy.

I remembered a story from my childhood, *The Girl from Lapland*. The girl lived in a white world. She was scared that the wolves would kill her dog. I wondered if those beautiful beasts were roaming nearby, looking for prey. I danced in the white softness thinking that maybe it was like dancing inside white, fluffy clouds.

They must have thought me insane, the guests who were looking out from their warm rooms, seeing a lanky girl, in a white nightdress and boots, her long, raven black hair flying as she danced.

Mina came out shouting, 'Daniela, Daniela, are you stark raving mad? You are going to get pneumonia. Get in. Quickly.'

She was right. Once inside, I felt the cold spreading through my body. I started shivering. My toes throbbed but I had no idea why.

Mina took me to their sitting room, told me to take my wet nightie off, and then wrapped a blanket around me. She sat me in an armchair by the fire and pulled my boots off, my toes looked white. Once again Mina was looking after me. I felt a comforting sense of familiarity, reminiscent of times past, when in our school days she had looked out for me.

'You are not even wearing socks. Do you have frostbite?'

'What's that?'

'Are your toes frozen?'

'Ah, so that's what it is. My fingers and toes hurt. They tingle.'

'Good thing you can still feel them. If they were totally frozen you would have had to have them amputated.'

'Don't exaggerate. You are scaring me. One cannot dance without toes.'

'You can joke as much as you like Daniela. My advice is, respect the snow, it is beautiful, but it could kill you.'

'My toes are hurting.'

'Good. That means that you are defrosting. Stay by the fire.'

'I have never sat by a fire. This is lovely. Warm inside, white outside, a book, a cup of tea, what more can I ask for? Thank you.'

She smiled. 'Stay here then. I'll bring you a nice hot cup of tea.'

She hadn't changed, calm, compassionate, caring, warm-hearted Mina. She had been the one I had run to when life at home was difficult, when my parents were fighting, then divorcing.

Mina came back with the tea, she pointed at my boots. I had put them by the fire to dry. 'Bad idea. You mustn't put wet leather too near the fire, the leather will dry too quickly, will split and become hard.'

She moved my boots. 'Your boots are beautiful, such soft leather. You'll ruin them going out in the snow. Listen, by the kitchen, there is an outer room where you'll find boots, snow gear and coats. People leave things behind. Help yourself.'

I looked at her quizzically. Knowing how I loved clothes and particularly shoes, she said. 'There is some good stuff there. The people who stay here are not short of a bob or two. Go and rummage. Borrow from my wardrobe if you like.' She paused. 'You've always been hard to please.'

'I know, I can't help it. I tell you what I would like to wear. In the film *Dr Zhivago*, Lara wears a coat with a military cut, nipped in at the waist then flaring out to a skirt, it has a fur collar, and on her head, she wears a fur hat, Russian style. I always wanted that outfit. In slate blue would be nice. But I don't think I'll find it here.'

*

Mina had to go back to work. I tried to read but my mind wondered. With a lot of time on my hands, I was quite happy to drift away, to lounge on the window-seat and be warmed by the fire. I stared at the white eerie world. Sometimes the wind blew snow dust from trees, the iridescent particles caught by the sun rays twinkled like diamonds, so pretty. At other times I would sink into the comfortable armchair and just look at the flames, mesmerised. They flickered and sparkled in vivid yellow mingled with red and purple. The fire hissed, the wood crackled and popped and threw up tongues of fire.

I imagined Benyamin coming in, walking noiselessly in his Hush Puppies shoes, his velvety brown eyes looking at mine and saying in his soft warm voice, 'my little one.' With my eyes fixed on the snow or the fire, I let the tears roll. I had cried and sobbed and even howled with pain after Benyamin had left. Mother had said that time was the best healer. I didn't believe it. I thought that I would never get over him. I missed him desperately, yearned for him as I sat alone by the fire place.

*

That night Mina and I sat by the fire and sipped brandy.

'You look tired,' I said.

'I'm exhausted. It was a very busy day. On top of which, the minibus got stuck in the snow and had to be rescued.'

'Would you like me to help?' I didn't really want to, but felt that I should offer.

She smiled wearily. 'It is kind of you but no thank you. It takes more time and effort to instruct someone than to do it myself.'

'You seem at home here. I would have never thought that you would end up living in an icebox.'

'Nor did I. But this icebox is my world now. I am happy here. It is cold, it is remote, but it is peaceful and it is my home.'

'I am glad for you. Looking after people is what you do best.'

She looked at me, catching my eyes. 'What's wrong Daniela? We haven't seen each other for a long time but I can see that you are unhappy. Last time you wrote, you were living with someone. You sounded happy.'

'I was.'

'What happened? Are you going to tell me or do I have to drag it out of you?'

'He left me,' I said with clenched teeth.

'All right. Have it your way. Have you talked to anyone about it? About how you feel?'

'No. You weren't there.' It sounded like an accusation. I don't know why I clamped down and behaved like a sulking child. Not Mina's fault that I had no one to talk to.

'I am here now,' Mina said tenderly. 'Let's start from the beginning. How did you meet him?'

The compassion in her voice was my undoing. Tears rolled down my cheeks. Mina took the drink from me, sat on the rug by my feet and held my hands.

'I bumped into a friend who was going to visit him and I just went along. Benyamin, that's his name, opened the door. We knew instantly. It was what the French call 'coup de foudre.'

'What does he do?'

'He is a photographer. Fashion and adverts. He had his studio and lab at home, so we spent a lot of time together. I've never shared so much love with anyone before. I thought it would last for ever. I wanted it to.'

She thought for a while, and then said, 'But I really don't see why you stopped going to university. You could have continued.'

'Maybe I should have. I wanted to be with him. He was all that mattered.'

'Don't be hard on yourself. You were hopelessly in love. It happens, even to you Daniela.' She paused. 'Then why take a job as a stewardess? That took you away from him.'

'It was his talking about moving abroad. He said that he felt stuck in a rut with no outlets for his artistic abilities. Clients wanted the same style, nothing innovative or unusual. As time went by, I saw that he really meant it, that he seriously intended to leave. I presumed that I would be going with him.' I paused. 'You know how expensive it is to fly. The job gave me a free ticket.'

'Did he know? Did you tell him why you took the job?'

'No. He never even asked why I left university, why I took the job. He was too absorbed in his work. Not the jobs that paid, but in taking photographs for his own satisfaction. You should have seen them. They are brilliant.'

He had said that his eyes were a camera. He saw the world through their lenses and shared the vision with me. He once said that taking a portrait was not just capturing the look of the sitter, it was more about getting the inner self to show through.

'How do you do it?' I had asked him.

'With dialogue. I get them to talk about themselves. Once they do, they are transformed, they become animated and that's what I aim to capture.'

Mina looked pensive. I knew that she was thinking that he was selfish. He was. But I had walked into his world.

'Look. I am not the one to advice you, she said, I've been with the same man since high school. But… well, I think that you should try to forget him. I hate to see you suffering.'

She looked exhausted. I insisted that she go to bed. After all those years we had so easily fallen into the closeness we once had.

*

I stayed by the fire. I couldn't brush away the memory that had haunted me. That day, that ordinary day when I had come back from work at the airport. He was in his studio setting up. He wore corduroy trousers, a black roll top neck and his Hush Puppies shoes. When he was working, he had a way of gliding rather than walking. I looked at him wanting to hug him, I knew better than to interfere when he was working. Usually, he would stop at some point, come to me and we would hug. I waited. He stopped and looked at me. I didn't like the look in his eyes. They were distant.

'I am leaving,' he said, matter of fact. 'I booked my flight.' He said it as if it was a given, as if I was expecting it and it had now come. It was not a bullet; it was a bomb. I felt myself and my life shutter into fragments. I waited. He carried on setting up, not looking at me. I couldn't move. I stood motionless for what seemed a long time, but probably wasn't. I staggered to the spare room, sat in a corner on the floor and hugged myself. In one minute, my world had collapsed, taken away. I've been discarded. I heard people come in. His soft voice giving instructions to the model. It was familiar, yet remote, unreal. Strangely, there were no emotions rising in me I was numb. I stared at the floor. I think I froze and stayed in that state until the day he left the country.

When I had felt like going to him, ask him to take me with him, I saw an image, as though from a film or a book, of a woman on her knees crying. She was clutching a man's knees, begging him not to leave her. He disentangled his legs and walked away. It was degrading to the woman; it was loathsome to me.

The fire crackled and sparked. I bent over and clutched myself, pressing the pain hard as if to stop it, to control it.

*

Mina and I spent many nights talking, just like we had done for years, all the way through high school and until, shortly after, Mina got married and emigrated. I realised how much I missed her. I never had a close friend like her again.

One night she said, 'You could have asked him.'

'What?'

'If he wanted you to come with him? If he wanted you to wait for him? You could have asked instead of agonising over it. But of course you wouldn't. Couldn't you have swallowed your pride just for once?'

I lowered my head. I couldn't have and Mina knew it.

After a pause she asked, 'Have you heard from him?'

'I've had a postcard. He was in France about to leave for New York. He wrote that he was filled with feelings of renewal and hope. He signed it, "Kisses, your Benyamin." That's it. Nothing more. What am I supposed to make of it?'

'Well then, he wrote. Perhaps you should wait and see? Maybe he thought it was too much to ask of you to leave your life behind when he himself didn't know where he was going, where he would settle down and be able to ask you to come?'

'Then he could have asked me to wait for him,' I said bitterly. 'What am I supposed to do? Live in limbo? Put my fate in his hands? Put my love on hold?'

'I'm sorry to say it Daniela, but I think he treated you badly. He should have talked it through with you.'

'Of course, he should have. I should hate him for the way he discarded me. But I still love him.'

Mina put a log on the fire and poked it about. Little red burning stars shot up into the chimney.

'Stay here as long as you like. Go back when you're ready.'

'I am not going back.'

She was taken aback. She just stared at me. I told her about my father, about the family. She was outraged. She called them narrow-minded bigots.

We were silent for a while.

'What will you do now? Where will you go?'

'I'll chase my dreams of living in London I suppose.'

She smiled. 'Always a dreamer. But why London?'

'Can't you see Mina? This is where it is all happening. New ideas, the questioning of conventions, the breaking of them, the rebellion of our generation. No one there would have frowned on me for living with Benyamin, would they?'

'I suppose not.'

'Even clothes. I see them in Vogue, Harper's Bazaar and I can't buy them. I have to get my dress maker to copy the designs. Just think how wonderful it would be to walk into a boutique and be spoilt for choice.'

She laughed indulgently.

'Mina. I am serious. I want to be there, live it. It is happening now.'

'I know you do.' She shook her head. 'Oh Daniela. Those are big ideas but… I worry about you.'

'You don't need to. I'm a big girl now. I can look after myself.'

She didn't look convinced.

*

On the night before I left, Mina came in to the sitting room carrying two glasses and a bottle of Armagnac. I was waiting for her. She stood by the fire looking harassed.

'What's the matter?'

'That man, this French visitor, is going to drive me crazy,' she spat.

'What did he do?'

'He had just waylaid me, complaining, always complaining. Nothing is good enough for him. I had to smile calmly, be helpful, all I wanted to do was ring his neck.'

'Do it. it'll make you feel better. I'll help.'

She smiled wearily.

'Do you ever get fed up? Want to give it up and go home?'

She poured the Armagnac, gave me the balloon glass and sunk into an armchair. Her brow furrowed. She turned to look at me.

'Of course I get fed up. Not often. It's hard work. Visitors are demanding and can be tiresome. It comes with the job. Normally I just deal with it, but there is always the one, isn't there?'

'Yes. Always. I came across it working at the airport.'

We were quiet for a while. I watched Mina's face aglow from the fire, relaxing.

'It is wonderful to be with you. I can see that you are happy here. I want to ask you something. Do you miss home sometimes?'

'Sometimes. I do visit, but I wouldn't go back. It is peaceful here. Israel is like a pressure cooker about to explode. We live on edge, on nervous energy.'

'Yes,' I nodded. 'It couldn't be otherwise in a place where war can break up at any time, where there is constant fighting on all borders, when we could be called up at any moment to join our units, put on our uniforms, fight and maybe killed.'

*

Later that night Mina asked, 'Do you know anyone in London Daniela? It is all right to dream but you need to be practical, prepared.'

'No. Don't look so worried. I am perfectly capable of looking after myself.'

Outside the moon shone on the white snow. I looked at Mina and knew that I would miss her.

'I can only wish you luck, Daniela. It is not easy to start anew in a foreign country. It wasn't easy for us. Yes, we both speak German and French, but we had to learn how things work here. No, it wasn't easy.'

'I don't expect it to be easy.'

Before I fell asleep, I thought about our conversation. I knew it wasn't going to be easy. It was the unknown, I didn't know what to expect, it made me feel apprehensive, but at the same time, excited and hopeful. I wanted to build a new life, and like Mina, a peaceful one.

*

The minivan was waiting. Mina and I hugged.

'I loved having you here. Write to me. I don't know where you'll be.'

'Nor do I. Thank you for letting me stay.'

In the transport van, I looked out of the back window and watched Mina slowly disappear as the road dipped down.

# CHAPTER 3

In our room on the second floor, I found Edna unpacking. She lifted her head and smiled. Her face was round and her eyes soft brown. She had dimples in her cheeks, they made her look cute when she smiled. She looked happy. She tossed her thick and shiny, longish auburn hair, her best feature.

'Isn't it exciting? Let's go exploring. We can unpack later. I can't wait.'

Her mood was catching and we sauntered out filled with curiosity.

I had met Edna in the Scouts but had lost touch with her. One day I bumped into her and we went to a café. I remembered her as vivacious and easy-going. At the café she seemed subdued and I had a feeling that something was weighing on her. We never had a close friendship like I had with Mina, so I couldn't ask her what was wrong. Had I known what had happened to her, I wouldn't have been unkind during our holiday.

She told me that she was going to the Club Med in St Moritz and asked if I would like to join her. She was getting a good deal through a relative of hers. Out of politeness I said I would think about it. I was taken aback when she told me that she was going there to look for a rich husband. As teenagers we had shared ideology. She was ambitious then; she was going to study chemistry at university and have a career. Something must have happened to her to have turned her back on all that we had aspired to.

'St Moritz is a good place to find one,' she had said.

But I was not looking for a rich husband and anyway, I thought the idea cold and calculating.

After I decided to leave, the idea of going to a place so very different to anything that was familiar to me and the distraction it would offer, attracted me. I said I'd go with her. She could look for a rich husband. I just wanted to have a good time.

*

I found the Club Med a pleasure playground for adults, rich ones only. It was what I was there for, so I might as well try to enjoy it. The long tables were always piled up with delicious food. Although, the sea was nowhere near, to my delight there was plenty of seafood; lobsters and huge, sweet tasting prawns, langoustines and scallops; which with French bread and salads I ate happily. I swam in the warm pool, had saunas and massages and read my time away.

One morning I was lazing in bed reading. Edna was painting her face, sitting at the dressing table.

'You won't find a husband with your nose in books.'

I stopped reading and looked at her. Her back was turned to me but I could see her face in the mirror. Her comment came out of nowhere. Maybe she thought that I was looking for a husband too. I found her obsession of finding a rich one puzzling.

'I am not looking for a husband Edna. I want a life, my own life.'

'Do you really not want a husband to look after you, children?'

'I have no intention of becoming a housewife, I don't want a husband to look after me, and as for children, I love them, but I am not the breeding type.' My tone of voice sounded confrontational. I didn't mean it to.

She lifted her eyes to look at me. 'O.K. you don't need to be unpleasant about it.'

'Sorry.'

'Getting married. Having children is the natural progression. What is expected.'

It sounded like a mantra. 'You sound like your parents. There is more to life than treading this conventional line.'

She quickly turned to look at me, her beautiful hair flying in waves. 'All this talk of freedom,' she spat. 'Where does it get you? So, you are free to have sex with whomever you want. What an achievement. Has it not occurred to you that men are using you? They get sex for free, and without obligation.'

Edna had been clever, a high achiever and at the same time fun to be with. In those days, we had shared our beliefs and exchanged ideas about how we wanted to live our lives and bring change to the old and stale conventions.

'Think about it, Edna. The word wedlock. It is comprised of two words, wed and lock. Is that what you want? Really?'

She sighed. She wasn't looking at me. She was busy choosing an eyeshadow. 'I want a husband, children and a home of my own.' She turned and looked at me. 'There is nothing wrong with that, is there?'

'No, there isn't, if that's what you really want.'

'Well, it is!'

Of course there was nothing wrong with it, that was what

having a choice was all about. But there was something in her voice that told me that behind those declarations was something deeper.

She got up and started taking her night dress off. She was still plump but in a cuddly sort of way. What about love I wanted to ask her, but I could see that maybe it wasn't the right time. She was entitled to her opinions. I got up and dressed and we went down to the restaurant. There was an awkwardness between us that I hoped would dissipate. Over breakfast I reflected that I hadn't been very nice to her. We had come on holiday together and I should have been spending more time with her. I suggested that we go to the dance that was planned for that evening. She smiled, her dimples showed and her eyes were lively. Sometimes it took so little to please people. I felt I should make an effort. It was not her fault that I was hurting, that all I wanted was to crawl into a dark hole that would consume me. Maybe I shouldn't have come. I couldn't find it in me to join the fun and the jolly mood of the holiday makers that were hellbent on enjoying themselves.

*

So I did make an effort. Edna and I had fun dressing up. We helped each other choose clothes and accessories and I was relieved that the awkwardness was gone. I painted my lips and fingernails red, put my hair up into a ponytail and wore a swirling, thirties black dress and added a red belt. We stood in front of the mirror, twirled and smiled at ourself with approval.

The evening was called *Temps Perdu,* and the theme was old fashioned dances. The D.J. played music that I was familiar with; old Italian and Spanish songs. Edna and I had no shortage of men to dance with. I waltzed, danced the Cha Cha to '*Bessame Mucho*' and Samba to '*Volare*'. It was great fun. Some of the older men were very good. It took me back to family gatherings, when the grownups had danced the Rumba, the Paso-Doble and the like, and we, the children, ran among their feet, got in the way and laughed at our aunts swaying their behinds with gusto. When I was a teenager, I danced with my uncles. They were good, they danced with style and I had learned from them.

'The next dance will be the Paso-doble,' the DJ announced. 'Take your partners.'

If I were to dance this, I needed a good dancer to partner me. I smiled at the one I had enjoyed dancing with the most. He was a handsome older man with silver sideburns. He smiled back and came over. We took our places. The DJ played '*Espana Cani*'. We danced well together. He led. I followed. We moved as one; our bodies were having a silent rapport. Soon we found ourselves alone on the dance floor. The other couples had left to stand and watch. We got loud claps and cheers at the end. The man bowed to me.

Later on, most of us danced the Charleston together and sang *Funiculi Funicula* at the top of our voices. It was exhilarating and I was glad to see Edna laughing and enjoying herself.

*

Back in our room, smiling and in a good mood, we had a laugh and a giggle as we reminisced over the events, people's remarks, their good or bad dancing, and went to bed feeling satisfied. In the silence I listened to Edna breathing softly.

There would be no more dancing with my uncles at family gatherings, I thought sadly. They too had lectured me, berated me and turned their backs on me. Not even one of them showed me any kindness or understanding. I had phoned my favourite uncle but his wife said that he didn't want to talk to me and not to phone again. I hadn't been made to feel welcome at family gathering, so I stopped going to see them with my mother.

The conversation I had with Edna was playing on my mind. I had heard those arguments before. It was true that some men took advantage of the new freedom of sex. There were those who said that if a woman slept with them, she was a slut, but if she didn't, she was a prude. They were not the men I had known, nor would I want to know them. It would be better, I thought to avoid those sorts of discussions with Edna.

I did spend more time with her. Every evening, after supper, we would sit at the bar. Men bought us drinks and we joined in the conversations, or rather Edna did. I was never good at small talk. A drink or two helped me to at least try.

Most of the guests were Swiss, French or Italian. Some came with their families for a skiing weekend. The women were immaculately done up, their hair, plastered with smelly hairspray, did not move, their strong perfumes mingled with the men's aftershaves. They talked about fashion, cosmetics, what they read in Elle and Vogue magazines, particularly about famous people. There were film stars who owned houses in the Alps and gossip about them, which I thought was guess work rather than facts, was rife. The men talked about business, the stock exchange, cars and sports. Later, as the alcohol began to take effect, there were jokes and silliness, and flirting.

I felt like a voyeur. I couldn't be a part of it even if I

tried, but I could pretend to join in. There were times when friends had said that I was too serious. I sought interesting conversations, exchange of ideas, more fulfilling discussions. I did not expect to find it in St Moritz.

*

On Saturday night, after the resort's staff performed a short, funny show, I stayed at the bar rather late. I had had a few drinks but felt very awake. From my seat by the window, I watched the full moon swim in clear skies full of stars. When I turned to look back at the bar, I saw that there was only one man left, an arms dealer from Colombia, a stocky man with dark complexion, who spoke with a thick accent in a loud voice and wore garish clothes. Tonight, he had a flowery shirt on and ill-fitting pink trousers. He seemed out of place with the sort of people who came there. He had often boasted in a loud voice about the source of his money, telling whomever would listen, how very lucrative it was. No one seemed to think badly of him, after all he was rich, and that was the name of the game.

He waved his hand and called me over to have a drink with him. It would have been rude not to, and so reluctantly I joined him. I asked for an Armagnac. He smelt strongly of aftershave. I thought I might as well tackle him about the way he made his fortune.

'I understand that you are an arms dealer. Very lucrative I believe.'

'Yeh. Very.' He winked and tapped his nose.

'Is it dangerous?' I wanted to see how he saw himself but I was going to tread carefully. The man did not fool me. He was dangerous. Considering what he did, he had to be.

'Most of the time it is not.'

'When is it dangerous? I hope you don't mind me asking.' I smiled so as to not look too serious.

Even though he had quite a lot to drink, he looked at me and hesitated as if to see what I was after. But the need to impress got the better of him. 'Well, there are things that I can't tell you. Some clients are dangerous, you understand.'

I pressed on. 'Like who?'

'Well, you know. All sorts of groups, factions, rebels.'

'Terrorists?' I smiled casually.

'No. Freedom fighters. They are dangerous and a little crazy, you know, locos. But I can handle them.'

I tried not to show him that I thought what he was doing was vile. I was certain that he was indifferent to whom he was selling, and what the arms would be used for. He was smiling at me, looking pleased with himself as if he was to be congratulated for his smartness.

He downed his drink and ordered another round. He lit a cigar; its fruity smell was quite pleasant. I waited hoping that he would continue talking. Soon enough he started boasting, telling me how he smuggled the arms, bribing officials to turn a blind eye, even the upper echelons. Then he chuckled, 'Sometimes we sell arms to both sides.' He paused and lowering his voice he said, 'I bought Uzis from Israel via a legitimate official in Portugal and then sold them to Arab fighters.'

I wasn't going to tell him that I was from Israel. I didn't think it was advisable. What an awful man. Maybe I should have made my excuses and left. But I wanted to know how he justified his actions to himself. I hesitated, but then decided that I would confront him. 'So why did you sell them, knowing what you know?'

'If I don't, somebody else will,' he answered as if that

justified everything.

It was obvious that he did not see anything wrong with what he was doing. He had absolutely no morals, no conscience, no scruples or decency.

I was incensed. People I knew had died, their blood soaked into the ground, their family and friends bereaved. They could have been killed by arms that he had supplied. The money, the currency of death from those deals had just paid for the drink he had bought me. I couldn't drink it. With great effort I swallowed my anger and said calmly, 'I think I'll turn in now.'

Lying in bed, I couldn't sleep. He had no compassion for other human beings. It was incomprehensible to me. To him, it was just business, a way to make lots of money and probably there was thrill in the danger. I could have told him what I thought of him but there was no point, he would have probably turned nasty. A bullet from one of his guns could have killed a cousin of mine. I was very fond of him. He was only eighteen years old. His blood was on that man's hands. I found it hard to understand why the other guests, listening to his boasting did not seem to see anything wrong with what he was doing.

# CHAPTER 4

Almost as soon as I had arrived, one of the ski instructors, a Canadian called Chris, took a shine to me. Blond, blue eyes, strong bone structure, tall and lithe and with charming manners, he reminded me of the male models that had come to Benyamin's studio. He told me that he had studied agriculture and during the summer grew cucumbers in Canada, then in the winter he taught skiing to supplement his income and have a holiday.

Chris was persistent. He'd come and sit next to me at the bar and try to strike a conversation, telling me that I was beautiful, how struck he was by my big green eyes, trying to tempt me to go skiing with him. My answers were laconic. I hoped that he would leave me alone. I had neither wish nor appetite for flirtations. Besides, what would I have in common with a ski instructor except for a light banter. I was not in the mood for that.

One evening he came up with this statement. 'You know that you are unapproachable, or at least it is the signal you give.'

'What if I am?'

'Attempting to talk to you feels like a challenge. You should give me credit for trying.'

I stared at him then smiled. 'Come in then. I promise

that I won't bite.'

'What a relief,' he laughed. 'Now then, answer me. Why aren't you skiing?'

'I don't know how.'

'I'll teach you.' He straightened himself. 'I am the best instructor here.' He looked proud and confident. 'You'll be safe in my hands. I assure you.'

'A, I am not interested in skiing and B, I doubt I'll be any good at it.'

I was not an outdoor person. At school I always tried to find excuses to be let off sports' classes. The best excuse had been having my period, but there was a limit to how many I could have a month without the teacher noticing.

Chris stared at me for a moment, laughed then said, 'I watched you dance in the club the other night. If you can dance then you can ski.'

'That was fun. Skiing doesn't look much fun to me. I don't like being cold. It is freezing out there. It is not for me.'

'I don't understand you. Why did you come here if not for skiing? People come here for outdoor activities, not to moon about.'

'To look at the snow? Because we got a good deal? What does it matter? Besides, I like mooning about.'

'O.K. if not skiing, come tobogganing with me. I am sure that you would love it. I'll get you ski clothes and boots. How about it?'

I was about to say no but something made me change my mind. Why not, I thought. I was staying at a ski resort and perhaps I should experience what everyone else was there for. I said yes. I remembered, as a child, watching children rolling down the hill inside large tyres screaming with excitement.

Edna came in to our bedroom after her skiing lesson. I was reading, curled up in an armchair.

'I ache all over. I'm going to have a long, hot bath.'

I carried on reading. I had nearly finished the book.

'How was your lesson?' I asked when she came out wrapped in towels.

'All right. I haven't got the hang of it yet. My instructor is patient with me. Talking about instructors, be careful and don't flirt with them. They are not husband material and they are after one thing only.'

She started putting on her bikini. Her exposed breast was firm and rounded. A good breast to suckle children with.

'Why didn't you get that man you lived with to marry you?'

I hadn't told her about Benyamin. She must have heard the gossip about us somewhere. The clue was in the "get". The implication annoyed me.

'It takes two to tango. Or do you mean that I should have trapped him? Getting pregnant is the usual way, isn't it? Do you really see me doing that?'

'You really think yourself special, don't you?'

There was a note of resentment in her voice.

'I don't believe in marriage. It is just a piece of paper. You can't hold people against their will.'

She raised her eyes to the ceiling as if to say 'I give up on you'. She put on a bath robe.

I remembered that I was going to avoid the subject. 'Have a good swim,' I forced a smiled.

'What are you going to do?'

'I am going to look for a book to read. I just about finished this one. I'll come and join you in a little while.' It was not the best olive branch to offer, but I couldn't think of anything else.

I finished my book, put my bikini on and went to the communal room where there was a bookcase full of books previous guests had left behind. They were mostly Mills & Boons, crime and detective novels in different languages. I had nearly given up when I saw it: Thomas Mann*, The Magic Mountain.* I rescued it from the unsuitable company it was with.

*

At the pool I put the book down on a lounger and joined Edna in the water. We chatted and laughed with the swimmers. I think Edna was pleased to have me with her, joining in and socializing. All I wanted to do was to start reading Thomas Mann.

Edna was back in the water and I was lying on the recliner. I watched her swim and flirt. I remembered Edna saying that the instructors were after one thing only. I thought about sex. That small word that had become the centre of my generation's revolution. No one had talked to me about sex when I grew up. It was one of the many taboos. We still did not talk about it, yet felt free to do it. I had just assumed that when the time came, men would know what to do.

Until I met Benyamin, I hadn't seen a man's penis except for in paintings and sculptures, and the toddlers on the beach; neither had erections. I had felt but hadn't seen one, when half-dressed, in the back of cars, in the dark, I kissed and fondled with boyfriends.

After Benyamin had gone, I had a one-night stand with a French pilot. In the morning, as he was leaving, he told me that I was frigid. I had no idea what he was talking about, or why he should mention it. We'd had sex, and for me, it was much the same as usual. I was hurt, but more than that, puzzled. In the past I'd heard women say, 'We are whores if we like it, frigid if we don't.' I didn't understand that, and I didn't know what he meant, and there wasn't really anyone I could ask.

I wondered whether Benyamin thought so too. We had had sex when he wanted, which was not often. He had never complained. He had said that he loved my body and told me, I had beautiful breasts, he had even photographed them. But what I loved was sleeping in his arms, waking up next to him. It was all very confusing. I did not know how often couples had sex. I wondered what the norm was, or if there even was one.

*

That night Chris provided me with a ski outfit. I looked like a stuffed bear. It made me laugh. Chris assured me that I would be warm. We took the cable car to the first stop and walked to the start of the run. It was a clear night full of stars. The moon was big and low. I thought that if I stretched my arms, I could touch it.

'We'll be taking a short run,' Chris said.

I looked down. The bottom looked far away. I hesitated. He took my hand and led me to where the toboggans were. He dragged one to the starting point and sat on it.

'Come on,' he said.

'Chris. I am not sure about this. It looks scary.'

'We are already here. Where is your sense of adventure?'

I was standing next to him, he took my hand and pulled me down. I sat between his legs, facing the slope. He put his arms around my shoulders and pulled me back so that I was leaning against his chest. He pushed with his legs and we started sliding. The snow was banked along the path, shining white. We were hurtling down at a dizzying speed. I thought that the toboggan was out of control. I grabbed his hands and screamed my head off. Chris laughed so loud that I could hear him above the noise of the toboggan loudly scraping through the snow.

Round the gentle bends we tilted and my stomach lurched. 'Stop,' I screamed illogically. 'Relax,' he shouted in my ear. 'Breathe.' I realised that I had been holding my breath. I took a lungful of air and exhaled a stream of transparent white mist. I looked up at the moon and resigned myself to my fate. That was when I felt exhilarated, my mind was clear and my spirit free. I screamed, but this time it was with elation, with a joy of freedom.

But as the end of the trail loomed near, I watched its rapid approach with horror. I couldn't see how we would slow down, how we would stop. There were no breaks. We were surely going to crash and die.

We stopped. I staggered to my wobbly feet.

Breathing hard and smiling Chris said, 'Wasn't it great? Do you want to do it again? Head first this time?'

'Chris, you are incorrigible.' I could hardly get the words out. My heart was racing, my legs shaking and I was breathing hard. I did not regret doing it, but once was enough.

Maybe it was because I felt euphoric, and in rapture that I went with Chris to his bedroom. It seemed natural to do so. I thought it was a good way to end a lovely evening. One that I would remember, a memory stored up to be looked at in the future. That was all it meant to me.

*

In the morning, when I entered our room, Edna said, 'That was a big mistake.'

'It was a nice mistake as it happens,' I said and went to have a bath.

I lay in a hot bath smelling the delicious scent of the Guerlain oil I had added to the water. I was glad that Chris had insisted on taking me tobogganing. I could still feel the thrill of it. Despite what Edna had said, I did not regret spending the night in Chris's bed. It was a one-night stand. It was nice. It didn't feel wrong.

Edna was sitting on the bed when I came out of the bathroom.

'Everyone knows that you are sleeping with him,' she said.

Here we go again, I thought. 'So what?'

'You are wasting your time with him. You do realise that you are not the first woman he has ever picked up, nor will you be the last. You are ruining your chances of finding a husband.'

Something snapped inside me, and before I could think I spat at her. 'What is your problem with sex, Edna?'

She went white and stared at me unblinking.

'What is it? What's wrong. Did something happen to you?'

I went and sat beside her on the bed. Her body was rigid, her face taut. She held her hands between her legs.

'It did, Daniela,' she said in a trembling voice.

I took her hands in mine and stroked them. 'Please tell me.'

'I met a guy at a party. We got on. He seemed lovely and I liked him.' Her eyes were wide open. She hardly blinked.

'I went out on a date with him. We went to a restaurant. Afterwards he suggested that we go for a walk on the beach.'

She stopped talking. I felt her shiver. I poured her a glass of water from the pitcher on the bedside table, pulled a blanket of off the bed and wrapped her in it. She calmed down a little.

I began to suspect what was coming but at the same time hoped I was wrong. Whatever it was, I had to be strong for her. Edna took a sip of water. I waited. I could see that it was difficult for her to talk about it.

'He started kissing me. I expected it to happen. I am not a prude you know.' She paused. She turned her head to look at me. 'But then he pushed me, he pushed me down on the sand and started pulling my skirt up. I told him to stop. I struggled.' The word caught in her throat.

'Have more water,' I said with a calm voice.

She drank, then put the glass on the bedside table. She pulled on the blanket and held it tight around her with both hands.

'There was no point in screaming, there was no one there. He pinned me down with his knees.' She lifted her head and looked into my eyes. 'Daniela, he was going to rape me.'

'Drink,' I said.

'I kept asking him to stop. He kept saying, 'It's what you want. I know you do.' He was grinning. Somehow despite my fear, I was looking for a way out. He managed to rip my underpants. He opened his fly and took his penis out. I've no idea why I did what I did. I said to him that I did want to, but not like this, not getting covered in sand. I told him that we would be more comfortable in the hotel up the road.'

'Did he go for it?'

'Yes. I still don't understand why, but he did. We walked to the hotel. He seemed pleased and eager. As soon as we got there, I left him standing at the entrance and ran to a taxi.'

I hugged her while she sobbed. Once she calmed down a little, I lay her in the bed and piled blankets over her. I didn't know what to do, so I did what my mother would have done and ordered tea from room service. I put a lot of sugar in it and made her drink it.

I lay on the blanket beside her. I tried to imagine what it would feel like to be pinned down, helpless and knowing what was going to happen to me. I couldn't. I had been harsh with Edna, I wished I hadn't. I was pretty certain that I was the first person she told it to. It had altered her. She was no longer the carefree person that I had once known.

*

I didn't stay the night with Chris again but I did spend time with him drinking at the bar together with Edna. We only had a few days left and on our last afternoon at Club Med, I went up in the cable car with Chris.

We got out at the last stop. The sun was bright, the sky intense blue. Skiers were standing further up at the start of the ski slope, ready to launch themselves. We went into the small wooden hut, sat on a bench and were served a delicious mulled wine.

Outside, we walked up and away from people. We stood in the vast wilderness in silence. The snow-capped mountains dotted with dark pines shimmered in the sun. Wispy fog floated lower down. I breathed in the pure, crisp air and felt the cold streaming into my lungs. It was the utter silence that struck me most. I heard a screech and looked up. A golden eagle was gliding, circling slowly above us. It suddenly flipped its wings and dived.

*

Edna had said that to find a rich husband you had to go to expensive places and invest for the future. Edna had not found a husband. St Moritz did not pay dividends and we were running out of money.

On the train to Zurich, she whispered. 'There is something I didn't tell you.'

'About that guy?'

'Yes. I can't explain it really. When he took his penis out. It was very, very small. A voice in my head was asking what was he going to do with it? It was so tiny. Don't you find it strange?'

'Yes, I do.' I paused, 'Why didn't you report him to the police?'

'No point. I went with him of my own free will. This is what I was trying to say to you. You are going to travel, a woman on your own. Don't be too free. Be careful.'

I understood Edna's reaction, her wanting a safe home and family. Yet, I wasn't going to let go of my wish to be free and independent.

I smiled at her. 'Yes Edna. I'll be careful.'

I swayed from side to side as the train negotiated the bends, ploughing through the prevailing white. Jagged mountains loomed against the sky. I watched the sentry-like, dark evergreen trees, appearing and vanishing. On the slopes were small pretty houses, painted and well-kept. An orderly looking countryside.

# Chapter 5

Dolly met me at Frankfurt airport. I had forgotten how doll-like she actually looked. She recognized me immediately and beamed at me. People turned to look at her, I have never, nor have I since, seen anyone wearing a fur trouser suit. She kept kissing and petting me to make sure I was real. Dolly was so obviously happy to see me that I began to suspect that she was one lonely woman. It was nice to be welcomed. She didn't stop talking all the way to the waiting car.

Dolly was about forty years old. She would never divulge her age and no man would dream of asking. She was short and plump, pretty with a round face, heavily made up, small velvety brown eyes adorned with long false eyelashes, dyed auburn hair, immaculately coiffured as if she had just stepped out of the hairdresser.

I had met Dolly at a nightclub my mother once took me to. She was there on a visit from Germany. I found her an intriguing character. She was vivacious and outrageously flirtatious. I watched fascinated as she sat on men's laps and made remarks that made them laugh and wink knowingly. I guessed what she was saying had a sexual connotation, but I didn't really understand.

She told me that if I ever came to Germany, I must come

and stay with her. I said thank you but thought that if I ever went to Europe, it wasn't the likes of her that I would choose to be with. I asked Mother about her. She told me that Dolly had made a living by sexually servicing men. She met Herr Schafferman when he came from Germany for a visit. He was a rich man who dealt in pelts. During his visit, he enjoyed her services and one day made her an offer of marriage and she took it. He knew that she had accepted him in order to have a rich and comfortable life, which he was happy to provide.

Mother had warned me that Herr Schafferman looked weird. He had been one of the many children that were experimented on in the concentration camps. She said that it had left him looking horrible, but he was a good and kind man. It should have prepared me for meeting him, but although I expected the worst, I was still shocked.

I found it hard not to show my revulsion. In my head I repeated over and over, 'He is a human being; he is a human being.' He was very short, bow-legged with a big head that seemed ready to topple from his thin neck. His face was crumpled like an old man or a new born baby. His oily hair looked like it needed a good wash and there was a faint unpleasant odour around him. I swallowed hard and said hello. He looked at me with inquisitive, pale, bright blue eyes and I saw that in this body lived a smart and quick brain.

*

The Schafferman's lived in a large apartment in a modern building in the centre of Frankfurt. I settled in to a comfortable life of luxury. Dolly could not do enough to make me happy as long as I was prepared to be her companion and captivated audience over endless cups of hot cocoa. Dolly didn't lift a finger; she had a cleaner, a chauffeur and a woman who brought supper every evening. I joined her lazy and leisurely life and it suited me just fine.

Everything was taken care of and all I had to do was to be, to let go and not think too deeply. I felt emotionally exhausted. Nothing mattered very much. I had no purpose and no particular aim and was not in a hurry to get to London. Sometimes I felt that there were two of me; one functioning and one grieving. The later was hidden in my bosom like a lump. A few times a day, the lump reminded me that it was there. It would rise to my throat and I would swallow it back down.

Dolly's taste, if I can call it that, was loud. Everything screamed that it had cost a lot of money, no subtlety, no finesse, brash, jarring to my eyes, but she loved it all. The living room was dominated by a large white sofa and matching armchairs. On the floor was a white shaggy carpet and the ornaments in the glass cabinet shone in gold and silver. She was proud of the décor, but then what else would one expect from a woman who wore fur trouser suits?

After supper, Herr Schafferman would go to bed and Dolly and I lazed on the comfortable but ugly sofas. She drank cocoa and chatted her head off in Hebrew. She didn't expect answers or contributions to her monologues. I nodded my head ever so often and said 'Mmm' several times to reassure her that I was listening. I did try to read a book but gave it up as she continually interrupted me. She trawled through German women's magazines telling me what she was reading; murders, robberies, sex scandals, fraud, officials embezzling money. She had an opinion about all the items. She too was fascinated by film star gossip. She would show me adverts for cosmetics, hair dyes, clothes and shoes and ask me if they would suit her. I always said yes because if I said no, she would argue. Sometimes she would point out an outfit and say that it would suit me. In the fear of her buying it for me, I would say that I didn't like it. She would tut tut and once, she even said that I had no taste.

I asked myself why I was staying there. Why was I putting up with Dolly? But just the thought of moving somewhere else, the effort required to do so, made me see that I had no energy to deal with anything or to make decisions. Better wait until I felt strong enough to leave and put up with Dolly for the time being.

Curled up in the large white armchair, I fought away memories of Benyamin. I pushed them to the back of my mind and escaped to dreamland. I fantasized, dreaming myself into a femme fatal in long black dresses, dark eye makeup, red lipstick, carrying a long cigarette holder, parlaying with poets, painters, intellectuals and thinkers in bohemian settings. We would discuss art and books, exchange opinions and engage in badinage. My long silver earrings would sway as I spoke, and the people around me would have their eyes fixed on me and listen smiling. At other times I would dance in great halls, wearing sumptuous ball gowns and surrounded by men in tail coats.

Dolly's voice droned in the background. Whenever I got too carried away in my story-weaving and forget to nod or mutter something, she would jolt me by demanding, 'Are you listening?'

'Yes of course.'

'So why didn't you answer me?'

'Sorry, I misunderstood. I didn't think that you wanted an answer. Shall I make you a cup of cocoa?'

There were the rare evenings when Schafferman stayed with us in the living room. He would put a record on, disappear into the large armchair, close his eyes and put his head back. To my surprise, he listened to classical music. Dolly hated it. He would shout at Dolly to shut up when she couldn't help herself and started talking. His favourite was Mendelssohn Violin Concerto and the Four Last Songs by Strauss. They were some of mine too. I would rest my head on the music's wave and soar with it. I wondered where and when he had developed his love for music. Did he hear it in the concentration camps? My family, being one of the oldest in the land, had not experienced the Holocaust. I couldn't understand the survivors, how they managed to live after such horror. I looked at the little man in the big armchair, abandoning himself to the music and felt admiration for him.

*

Dolly and I got up late, dressed, breakfasted, then went shopping in the comfortable chauffeur driven car. We shopped a lot. She was insatiable. She never tired of trying on clothes and shoes, she bought makeup brands recommended in the magazines and threw the old ones away. We always stopped at the confectionary shop to stock up on chocolate and bonbonnieres that she consumed with her hot cocoa in the evenings. I had to fight her when she decided that a garment would look good on me. I refused to try it on, and sometime walked out of the shop. There was no point in trying to improve her garish taste.

I was relieved when we stopped to have lunch. Dolly was a generous tipper and they showed their gratitude by fussing over her. Doors were opened for us, chairs pulled back, napkins gently laid on our laps, and every little wish attended to promptly.

She wouldn't let me go off on my own. If I wanted to go somewhere, I had to be driven. There was no point in trying to get Dolly to take me to art galleries. I did ask her once, and all she said was 'What for?'

When we went to Berlin, I had a glimpse of the city during the taxi ride to the hotel. I wished I could go out on my own and look at it. Herr Wagner, the owner of a fashion house and a client of Herr Schafferman took us out to dinner. He was a pleasant man, well-mannered and spoke good English. Sometime during the evening, he said that I had the making of a model. I laughed, thanked him for the compliment and thought nothing more of it. Dolly's face darkened. She looked suspicious. She said, 'She is no model.' What niggled her I couldn't tell. We flew back the next day after Dolly shopped. Sightseeing was not something she was interested in.

*

On a very cold winter day Dolly took me to Herr Schafferman's warehouse in the industrial part of Frankfurt. It was the first time that Schafferman showed any interest in me. The room was huge and there were piles of pelts on its floor. I knew nothing about fur, it was not cold enough to need one where I came from.

He took me around the store and gave me a most valuable lesson about furs. We had no language in common. He spoke German, Yiddish, pigeon English and biblical Hebrew. I had picked up a little German at friends' homes where it was the language spoken by their immigrant parents. Herr Schafferman and I talked in a mish-mash of languages. It wasn't difficult to understand. It was basic language; it was not sophisticated.

I loved the beautiful colours of the pelts and their softness to the touch. He laughed when I said that I liked the ermine. 'You have royal taste,' he said, holding his hands up like a crown on his lolling head. Then he guided me to a room by his office and stood me in front of a rail loaded with fur coats. 'Choose,' he gesticulated with his hands. I looked at him in surprise and he, in turn, looked at my coat and said, 'Schmatte.' O.K. it was an old coat but I liked it.

I chose a long, silver fox and tried it on. Schafferman started jumping up and down, his head lolling on his thin neck.

'Schone!' he shouted, 'Wunderbar, beautiful. Dolly come, look!'

She came in and looked me up and down. 'With your green eyes you look like a fox.'

It sounded nasty. I heard something in the tone of her voice, I couldn't quite put my finger on it. It was clear to me that she was not as pleased as Schafferman was. He looked at her puzzled. She ignored him. She told me to put my arms out and piled them with rabbit fur jackets that she pulled out of a box. Herr Schafferman left. She then told me to follow her. We walked out of the warehouse. And into the car. I wondered what I was supposed to do with these jackets. Surely, she wasn't gifting them to me.

Dolly instructed the chauffeur to drive us around the warehouse industrial area. It looked bleak. On two of the streets that we drove past, I saw prostitutes standing in clusters. They wore as little as they could get away with in the cold, freezing day: short miniskirts, tops. that showed a lot of cleavage under open jackets. Their faces were heavily painted. They were chatting, shifting their weight from one high heel to another, hugging themselves.

There didn't seem to be any customers. Then, a car appeared from the other end of the street and slowed down. The women spread out. The driver, a wrinkled-faced man, scrutinised the women through thick glasses. He took his time. He then opened his car window and beckoned to one of the women. She approached his car. They had a brief conversation and she got in.

We turned into another street, the nearest one to the warehouse. Dolly told the chauffeur to stop. We got out of the car. The girls were standing together smoking. They were wearing fur jackets. When they saw Dolly, they ran to her smiling, welcoming. They told her how well she looked, how much the new shade of auburn hair-dye suited her, and giggled a lot. She basked in their admiration and the fuss they made over her. I could see that.

I stood slightly behind Dolly leaving her the stage. I was warm for the first time since I arrived in Europe, and came to the conclusion that in European winters, one should not step outside without wearing fur. What I didn't register at the time, was that the dynamic of my staying with the two of them had changed.

One of the women introduced a girl to Dolly. 'She's new,' she said.

The girl looked under sixteen to me and had no fur jacket.

'Just starting, eh?' asked Dolly.

The girl smiled shyly. Her pale blue eyes looked at Dolly like a pupil looks up to a teacher.

'You'll get the hang of it,' Dolly told her, then to the rest of them, 'Men are like children, aren't they?'

They laughed and giggled nodding their heads in agreement as if she had said something really clever and profound. I looked at their heavily made-up faces, the cheap clothing, the very short miniskirts, the ugly white legs in high heels and felt revulsion. I knew I shouldn't have, but I couldn't help it. It was all so seedy.

'You'll show her the ropes, won't you?' Dolly said whilst pulling out a fur jacket from my arms.

She held it up, looked at the girl, then at the jacket sizing it up and said that it was too big and then told me to choose one. I chose the nicest one I could find that I thought would fit best. It was obvious that Dolly had given furs to all the girls who worked on that street. She had adopted them and they responded by making her feel important and generous.

'Try it on,' I said to the girl. She did, and all the girls admired it, too vociferously I thought.

'You need a stronger coloured lipstick,' Dolly told her.

One of the girls obliged and fished one out of her bag and a small mirror. The girl put the strong red coloured lipstick on and Dolly said, 'Much, much better.'

The girl looked like a child trying her mother's make up on.

A car drove by and slowed down. The girls ran to take their positions. The man looked at the merchandise on offer; maybe it was because of the new coat, maybe the red lips or maybe the innocent look of the very young girl, that he chose her. Before she got into the car, she looked at us with what I thought was fear and a plea for help. She got in and the car drove away.

Dolly said, 'She'll do well. So pretty and young.'

I felt sad. I wondered if it was her first time.

Back in the car, Dolly said to me, 'I never hustled on the

streets. I worked the clubs. You get better punters there. But then I had my regulars, it is safer that way.'

She said it as if it was a profession like any other. There was no shame in her voice, it rather sounded like she was boasting, putting herself above the girls on the street. I wanted to ask her how and why she became a prostitute. I knew better than to ask.

*

Once a week, on a Friday, there was the bath affair. Usually, I would disappear to my room to avoid this ritual. It was the Friday before the evening that Dolly was to give a party for her birthday. We were in the kitchen sorting out serving dishes when Schafferman came home. Dolly looked at him in a peculiar, meaningful, sort of way, her hands on her waist. The little man ran to his room and closed the door. She went to the bathroom. I could hear the bath tap running and smelt the pine scented bubble bath. I stayed standing by the kitchen door.

Dolly came out of the bathroom shouting, 'Where are you? I'm coming to get you.'

She walked straight to his bedroom pushing the door open. A few seconds later, he shot out, ran and hid behind the sofa. She came out and marched towards it. As she approached, he ran away screaming and yelling. She chased him, caught him and dragged him to the bathroom.

It was comical but sad. I should have retreated to my room and gave them privacy, but I was fascinated. They were totally oblivious to my presence. It was a game they played. In this one, she was the domineering one and he the child. Maybe he liked playing the game or maybe he genuinely didn't like to have baths.

I heard the water splashing, him whining and pleading with her to stop.

'Shush, shush. You need a bath. you smell. You will feel nice and clean afterward. Stop fussing.'

'Enough Dolly. I'm clean now,' he whined. Then he stopped and said, 'Dolly, I have one of those headaches.'

The next thing I saw was Dolly gently walking him back to his bedroom wrapped in a large towel. That was odd, I had never seen her being gentle with him before. I wondered why he hated having a bath. I had my suspicions. It must have something to do with the concentration camp. Being marched to have a shower, meant death. Maybe subconsciously he felt that not washing meant life. Again, I couldn't ask.

*

Before the guests arrived, Schafferman retreated to his bedroom and closed the door. I wasn't feeling too well; I felt hot and my body was aching. I told Dolly but she insisted that I stayed. I sat down in a corner waiting for the celebration to be over. A man wearing a three-piece suit and looking respectable came to chat to me. He introduced himself and started asking questions. In order to get rid of him I told him that I did not feel well. He said that he knew what I was suffering from and had a remedy for it. He went away and returned with a sugar cube in the palm of his hand. He dug in his pocket and produced a little phial from which he put a drop onto the sugar cube. He gave it to me saying that it would make me feel better.

I sat in the armchair, sucking on the cube, waiting to feel better. I thought that whatever he had given me did not work. That was until the world flipped from underneath me and I found myself on the floor crying hysterically. I was scared, nothing was stable, everything was shifting, I could not get up. I put my hand out to support myself but could not find the floor.

Almost instantly Dolly was there towering above me. 'Did someone give you something? A sugar cube? Tell me!'

I nodded my head. I felt hot. My body was drenched in sweat. My head was spinning. Shudders ran through my body. I wanted to throw up.

'Who was it? Was it him?' She pointed the man out.

I nodded.

She shouted for someone to get a doctor, then marched straight to the man and screamed at him as she pushed him out of the apartment. Someone carried me to bed. I must have been delirious. I do not remember the next two days. What he had given me was morphine in a liquid form.

I recovered and life with the Schaffermans settled back to shopping and Dolly's evening monologues. At night I would cry myself to sleep, and in the morning, my first thought was of Benyamin and the lump I carried in my chest felt unbearably heavy. With all her faults, Dolly was a constant distraction since she wouldn't leave me alone, didn't stop chatting, not leaving me much time to nurture my pain.

*

It was a surprise to me when one day Dolly announced that she and I were invited for drinks at one of Herr Schafferman's clients. The invitation was for herself and specifically for me. Schafferman never socialised outside his home. He told her that she shouldn't go. She was having none of it. Dolly said that they were important clients and that it was the first time that they had invited her to their home.

'How did they know about me?' I asked her.

'The fur trade is small. People know people,' she explained.

She spent days on end agonizing on what she should wear and what gift to take with us. She swore me to be on best behaviour and stressed how important it was to her. I did intend to be on my best behaviour. What reason could there be for me to misbehave?

The chauffeur deposited us at a large house on the outskirt of town. We mounted the steps and Dolly, carrying an enormous box of chocolates, rang the bell. 'Very rich,' she whispered. 'Family money.'

A corpulent man in a well-made suit, with a ruddy face, opened the door. He smiled, welcomed us, took our coats and showed us to a drawing room. It was decorated with damask and oil paintings, the tall ceiling hung with a crystal chandelier and the antique furniture shone with years of polish. Two people rose up to greet us. The husband introduced his wife and son.

'Please sit down,' he said. 'Dolly, what would you like to drink? Sherry? We have liquors if you prefer.'

'Do you have banana one?' Dolly asked.

'Sorry we don't. how about a Cointreau? It tastes of orange.'

'I never had one but I'll have it.'

'For you Daniela? What would you like?'

'A glass of wine please.'

'Red or white?'

'White please.'

He walked across the room and opened a drinking cabinet. He poured a drink for Dolly and gave it to her.

The wife smiled at Dolly. 'Do you like it?'

'It's nice,' she smiled back.

I was sure she didn't.

The parents had a conversation with Dolly and from the little German I had, I gathered it was about pelts and the business.

I sipped and watched them. I couldn't help wondering why we were invited. Dolly looked very out of place in her shiny lurex dress with silver shoes and heavy gold jewellery. By contrast, the wife was immaculate in cream twinset and pearls. The son who was about my age was blond, blue eyed and did not smile. He wore jeans and a corduroy shirt and his hair was longish. He too, like Dolly, looked out of place. He had a sullen expression and seemed uncomfortable, I suspected that he didn't wish to be a part of this affair. He said very little, mainly yes or no. I could tell that his parents insisted on him being there. But why? Why would they be interested in Dolly, or me come to that?

The parents turned to me and switched to English. That left Dolly out of the conversation altogether. She was happy to sit there, sip and smile, be their guest as if they were bestowing honour on her. It irked me somewhat.

The husband turned to me smiling politely. The sort of smile that had an agenda behind it. 'Dolly told us that you came from Israel. Were you born there?'

'Yes, I did.'

'We admire your country, young, full of idealism. Secular I believe. Socialist?' asked the wife.

'Not pure socialism. A hybrid. Maybe you can call it social capitalism.'

'Are you a Sabra then?'

'Yes. My family is one of the oldest in the land.'

'The Sabras are very unlike our Jews, don't you find?'

I saw the boy wince. I thought I'd change the subject. 'Are you from Frankfurt?'

'I am. My husband is from Berlin.'

'Beautiful city. Dolly took me there.'

'They are not like the Israelis. Are they? Very different,' said the wife.

'Who?' I asked.

'Our Jews. Here.'

I didn't like the way she said, "our Jews".

'They wouldn't be. They are brought up here, their culture is German.' I paused, then added, 'I don't really know the Jews of Germany.' I thought that that was diplomatic and would put an end to this line of questioning.

They looked at their son. No reaction there. 'Of course, they are Germans,' she said. 'But they are not as free and courageous, not as liberal as the Israeli Sabras. All I am saying is…' her voice petered out.

They both looked at their son as if seeking something. The show was for him, I thought. I was expected to perform. But what was my role? Did they expect me to agree with them? But on what?

The husband coughed. 'Another drink? Dolly? '

I declined. She took one.

'We are liberal. We know all kinds of people. Our son knows that we welcome them here.' He said looking at him.

'But they are different. Don't you agree?' She looked at me with an expectant smile.

"Them." "They." Obviously, this couple didn't think that "our Jews" as they called them, were Germans too. I realised what their agenda was. They wanted to prove to their son that they were not racists. All they proved to me was that they were.

I got up, looked at them up and down and said: 'Do you expect the Jews of Germany, what's left of them, to try and erase their individuality and copy you? The master-race? I am an Israeli. I do not kowtow to anybody; I can see your ugly souls.'

The wife went pale. Her husband's jaw dropped. The son smiled.

*

I left. I walked the streets without seeing where I was going. I felt violated. They must have been very young during the war judging by their age, yet here they were, still holding on to old prejudices. And as for their German Jews, why hadn't they left? What I had stopped short of saying to them was that Israelis would never have gone to the concentration camps or the gas chambers without resistance.

I stopped walking and sat on a low wall. I had never come across antisemitism before. My family, having lived in Israel for centuries, during the Ottoman Empire and then the British Mandate, had never been exposed to it. I saw that it was so deeply rooted, that it wasn't even a conscious state of mind. It couldn't be the case in England I assured myself.

When I got back, I heard Dolly arguing with Herr Schafferman. I walked in. She let me have it there and then. She shouted that I ruined their relationship with their client and that they would never ask her for a drink again.

I let her go on and on before I interrupted her and said, 'They were not going to ask you again anyway Dolly. We shouldn't have gone. They are not your friends and they don't like Jews.'

She started contradicting me when Schafferman cut her short. 'They are anti-Semites. I know one when I see one.

They fooled you but they don't fool me. You shouldn't have gone.' He left the room.

Dolly was a sourpuss all the next day. She stomped around the apartment, hardly said a word to me. At around noon, she disappeared into her bedroom. She came out all dolled up and shouted at me, 'How could you do this to me? How could you?' She left the apartment slamming the door.

She must have thought that I had taken Herr Schafferman's side. I didn't want to get between the two of them. I began to think that the time had come to leave this strange couple, but the very thought made me want to curl up under a blanket. I wasn't ready to move, having to find my way alone in countries where I had no one to go to, scared me. I didn't like this weakness in me. I wished that I could be angry instead, angry with Benyamin, angry with myself. That would have galvanised me, and given me the drive to go on and continue my journey. But I didn't have that anger. I told myself to wait, gather my strength and find my courage.

# Chapter 6

Herr Schafferman's interest in me grew. He had started talking to me about his business. I listened and asked questions because I saw that it pleased him.

'You like furs?' he asked me one evening during supper. I nodded my head.

'Ich can lehren you all furs business.'

I could see Dolly stiffen, watchful as she sensed something was on his mind. 'She doesn't need to know about pelts. For why?'

'She clever. I lehren her mine geschaft.'

I think, Dolly and I realised at the same time that Schafferman had plans for me. Let him talk, I thought. It gave him pleasure. It would come to nothing. But Dolly worried me. she was possessive and liked to have her own way.

One morning the chauffeur came to say that Herr Schafferman had told him to drive me to the factory. Dolly was furious. She forbade me to go and had a fight with Schafferman that evening. I listened to them arguing. I understood enough German to follow the gist of it.

Dolly was obviously getting worried that she was about to lose control over me. It didn't look like Herr Schafferman was going to give in.

'She is better off modelling for Herr Wagner,' she said to him. Then to me, 'You are tall, the coats look good on you and it pays well. Remember what Herr Wagner said? He said that you have the making of a model.'

Both Schafferman and I were taken aback. I had forgotten all about him. The idea appealed to me, a break from Dolly, time in Berlin and I'd be earning. Having money was important for my independence. I didn't like to rely or depend on people.

'I have other plans for her,' Schafferman objected.

'Like what?' Dolly said putting her hands on her waist.

'She clever. She can learn the business. Better than modelling. You just want her to waste her time with you, doing nothing. No future in that.'

'What?! You think she wants to work in a warehouse? What do you know? Herr Wagner wants her to do the show in Paris.' She turned to me. 'You want to go to Paris? don't you?'

It was the first time I heard of it. When did she plot this? But before I could answer she turned back to Schafferman. 'Her mother asked me to look after her. It is none of your business what she does.'

I watched them fighting. They totally ignored me. I wanted Dolly to win, I wanted to go to Paris.

Dolly wouldn't leave off, and in the end, Schafferman reluctantly gave in on condition that when I get back, he would teach me the pelt business. Dolly agreed. I was suspicious. She was plotting something. It was unlike her to comply so easily. But I was going to Paris and that was all that mattered.

Herr Wagner was happy to have me. Schafferman negotiated my fee for the Paris show. He looked pleased with himself when he told me. It was a lot of money, far more than I expected. I smiled to myself knowing that I would have done it for nothing as long as all my expenses were paid. I had spent too much in St Moritz. This windfall would support me on my travel all the way to London.

*

Herr Wagner and I walked into pandemonium. Backstage, models were being made up in front of mirrors surrounded by light bulbs. Clothes rails were being pulled in and out. Designers were shouting orders. People were running around or pacing up and down for what reason I didn't know. It was noisy. The air buzzed with nervous energy. There was a mixture of odours from shampoo, hairspray and cosmetics mixed with cigarette smoke that swirled up the light bulbs around the mirrors. It was all new and fascinating.

Wagner told me to wait and I saw him having an animated conversation with an icy blond model. They walked towards me. She looked at me with pale blue eyes. She seemed confident and aloof. I felt incompetent, a fraud.

'I asked Anne to show you the ropes.'

Anne smiled. 'I understand that you have never been on a catwalk before.'

'I'm afraid not. It looks terrifying. So many good-looking models. I don't know what I am doing here, or what I'm supposed to do.'

'Don't worry. I have all morning to spare before I'm needed. Come with me.'

We left the backstage area and followed a long corridor avoiding people who were pushing clothes rails and carrying boxes. We turned right then left into an empty corridor.

'We can do it here,' Anne said.

She taught me all that I needed to know. There was a lot more to it than I expected.

'Stand straight, shoulders back.'

I did.

'Now walk.'

I walked.

'No, no, no. Small steps. Don't run. Take your time. They need time to look at you, or rather at what you're wearing.'

I started again.

'Good. Now turn to the left.'

I did.

'Don't turn your head on its own. Turn your head and body together. Keep your head and spine as one line.' She showed me.

I copied.

'Good. You learn fast.'

I smiled. I found it easy. In my teens I had attended contemporary dance classes. I had enjoyed them but had lost interest when I lived with Benyamin.

'Don't smile.'

I was once told not to smile at chimpanzees, they take baring of teeth as a sign of menace.

'Are you listening Daniela? Concentrate.'

We practised the walk and then she said. 'Don't blink.'

'What?!'

'Don't blink. Keep an open stare, blank face. Vacuous expression.'

I could do vacuous; I could do hauteur very well. I thrust my chin up and stared straight ahead. I had been accused of being aloof, even a snob by people who misread me, or when I put on a remote expression on purpose.

'That's very good. You'll be all right.'

At the end of the day, Anne told me that I did really well. 'You are a natural,' she said.

During supper, Herr Wagner praised me. He said that I looked great on the catwalk, that I did a good job and he was very pleased. I felt confident, all I had to do was walk in a certain way and that was not difficult.

*

On opening night, my hair was styled and then I relaxed in a chair and let my face be painted very skilfully. I watched the makeup artist work and tried to memorised what he did. I asked for the names of the products, and bless him, he gave me samples.

All the while they chatted, the hairdressers, the makeup artists and the models. They gossiped, maliciously at times, about photographers, agents and other models. They related stories and anecdotes from their engagements all over the world. It was interesting to have a glimpse into the life of models. It didn't matter that I had not a clue whom they were talking about.

My hair and makeup dealt with; the dresser took me over. She slung a chiffon scarf over my face to stop the makeup staining the minidress that she slipped over my head. All I had to do was walk onto the catwalk.

The show was organised in a military, efficient fashion. The music was blurring. The machine backstage was in full swing, girls walked out, walked back, had a quick change and walked out again and so forth. I felt confident that I can do it. I had done well during the dry runs. I thought it was easy. That was until my turn was approaching. I began to feel nervous; my confidence was ebbing away. I worried that I would wobble, trip, or that the people out there won't like me.

My dresser came and stood by me holding the fur coat I was to wear. I felt sick. I was petrified, but I had no idea of what. All I knew was that my legs were not going to obey me and I would not be able to walk out there. I told Herr Wagner and collapsed on a chair. He looked at me horrified. He talked to me, cajoled me, but it did not work. I knew he had a lot riding on this, and I, his only model, was paralyzed.

Herr Wagner called Anne. She bent, putting her face to mine. 'It is only stage fright. Exactly that had happened to me on my first show. It'll pass once you're out there.'

But I could not move.

Anne took my hand and gently pulled me of the chair. 'Now Daniela, walk.'

I let her walk me to the curtains. My body did not hold the posture of a model. Herr Wagner had followed us, he looked pale. The dresser got me into the fur.

'Stand straight Daniela. Chin up,' Anne said.

'Anne. I can't do it,' I whispered.

'Yes, you can, and you will. Trust me.'

My cue came. Anne shoved me out. I stumbled, the lights blinded me, I could not see the audience. I knew I just had to do it. I threw my head back, lifted my chin and walked. Maybe my heart was pounding too hard, maybe inside I wanted to turn and bolt, but my body followed the routine that it knew from the many rehearsals. My hair, piled up in an artistic arrangement revealed my long neck. The full length, open fur coat waved and flowed behind me catching the light. I walked to the end of the catwalk, paused, turned one way and paused, turned the other way and paused, elegantly turned and walked back.

Whether they liked me or the look, I have no idea. They clapped and cheered me on, and I held my head high, keeping the stony expression on my face like I had seen the others do and walked back into Herr Wagner's arms. He was beaming and praising me and then he shoved me into the arms of the dresser who quickly changed my outfit.

After the show Herr Wagner, Anne and I walked down the boulevard to a restaurant. I felt exhilarated. I didn't need to drink the fine wine to feel drunk. Yet, all I had done was to walk down a catwalk wearing fur. It didn't seem to warrant such elation.

Herr Wagner ordered steak tournedos for us. He kept hugging me and smiling. 'Thank you. I wasn't wrong about you. You are a natural. Isn't she Anne?'

Anne smiled at me knowingly. 'She learns fast. Had I not known, I'd say that she had done it before.'

'It is all thanks to you Anne. I was so scared. I was shaking. Did it show?'

'Not at all. Honestly Daniela, you looked professional. It's only natural to feel that way on your first walk.'

It felt good to be praised, to be the centre of attention. I had earned it.

The steaks arrived. I was hungry. The meat was tasty, tender and succulent, I could have sliced the steak with a butter knife.

After the meal, Herr Wagner left us. Anne and I walked to the hotel.

'Anne, I owe you. If it wasn't for you, I would not have walked it.' It was true, but then, why did she help me? 'Anne, I want to ask you something, I hope you don't mind.'

'Go on.'

'There is a rivalry between the models, isn't there?'

'Of course, there is. It's a competitive business.'

'But you came to my rescue. Why? I don't believe that the others would have done so.'

She laughed. 'Probably not. I was happy to help you. Really I was.'

*

The show lasted a week. I began to think that modelling was an option. It was not my life ambition, not that I had one, but perhaps a mean to an end. I asked Anne about it one afternoon. We were sitting in one of those cafes with large windows and rattan seats.

'Sorry to say it Daniela, it is not easy. It is very competitive, nor is it a glamorous life. The models walk from one audition to another, from one photographer's studio to another, lugging their heavy portfolios, selling themselves, putting up with being treated like pieces of merchandise. Some of them compromise themselves to get the job. Don't think that the people who can give them a job don't try it on.'

'I see.' I didn't really. Not being easy should not deter me. 'How did you get into it?'

'I had a lucky start. One night at a discotheque a photographer approached me. He said that I had just the look that he was after for a photo shoot. He's been using me ever since. It does help that he is gay.'

I hesitated but then said, 'But both you and Herr Wagner thought I was good at it. I could try.'

'Yes, you are. Herr Wagner gave you the job instead of engaging a professional model. He took a risk. I don't think you understand. It fell into your lap without you even trying. Many would give their right arm to be here

69

modelling. You don't even realise it. On your first show you walked the catwalk in Paris. Have you any idea how prestigious this is?'

'I didn't, but I am beginning to see how lucky I was.'

At the end of the run, Anne gave me her phone number and said to get in touch when I came to London. Maybe I could fall into it in London. Maybe Anne would help. It was a thought, a possibility.

# Chapter 7

Immediately after my return from Paris, Schafferman started training me in earnest. I felt guilty as all I could think of was how to get out of this situation that I found myself in. I didn't see myself as a pelt trader. Schafferman was enjoying teaching me. He laughed more than he usually did. I didn't know how to disappoint him. There was no way I could tell him without hurting him. I kept putting it off.

He hired a teacher to come and teach me German, took me with him to auctions, to see clients and introduced me as his right-hand man. He told me that I was a natural but needed training and guiding and he was the man for the job. 'Mine assistentin,' he kept calling me with delight.

Dolly, to my surprise, seemed to accept the situation and even got involved. She sat in on all my German lessons. My tutor tried very hard to put up with her constant interruptions. She would comment that I did not need to know this or that, that no one talked like that, and as for grammar, what was the point of it.

She was too enthusiastic, too helpful and too jolly. We still spent the evenings together, but sometimes I caught her looking at me as if weighing something up. When our eyes met, she would smile or laugh and start talking fast as if to hide her thoughts. I didn't believe that Dolly had given up.

One evening, with a satisfied look on her face, she told Herr Schafferman that Herr Wagner phoned to offer me a contract modelling for him in Berlin. It included accommodation and a good salary.

Schafferman was incensed. His face was red but all he said was, 'It'll never happen.'

At that moment, I understood that Dolly felt threatened. Schafferman was taking me over. She was not in control and she didn't like it. I suspected that she had talked to Herr Wagner and instigated the offer.

'You like money. I know you do,' she said to me.

It sounded like an accusation. I didn't know how to answer.

She was staring at me. 'It's a necessity. Everyone needs money. All women like money. They want rich husbands. You do too.'

She would never understand me. She saw the world from a narrow point of view. It occurred to me that maybe she was also worried about losing her husband. And why not, after all she had married him for his money and in the simplistic way that she saw people, to her mind, all women would do the same. She probably suspected that he might be falling in love with me and I with his money. She had a lot to lose and she was not going to let it happen.

'Modelling for Herr Wagner,' she insisted to Schafferman, 'is a good opportunity for her. You are standing in her way. She should sign the contract and move to Berlin.'

I sat in the white armchair and watched them fighting over me as if I was a possession, as if I would do as I was told. But again, I wanted Dolly to win. I wanted to go to Berlin.

'She will sign the contract with Herr Wagner. I'll arrange it. it is not for you to say.'

He laughed at her.

'She doesn't need your permission,' she shouted.

'Nein. Nein. Nein. Not going to happen. I will stop it. Herr Wagner will not take her without my permission.'

She laughed. 'As if anyone asks you.'

'Laugh. Laugh as much as you like,' he shouted back. 'I own Herr Wagner. The man owes me tons of money. How do you think he buys pelts? You know nothing of mine geschaft. You just like the geld…'

'Rubbish. I don't care how he buys. What does it matter?'

I felt like being a spectator watching a farce. I wondered who was going to win this time.

'I'll explain you. He buys pelts on credit. I ask for money back. He ruined. No more pelts for Herr Wagner. No contract for Daniela.'

Shrewd, I though. I wondered what she'd do.

She stared at him. He stared back as if to say, got you.

'You are not going to get away with this. She is going to work for Herr Wagner whatever you say.'

As I listened to the arguments, the shouting, I thought that to them I was the same as the washing machine they had argued over. If Dolly didn't get her way, and I didn't go to Berlin, I would have to leave.

Schafferman locked himself in his room. He shouted and screamed that he wouldn't come out until she stopped this nonsense.

*

He had done it once before when Dolly wanted a new washing machine like the one her hairdresser had bought. He argued that the machine they had was a year old and nothing was wrong with it. Screaming and shouting he stormed to his room and slammed the door shut. Dolly went to the kitchen, got a large pot and boiled bones. I thought that she was making broth. Considering she hardly ever cooked, I thought it strange. The apartment filled with the smell of meat.

That night I had trouble sleeping. About three in the morning, I gave up and left my bed intending to get a glass of milk. I could smell the broth as soon as I opened my door. It was dark in the apartment except for the dim light that came from the kitchen. My feet on the shaggy carpet made no sound as I approached the kitchen. I could hear strange noises. It sounded like a dog sucking and grunting. I felt a little scared and holding my breath I approached with caution.

What I saw was strange, unnerving and painful to watch. Herr Schafferman was sitting at the kitchen table facing the door. He hadn't heard me. In front of him was a bowl filled with the boiled bones.  He was sucking them, teasing the marrow out, his eyes were glazed over.

I backed away and watched him from the dark corridor. I should have gone back to my room, I should have given him his rightful privacy, I don't know why I stayed and watched. All I knew was that I was seeing a man who had been through an unimaginable trauma, a man who survived the Holocaust, and here he was, losing himself in bones. I had no experience to even try to understand the mind-set of a survivor.

I did not get a glass of milk. I went back to bed and curled up pulling the duvet to my chin. The scene had left me wretched and shaken. It had been unbearable to watch. Yet I did. I wanted to understand what was buried in him that those bones could sooth. I could not ask. I could not begin to imagine the horror he had lived through.

I felt lost and lonely. Yet again I wanted Benyamin's arms around me. I wanted him to comfort me as he had done after I came back from being told off by my grandparents. I had cried in his arms. He had held me tight and said, 'Never mind darling, you have me. I'm here.' He then took me by the hand and sat me on a chair in the studio. He lit me and took photographs. 'You look beautiful when you cry,' he had said.

In my bed, I stifled my sobs. To calm down, I imagined my empty self, floating on the wind like an autumn leaf, rising higher and higher without resistance, then gently floating down, coming to rest on a bed of golden leaves. There was comfort in this floating. I started doing it after Benyamin had left me, and for some reason, it was soothing. Herr Schafferman found comfort in bones. Perhaps my floating was my bones.

Dolly's bones had worked. She bought a new washing machine.

*

This time round, I knew what Dolly was up to. After Schafferman stomped to his room, she went to the kitchen and made a racket with pots and utensils, slamming the fridge door and cursing him. The apartment filled with the smell of meat.

The following morning, I saw the evidence of Herr Schafferman's night time activity. The bowl on the table was filled with a pile of sucked clean bones. Dolly was clearing them away when he came out of his room dressed to go out and stood at the door.

He stared at Dolly and shouted, 'She will be my assisetentin! I am going to adopt her!'

He turned and left. Dolly and I were shocked. I had no wish to be adopted by Herr Schafferman.

Dolly was quieter than usual. She did not discuss the matter with me. She did not sit in on my German lesson. The chauffeur did not come to take me to the factory.

As it stood, Schafferman was preparing me to be his assistant and daughter, Dolly was plotting to get rid of me, and I? I wanted to get out of there. I decided that I would tell them that evening that I was leaving.

I didn't have to. the outcome was not determined by me. I had underestimated Dolly's cunning. That evening, when Herr Schafferman came back, we had supper. No one spoke. We moved to the living room. I could feel the tension in the heavy silence.

'Is it what you really want?' she asked.

No screaming. How odd. I think that Schafferman was surprised too.

'Ja. It is.'

'You can have her.'

He was taken aback and I was gathering the courage to tell them.

'On one condition,' she said.

'What is it?'.

'I want to take her for a holiday to Amsterdam.'

'For how long?'

'A week.'

'Then you come back and I train her?'

'Ja.'

I felt a coward. I had planned to tell Schafferman that I wasn't ready to settle down and that I wanted to travel. I didn't. I thought I would do it when we got back.

## Chapter 8

The car was packed. The chauffeur and I waited outside for Dolly. She had said, 'Pack lots of clothes. We'll be going out to restaurants and clubs. We can wear our pretty clothes. We'll have fun, eh? Good times.' I had packed my vanity case and my red suitcase. When Dolly showed up, she told the chauffeur to go and collect another one. He came back with a medium size brown leather valise and drove us to Frankfurt airport.

Dolly seemed happier than she'd been lately. We spent the afternoon shopping and later supped at the Hotel. Saying that I was tired, I went to bed early. Dolly stayed at the bar drinking.

Early morning, I rose, dressed and went down for breakfast. Dolly was not there. It wasn't unusual for her to sleep late and then take ages over her toilette. In any case, I welcomed a quiet time without her.

She still had not come down by the time I finished breakfast. I left a message at reception to say that I was going for a short walk. I didn't walk far for fear of losing my way back to the hotel. Outside was a city full of canals but no gondolas. I stopped on a bridge and looked down at the flowing water, at the wobbling reflections of the tall, narrow houses. A barge passed by scattering them into fragments. A sense of freedom seeped into me; an old friend, a familiar and comfortable one. I smiled. I really had to leave Germany and the two of them. I would tell them as soon as we got back.

I returned to the hotel and phoned Dolly's room from reception. There was no answer. I looked for her in the breakfast room, she wasn't there. I asked reception if she had come down. The receptionist gave me a strange look, then told me that Mrs Schafferman had left. She had paid the bill including three more days for me. It was my turn to give him a look of disbelief. I asked him if he was sure that we were talking about the same person. He assured me that we were.

On my way to my room, I was trying to digest or understand this turn of events. Maybe she had left me a note. Maybe there was an emergency and she had to go back. I would have to call Schafferman.

There was no note in my room. Then I saw it, the suitcase, the brown leather one. I opened it; inside were my clothes. Why had she packed more clothes for me? Were we going somewhere else and she hadn't told me? I wondered if it was meant to be a surprise. Maybe she intended to give me a few days on my own before Herr Schafferman started training me. But no, unlikely, Dolly was selfish, she didn't have it in her to be thoughtful and considerate.

I opened the suitcase. It was full of my clothes, shoved in unfolded. The message was clear. Herr Schafferman saying that he was going to adopt me had been the last straw for Dolly.

I didn't have to find a way out. I admit that it irked me that this woman, silly, stupid and simple-minded, had managed to outmanoeuvre her husband and myself. But she had made it easy for me. She had given me my freedom back.

I put on my old coat. It reminded me that I had left the fur coat behind because it was not cold enough to wear it. Dolly hadn't brought it. She did it on purpose. I was sure of that. The loss of it did upset me. It was a beautiful coat and I didn't relish living through the winters without it. I went out.

It was a cloudy spring day and there was a chill in the air. I walked about or just sat and watched the passers-by, the cars, the bicycles, drank in cafes and ate when I felt like it. Most of all I enjoyed being alone. A delicious sense of freedom took a hold of me. I felt sad for Herr Schafferman. He was special, courageous and he cared for me. He would miss me. The fur coat was a high price to pay for my freedom, but it was worth it.

*

The next day, sitting on a bench in the Vondelpark, I weighed up my options. I could fly to London or I could go there via Paris. Then I had an idea. I wanted to arrive in London with as much money as I could to keep me going until I found my way.

On my return to the hotel, I phoned Herr Wagner. I told him that since I was no longer with the Schaffermans I could come and work for him. He let me down gently. He said that he would have loved to have me, but he couldn't employ me as we both knew very well how vindictive Dolly was. She would not let Schafferman rest until he stopped supplying him on credit and call in his debt. I knew he was right. However, he said he would make enquiries and see what he could do for me.

He was as good as his word. That evening I received a

phone call from a fashion house in Geneva. They needed a house model urgently. On offer was a good salary and accommodation. They said that if it was agreeable to me, they would get me a flight. It was very agreeable to me indeed, so the next day I flew to Geneva.

I settled into the work routine. All that was required of me was to look good and to display their clothes to their best advantage. The immaculate looking women scrutinized me as I modelled for them, while the House's elegantly dressed vendeuse was skilfully doing the selling. Aloof and sophisticated, I glided and smoothly turned with my chin up as Anne had taught me. I did it automatically. My body knew the moves, it didn't need my brain. I didn't have to smile or to interact with the buyers, I was a walking mannequin. My mind though was elsewhere. Soon I would be in London, where my journey would end and my new life would begin. But first I would be crossing the border into France on foot. I had wanted to do it for a long time. I was in the right place.

I couldn't do it carrying a heavy suitcase. I was wondering what to do with it when I heard that one of the assistants was going to London. Not only did he agreed to take my red suitcase there, he also offered to leave it at a friend of his until I arrived. I bought a small holdall and packed it and my vanity case to take with me.

I was about to cross a border on foot. I had longed to do it for many years. This was something that most people took for granted. To me it was a novelty. I wanted to know what it would feel like to walk to another country. Israel is small and narrow. Every land border, and there are four of them, lead to enemy territory. The one and only way out is across the Mediterranean Sea. I was about to feel the freedom of walking from one country to another.

## Chapter 9

Next morning, I took a taxi to the busy major road that led from Switzerland to France, then hitch-hiked to the Swiss border. I got out, walked to the check point and handed my passport to the official. He looked at it, looked at me, put an exit stamp, smiled and said goodbye. I smiled back. It was so easy.

I could see the French border crossing further ahead. I walked towards it. Along the side of the road was a vast and empty space. I took a deep breath and raised my head to the warm sun. I was filled with joy.

I approached the French post. The customs officer was watching me. I smiled at him. He didn't smile back. I said bonjour and handed him my passport. He scrutinized it, turning the pages, taking his time. I was afraid that he wouldn't let me through. He called for another officer. He too scrutinized my passport. My fear grew. They looked at me suspiciously. The other officer went away.

'What is the purpose of your visit?'

'A tourist. Visiting a friend.'

A chill ran through me. Something was wrong.

'Where are you going?'

'To Paris,' I mumbled.

He raised an eyebrow. 'How are you getting there?'

I wasn't sure what was the right answer. 'Hitch-hike.'

He stared at me. 'Have you any idea how far Paris is?'

'No.'

He looked at me saying nothing. My heart sunk. I could hardly breathe.

He stamped my passport and handed it back to me.

I was relieved. My whole body sagged as it released the tension that had held it taut. I thanked him. He did not react. I walked away. Slowly the joy I had felt returned. I was exhilarated. 'I did it! I crossed a border on foot!'

I stood on the road and stuck my thumb out. A car stopped. 'Paris?' I asked.

The man looked at me baffled then nodded his head and said what I thought was a name of a place. He did not speak English. On the way, he listened to a talk show in French and I was pleased not to have to try and make conversation. By the time he dropped me, it was late afternoon.

I waved down another car. It stopped. The driver wound down the window.

'Bonjour. Paris s'il vous plait?'

'Qui. Qui.'

I put my luggage on the back seat and got in.

He was a middle-aged man wearing thick-lensed glasses.

'English?' he asked. 'I am going to Paris too.' He spoke English with a thick French accent.

I couldn't believe my luck. I was getting a ride all the way to Paris. But it was not the case.

'Paris is very far away. It is getting dark. You better stop hitch-hiking.'

'Didn't you say that you are going to Paris?'

'Well, not exactly.'

I felt worried. I wasn't sure what he meant. 'Where will you be stopping? I'll have to hitch-hike from there then.'

'I'll explain. I am driving to an airport to board a small plane carrying medical staff to Paris. It's not too far. I think that there will be room for you on the plane. There usually is.'

'That's wonderful. Thank you.'

It seemed too good to be true, and as it turned out, it was.

We arrived at a small airport. He parked and walked me to a single-story building. Inside was one big room where he said I should wait for him to come and get me.

I sat down to wait. It seemed to be taking him a very long time and I was getting anxious. A man came in and asked what I was waiting for. I told him that I was waiting to go on the doctor's plane.

'They've already taken off.'

'The doctor.' I mumbled, 'he…he was getting me a seat…'

'There was no room on the flight.'

I stared at him in disbelief. He must be mistaken. I couldn't believe that that nice man didn't have the decency to let me know and just left me waiting in vain in the middle of nowhere.

'There are no other planes,' he said.

I panicked. My feet wobbled as I stood up. I was shaken, and embarrassed about being dumped. All I could think of was that I needed to get out of there. I said, 'Merci.'

I was in the middle of nowhere and it was getting dark. I walked towards the main road feeling lost and scared. There were no cars passing. I walked for a long time then saw lights and walked towards them. The lights receded, then disappeared. There were no more lights, no cars, the silence was absolute. I must have been walking for what seemed like hours, carrying my luggage, following imaginary lights that moved away from me, and roads that led nowhere. It was getting cold and dark, I was getting tired, I started to cry. I turned into another road. I was surrounded by fields.

I heard a car. I stood in the middle of the road determined to stop it or die trying. It did stop, almost running me over. The driver rolled down his window. I approached. I was crying, I was hysterical, I tried to speak French, but had no idea what I was saying and I am sure neither did he. The poor man must have figured out that I was a stupid hitch-hiker and kept saying 'pas grave' and motioned me to get in the car. I did. I couldn't care less where he was taking me.

My school French was stored somewhere in my brain, but I couldn't find the words. I kept repeating 'Paris.'

We arrived in a town and he stopped at a train station. He pointed to it and said something in a thick accent. I stayed sitting and just looked at him through tears. I was not going to let go of my saviour. After trying to explain something to me in rapid, guttural French and my shaking my head in despair, he started the car, drove me to a pensione and handed me over to the lady behind the desk. She led me into a room, laid me on the bed, took my off my shoes and threw a blanket over me.

*

When I opened my eyes, I was in an unfamiliar room, discombobulated, not knowing where I was or how I got there. I was fully dressed and under a blanket. My body was aching, my head hurt. Then I remembered. In the mirror I looked dishevelled, my clothes were crumpled, my yesterday's make up smeared. I couldn't go to Paris looking like that. I washed, dressed and went downstairs. The kind woman from the night before gave me coffee and didn't stop talking to me, calling me 'Englishe lady'. I didn't understand what she was saying except for, 'le train'. All I said was 'Paris'. I felt shaken, disorientated and helpless. The thought of finding the way on my own, scared me. I did not move. I think she took pity on me. She shrugged her shoulders, smile kindly, took me by the hand and led me to the train station. I was happy to be manhandled. I didn't let go of her until she had put me on the train. She smiled and said, 'Bon chance Englishe lady.' I nodded my head, smiled and said 'merci beaucoup' repeatedly.

*

Gare Saint-Lazare was busy and noisy. Outside it was mayhem, people rushing, talking, laughing, cars hooting impatiently. The spring sun was shining and somewhere a pigeon was cooing. In my head I was singing, '*I love Paris in the springtime*'. I felt that I should have a top hat and cane and tap dance along the pavement. The smells of garlic and olive oil, the sweetness of cakes and pastries and of freshly baked bread made me feel hungry.

The Parisians were not going to take me by the hand and lead me anywhere. I asked for directions to the metro. I could understand the clearer spoken French of the Parisians. At the metro all I had to do was to press the button for my destination on the map and my route was lit up. I had never been in an underground train before, I wondered who could have possibly thought of putting trains in tunnels, maybe that person got the idea from the moles in his garden that drove him mad.

I booked into a small hotel near the Place de l'Opéra and set out to enjoy Paris. Spring brought hope and lightness to my heart, I felt ready and eager to get to London. But I was not going to leave Paris without shopping. The only way for me to buy the latest fashion, had been through the air stewardesses I had become friendly with when I was working at the airport. The thrill of being able to go to boutiques and choose for myself was too tempting. I could have filled another suitcase with beautiful clothes, but restricted myself. And even if I didn't buy many, the pleasure of looking, touching, trying on, was a new sensation.

In the garden of the Musee Rodin, the trees were adorned with fresh new leaves bathed in sunlight. The statues looked at home nestling in the greenery. I sat on a bench and listened to the birds chirping, happy that spring had come. I watched a group of people doing Tai-chi; moving in slow motion, elegantly, weightlessly. The green enclave was in the middle of the bustling city yet somehow, removed from it, filled with peace and quiet, not affected by time.

Inside I looked at The Gates of Hell. It was monumental. I had read Dante's Inferno and remembered that in the canto, above the gate it was written: *"Abandon hope all ye who enter here."* I looked at it for quite a while. I could have sat in front of it for hours looking at all the figures. I was thoughtful when I left. It had left an impression; it had stirred something in me. I would remember it on the day when I, would abandon all hope.

*

However much I was enjoying Paris; it was time to leave. I hadn't seen the Mona Lisa, there were always big queues, but she was not going anywhere. I would surely come back one day and let her eyes follow me.

# CHAPTER 10

I had no plan in mind when I reached Le Havre. I had no ticket either. There were many ships, some were surely bound for England, but I had no idea which ones. A group of men in uniform were standing nearby chatting in French. I approached and asked them which boat was going to England.

'Do you have a ticket?'

'No ticket. Where can I buy one, please?'

They looked at me and laughed. I was sure that I had managed those simple sentences in French perfectly well. Then one of them said something. They roared with laughter slapping their hands on their thighs.

I understood only two words, "passage clandestin". It was enough. They were making fun of me. I couldn't think of a cutting thing to say in French so I gave them a haughty look and turned to go.

They fell silent. One of them followed and caught up with me. 'Pardonnez-moi. Je suis désolé. S'il vous plait, laissez-moi vous aider. S'il vous plait.'

I looked at him. His apologies seemed genuine enough so I let him help me.

*

I climbed up to the deck and stood in the sunshine. It was my first time on a ship. Soon it coughed, shuddered and started moving. France receded. I was going to England; the country where people were civilised, polite, reserved, formed queues and carried umbrellas; and of course, they all spoke English. To be young and in London was not a dream anymore. I was at the beginning of a life, a life I had dreamt and wished for. It was not that I knew what to expect or what would unfold, all I knew was that I wanted to be there. I stayed on deck for quite a while. The wind was whipping my hair around. I tied it back with an elastic band trying to keep my balance. The smell of the sea was a powerful reminder of a long-forgotten smell that used to be on my doorstep, a place that was getting farther and farther away. But this smell was stronger and more pungent than the Mediterranean Sea.

Below deck, I sat by a window, drank my coffee and tried to read a book. The journey would take five and a half hours. I was too impatient. I couldn't concentrate on reading. I went up again, but this time I walked towards the prow of the ship. I swayed and stumbled as I tried to keep my balance and resist the strong wind that was trying to push me back. I reached the railing and held fast. I was alone. I looked down at the choppy sea, it was rushing backwards along the boat crowned with white foam. It heaved and sunk and rocked the deck and me with it.

He came and stood next to me. He was not so close as to invade my space or to make me feel uncomfortable. I ignored him. I felt the fine drops in the air on my face. He said hello. We fell into a sparse and polite conversation. We talked loudly in order to be heard above the roar of the sea.

I listened to his voice first, and only later did I look at him. I was aware that he was taller than me, he spoke English with an accent that I did not recognise, a pleasant voice.Clouds were gathering. I looked up. There was a definite line up there; behind us, sunny, ahead, we were sailing into greyness.

'The sun is not coming with us,' I said sounding sad.

'Welcome to England,' he smiled. 'Would you like to have a coffee?'

I looked at him. He had a plain, bland sort of face. I nodded my head. It would pass the time I thought. Over a coffee Verner told me that he was Swiss and worked and lived in London. That was all I found about him because I did most of the talking. I didn't usually talk about myself, or open up to people easily, but there I was, telling a stranger about my journey and my wish to live in England. He listened attentively.

Over another cup of coffee, Verner asked where I was staying in London. In response, I looked at him and chuckled. He looked puzzled.

'I have no idea,' I said. 'I haven't thought that far. There are people I intend to call. Maybe I could stay with them for a little while.'

'You don't know London. No one is meeting you, but you intend to get there and find your way?'

'Yes, it's a city like any other city.'

He laughed. I was offended. He must think me stupid.

'Do you realise that London is a large city, which you don't know, much bigger and more sprawling than Paris. It is courageous of you, but you will not be safe and you'll be lost.'

I didn't need a lecture; I was capable and resourceful. 'Oh well, I'll find a hotel for tonight, that can't be difficult.

There are always hotels near stations.'

'So, you'll take the train to London. Then what? You'll walk around looking for a hotel carrying your luggage? How would you know what sort of a hotel it is? There are prowlers who prey on new comers. Believe me, it is not safe.'

He was right of course, but I was not going to admit it. What choice did I have? 'I'll find somewhere. I'll manage.'

He looked hesitant before he spoke, 'Look, I have a flat, I have a spare room and if you feel that you can trust me, you can stay until you sort out a place to go to. I work during the day and go home to Switzerland at the weekend.'

I looked into his eyes. They seemed honest and unthreatening. I decided that I did trust him. It was a gut feeling rather than reasoning. It was all I had to go by. Perhaps, I thought, one man was less dangerous than a whole unknown city.

'Thank you. It is very kind of you. I appreciate it. I can even say that you are a godsend.' I smiled.

*

It was grey and drizzly. I followed a man I didn't know, to I don't know where, on a train, in a taxi, into an apartment block, up dim-lit stairs and through a door into a stranger's home. Verner carried my holdall into a bedroom. I followed. He showed me where everything was, said goodnight, sleep well and left me to it.

In the morning I found a note with information by the kettle. Apparently, I was in an area called Chalk Farm, I was to feel free to use the phone and he would be back late. There was also a set of keys and a book called *AtoZ* to help me find my way. A book! That should have told me how big London was.

I couldn't wait to meet London. I went out intending to find a café or a bar, drink and have a croissant. I walked along a road with terraced houses painted white. Their front gardens were burgeoning with flowers. It didn't look like Paris and I didn't see any shops or cafes. I asked a passer-by. She told me to turn around and follow the main road. 'Not far,' she said and pointed me in the right direction. I reached a canal. I stood and watched the ducks for a while. There were people in the house boats. Someone was watering their pot plants. I could see the shops across the bridge. They looked run down and there were no cafes or bars to sit in.

After asking, I found the bus station and took a ride to the West End. The bus drove through Camden Town, then Kentish town and Tottenham Court Road, it all looked run down and uninviting, but Regent Street looked grand. I got off and walked to Piccadilly Circus and happily got lost in Soho. Later, I tried to find my way to collect my red suitcase. Getting there was not simple. There were buses but it was not easy to find where they were going or which direction to take. Then there was the underground but it was not as simple as the metro, no maps that lit up to indicate the routes.

Verner was in London for two days. He took me out to an Italian restaurant in Belsize Park, and told me that he had work to do in Switzerland and would be away for a few weeks. He said I could stay in his flat.

\*

It took a few phone calls to track down an acquaintance of mine called Ella. Both of us had frequented Mandy's club in Tel Aviv. Everyone who was anyone went there. It had a bar, a Chinese restaurant and a disco.

Number 20 Abbey Road was the address she gave me. 'The Abbey Road?' I asked in amazement. It was, and it was very near The Zebra Crossing in the famous Beatles picture. The flat was on the third floor. Ella opened the door. She looked as beautiful as ever, dark almond eyes, black curly hair, olive skin, petit and perfectly formed. It was good to see a familiar face.

She greeted me warmly and then introduced me to a man with salt and pepper longish hair, who seemed to be calling the shots. He wore a fitted flowery shirt with its first few buttons undone, revealing a chunky gold chain with a medallion attached, and an expensive watch on his wrist. He was not subtle, but loud and ostentatious.

More people arrived and Ella said that we would be going out later. I settled myself into an armchair and watched people coming and going. I listened to them chatting, laughing and cracking jokes. They were all Israelis and spoke Hebrew. They were rowdy, their jokes a little vulgar. A young woman sitting at the table caught my eye. She was leaning on her arms. Her skin was smooth and very pale, her elongated face with slightly slanting brown eyes, rested on a long neck. The low-cut top showed a pronounced cleavage. She looked surreal and made me think of Modigliani's paintings. She never said a word. Later, the man with salt and pepper hair nodded to her and she went to him. She was the woman in tow, the flower in his buttonhole.

*

We were on the move. I squeezed into the back of a yellow E-type Jaguar. The man with salt and pepper hair was driving fast, overtaking and swerving like a maniac. From my crumpled position, half sitting half lying in the back,

I watched the streetlights, houses and trees speeding by.

We went to a restaurant, then to a venue called The Speakeasy. It was packed, dark, filled with smoke and music. Someone put a drink in my hand. The place was buzzing, people laughing, smiling and enjoying themselves. Not very different to Mandy's, only there I knew many people to talk to. The band came on stage. It was better than I had ever imagined. The solid sound, the energy, the power of it, all poured into me. I was still elated when we went to a discotheque called La Valbonne. I was on the dance floor till almost dawn. I didn't need a partner to dance rock and roll with, I didn't have to wait for a man to invite me to dance with him. Every so often someone would dance with me. I liked it that there was no touching, no intimacy, just the joy of dance.

This happened every night. I tagged along with Ella's crowd. I was not expecting interesting conversations with them. Their girlfriends came and went, all that was required of them was to be pretty and obedient. None of the men tried it on with me, I think they knew that I was not interested, or as Chris had said in Switzerland, I looked unapproachable. But I got to know the night life, to dance, to hear live bands and eat in good restaurants. I was in London, I felt the excitement, the raw energy and the new freedom of the youth, it was intoxicating. The man with salt and pepper hair and his friends paid for everything and tipped generously. Their money made them welcome everywhere we went. They drove flashy cars, gambled at the casinos and carried wads of cash, but they didn't seem to work.

*

The accident happened one night when I was out with Ella's friends in the Marquee. She pulled me away saying that we were going somewhere else. I wished that I hadn't gone with her. I squeezed into the back of a sport Alfa Romeo. I thought that we were going out to another night spot. James drove us to his flat where we reclined on large carpet cushions, had a joint and listened to loud music. Ella and James started kissing.

I felt embarrassed, uncomfortable and pissed off. She used me; she didn't want to go with him on her own, she had put me in an awkward situation. I worried that they would disappear into the bedroom and I would be left alone not knowing what to do. I didn't know where I was or how to get back late at night. There was nothing I could do. I closed my eyes, lay back and listened to the music, at least it drowned their kissing noises. I was going to tell her off, but I never got a chance to do so.

Near dawn I was again in the back of the car. James was driving too fast for comfort, but at this time of the morning, the roads were fairly empty. The collision was loud, the car spun for what seemed for ever, finally hitting a brick wall and coming to a stop. Ella staggered out in shock with blood on her forehead. I found myself on the back seat, curled up in a ball with my arms covering my head and face. I crawled out and felt a sharp pain in my chest. I looked at James, he was slumped on the steering wheel, his eyes were closed and his face bloody. The driver of the other car was standing next to his in a daze. Both cars were crumpled and bashed. The ambulance and the police arrived within minutes. The three of us were taken to St Mary's hospital, James on a stretcher. Ella had a big scratch on her forehead. It was bandaged. I was told that I had cracked ribs, that they would heal by themselves, not to laugh or cough because it would hurt. James was seriously injured.

Before we left the hospital, a policeman interviewed each of us separately. They wanted us to verify that James had not stopped at the Give Way sign coming from a side road into Abbey Road. The truth was that he had not stopped, but I said that I couldn't see from my lying down position. Ella told me later that she had told the police that she thought he did but was not sure. I thought that she had lied to help James.

*

Maybe it was the accident that sobered me up, reminded me that it was all very well to dance the nights away, but I needed to get on, find somewhere to stay and a way of earning. I reminded myself that I was not on holiday.

I made phone calls to the English people whom I had met in Tel-Aviv. They had said to call them when I got to London and that they would love to see me. I met them for tea or a drink in a pub. I soon realised that they had meant what they had said, nothing more. They did not offer to help me settle down, find work or a place to stay. They shared rented flats and even shared rooms. I checked up hotels only to find that even the cheap ones were expensive. The one person I hadn't phoned was Anne. I didn't feel that I knew her well enough to ask for help. I felt that it would be an imposition. She had already told me that getting modelling work in London was extremely difficult and competitive.

## CHAPTER 11

I had been ringing Guillaume, a friend of Benyamin's, for days, but there was no answer. I was beginning to think that he had moved away. One day, I was just about to put down the phone when there he was, a familiar voice, happy to hear from me. They'd been away, he said and invited me to have supper the next day. They lived in Swiss Cottage. I descended the stairs to the basement. The sun was shining but it was dark in the flat. I thought it a strange thing to live underground. A basement's function was to store things and good bottles of wine, or to be used as a bunker when bombs were falling.

Guillaume's girlfriend was a ballet dancer. They were interesting people and I enjoyed their company. During the evening, they told me that shortly, they would be going away to work in Paris for two months and offered me the basement for the duration. So despite the fact that it was dark and sunless, I said yes please.

*

I moved in and just like I had done at Verners', I left my clothes in the red suitcase. The flat was cosy, full of old furniture, rugs and cushions. In the living room was

Guillaume's work desk, and there I saw his drawings, skilfully done and full of imagination.

In the kitchen, under the curtained counter, I found large sacks. They were full of used ballet shoes. She must have kept all the ones she had ever danced in. I had gone to contemporary dance classes in Tel-Aviv, not on a regular basis, not in view of becoming a professional dancer, only because I enjoyed them. There, we wore jazz shoes. I sat on the floor and put a pair of her shoes on. It fitted. I tried to stand *en pointe* but I wobbled so much that I nearly fell to the floor. It wasn't as easy as it looked. I tried again, this time holding on to the door handle. I managed to stand for a short while, then my toes began to hurt. Doing a pirouette was out of the question.

*

Benyamin had given me the phone number of Jerry, a friend with whom he had studied photography in London. I thought that he might be able to give me work or introductions and advice. Maybe I could model a little just to make money until I found my way, until I could work out what to do.

I painted my face skilfully in the way I had learned during the Paris fashion show, only the makeup was different. I had bought it from Biba, dark purple eyeshadow and dark lipstick. I wore a minidress and my red shoes. Armed with the photographs that Benyamin had taken of me, I went to his studio in Covent Garden. A feeling of recognition mixed with pain came over me. The coloured rolls of the backdrops, the silver umbrella, the lighting, the Hasselblad on a tripod, all so familiar. On a table was a Rolleiflex and a Leica camera, and on the floor a pile of

*Vogue, Harpers Bazar* and *Elle* magazines.

We stood talking in his studio. I was offended that he didn't offer me a seat. He was polite but made me feel that he was too busy to give me his time. We had a short chat about Benyamin and then I gathered my courage and asked him about modelling work. I said that I had photographs to show him. He took his time looking.

'Benyamin is good. He always was. I am impressed.' He paused. 'You photograph well.'

He had looked at Benyamin's work, not at my potential. I waited. This was the moment. But no, he handed them back.

'What do you think?' I didn't want to sound desperate but I had to ask. 'Could I get modelling work?'

He rubbed his chin and looked at me intently as he said, 'I'll be honest with you… Not easy.'

He was not going to help or photograph me himself. It would have been easy for him to give me some contacts to follow. How unkind and unhelpful.

'Bad idea? It was just a thought,' I said. 'Anyway, I think it's time for me to go and let you get on with your work.' I didn't care if I sounded rude.

'I have something for you.' He fetched a letter. 'Benyamin sent it, he thought I might be seeing you.'

I had failed. I felt embarrassed for asking. I took the letter. We said good bye and I left.

On the way back to the flat, I tried not to raise my hopes. But by the time I arrived I was already dreaming that Benyamin had written asking me to join him. He would meet me at the airport in New York, He would take me home with him. What other reason did he have to write to me?

\*

I stood in the living room. My hands shook as I opened the letter. It was long. I started crying after the first sentence. *My dearest love. I am alone in the house; it is late at night. This is the first time that I've cried in years. I'm saying only one word over and over – Daniela. How could I had left you after bringing you up my little one? My dearest. I am so very tired.*

I stopped reading. The letter dropped from my hand. I sat on the sofa and tried to calm down. I picked up the letter. I skimmed through the paragraphs he wrote about the people we knew that he met in New York and what they were up to. About the guy who had introduced us who was visiting him and had dragged him out to listen to excellent jazz musicians. He had not done that since he arrived in New York. All he had done was work.

I read on. *I've learned everything I could from the great photographer I am assisting. Now the work is just routine. I could strike out on my own, but to establish myself here will take years, hard work and luck. Not only that I am not prepared to stay here struggling, even a few more weeks would be hard for me. I don't regret my time here. I learned a lot about photography and about life. But I value my life too much to want to stay. I miss all that we took for granted; sun, air and the sea. From here they feel like a dream. This is a city of concrete, smoke and disturbed people. this is not a place for a little Hush Puppy.*

I saw us in the house playing at being little Hush Puppy dogs, running around chasing each other, being playful. I winced.

*I will soon be leaving for Israel. I intend to stay there for a short while, refresh, get healthy and be able to think clearly and to decide where to go next. I will see my puppy and take you for walks. This time I shall not be afraid.*

*Thank you for the time that we had lived together, that now I am able to see how wonderful it was, and even though I did know it at the time, I truly know it now.*

*Write to me. tell me how you are enjoying the wonderful city of London.*

*Yours Benyamin.*


I felt sick to my stomach. I didn't know what to make of it. He talked of me as if I was in his past and at the same time seeing me in Tel-Aviv even though I was not there. He was not asking me to come and meet him. He was not asking me to wait for him.

Pressure was building behind my eyes and the lump rose to my throat again. I braced myself and tried to harden my heart unsuccessfully. I had lost him. I lost all that was us, all the future we could have had, we should have had.

I closed my eyes. A flood of memories raced through my mind accompanied with waves of emotions. There, was that sunny day when he had taken pictures of me lying in a field of ripe wheat. I see us walking on the sea shore, the sun is setting, we are holding hands. I could smell him, the Ambre Solaire sunscreen I used to rub on his body when we lay on the beach getting tanned, the Old Spice aftershave he used. But most of all I remembered the times we sat together looking at fashion magazines, not at the clothes, but the photographs. I learned to see them through his eyes; how they were lit, the angle, the composition and the quality of the prints.

He had taken me to movies by Fellini and Truffaut. I remembered going to see the film Cries and Whispers. People upped and left during the screening, but we stayed right till the end and we loved it. He gave me books to read, always in English, and took me to lectures at the university. Yes, he had been bringing me up. He said that I was a bud that would turn into a beautiful flower. He was a few years older than me, he had studied and travelled abroad: I looked up to him.

Those memories were replaced with painful ones. There had been those two weeks when he had been getting ready for his travel, making arrangements, printing photographs for his portfolio, packing. He was excited. I was holding on, trying not to collapse. I was feeling like a wind-up doll going through the motions; I went to work, I came back, I had even helped him pack. Dead and empty inside, I watched life going on from afar, letting nothing penetrate my protective shell. Even when he held me to him, which he did often, I felt alone. There was a distance between us. The closeness had gone. Not that he felt it: his mind was on his preparations and probably on his dreams. Sometimes, I wished that the end would come quickly, that it would happen and he would be gone, that this situation would come to an end.

We said goodbye in the house. He pulled me to him, his breath warm on my ear as he said, 'I love you.' The words chilled me. What use were they? I stood at the front door and watched him get into the taxi. It drove off. He turned to look at me out of the car's rear window. The taxi turned the corner.

I went inside and stood in the empty studio. It was just an empty room. In the bedroom the wardrobe doors were open. Next to my clothes was a big gap where his had hung. In the living room, I sat in the armchair where many times I had sat on his lap. All the pain and the hurt I'd managed to keep at bay came forth. My sobs had echoed in the empty room.

*

His letter slipped from my hand. If only memories were like undeveloped rolls of film: once exposed to light, they fade, they vanish. I staggered to the bedroom. On the bed, the tears came, hot and in torrents. They were tears of pain, tears of loss, tears of loneliness and tears full of sorrow. I stayed in bed for two days. I was not ill but I felt cold and shivery. I didn't want to get up. I was lonely and scared. I didn't see how to find a life in London. The city seemed impenetrable to me.

*

On the third day, I forced myself to get up. I looked at myself in the mirror and did not like what I saw. My hair was dishevelled, my face streaked with old makeup, and my eyes puffed and red. I had to pull myself together. Wallowing in my pain was not going to get me anywhere, I couldn't afford to do it. I had to shake it off. I got up, dressed, made up my face and went out. I wanted to see people, to hear voices, music, to dance, to forget.

It had rained, orange light glittered on the road and the air felt damp. I passed a red phone box. I wanted to call my mother. I got all my coins out and started dialling. I stopped. What was I going to say to her? That I was doing badly? That I was unhappy? I gathered the coins and put them back in my purse.

Before I rang the bell of the flat in Abbey Road, I composed myself and forced a smile. Ella opened the door. She smiled sweetly. 'Hi, good to see you. where have you been?'

I followed her in. It was like any other night there. The crowd greeted me with smiles, said hello and continued chatting, laughing, smoking. The Modigliani woman was sitting at the table, she turned her head to look at me then looked away. There was a comfort in this strange normality. No one there would have believed that I had spent days in bed feeling morose and still did.

*

Sometimes help comes unexpectedly. Meeting Zack did just that. He was the brother of the man with salt and pepper hair. He looked like an accountant, or a teacher. He had dark skin, wore glasses and sober clothes. Once we started talking, I found that he was intelligent, interesting and nothing like his brother. He suggested that we go to the pub for a drink.

There, Zack told me that after he had finished high school, he was called up to do his military service. He was intending to go to university when he was released from the army, but the war left him shell-shocked.

'My tank was hit,' he said. 'I was the only survivor.'

We were silent for a while.

'Where you injured?'

'Yes. Badly.'

We sat through another silence. I knew he didn't want to talk about it. Those who'd been through the war never did.

'After the war,' he said, 'I changed. I could not go back to civilian life. Normality seemed unreal. It's hard to explain.'

'I understand.' I did. We had fought in the same war. I was not front line like he was, but I had seen the burning tanks, the charred bodies covered in flies, the rotting smell that I would never forget.

'I had to get out of the country, to be somewhere else, to travel, to breathe. So, I went traveling.'

He told me that he had intended to go back and continue his studies. But in London he had met a girl, fallen in love and stayed. They had separated. 'But by then I loved living in London and decided to make a go of it.'

I told him a little about my travels in Europe. He was easy to talk to, a good listener and I found myself telling him about my worries.

'I don't seem to meet anyone, to make connections. I need to find work. Find a place to live. I just don't know how. I don't know where to start.'

All around us people were loud, downing their drinks as fast as they could before the bell rung.

'Yes, I know, it is not easy but it could be done. Don't be too hard on yourself. Give it time. You will meet people.' He paused. 'Where are you staying now?'

'A friend lent me his place while he is away. He'll be back soon.'

'Then what?'

'I don't know. I can go to an hotel, but my money won't last long.'

He cleaned his glasses, drank his beer, then looked at me and said, 'I have a café; you can help me. It's probably not what you hoped for, but it is something.'

I wasn't expecting that. Did I want to make sandwiches? Not really. But it was the only option I had and maybe something else would turn up. I said I would.

\*

His café was in a side street near Bakerloo underground station. I made sandwiches, served customers and kept the counter and the tables clean. They were mainly office workers. Many were regulars who chatted to Zack and me over a sandwich and a cup of tea. He was amiable and his clients liked him.

I did too. He was comfortable to be with, and when there were no customers, we sat at a table with a cup of tea and talked.

Soon Guillaume and his girlfriend would be coming back. I wasn't earning enough, even with the generous tips to rent a room. This time, I was heading for a cheap hotel. Zack asked me what was wrong. Maybe I looked worried, maybe he noticed my silences, or that I spent my lunch breaks looking through the ads in the newspapers that customers had left behind. I told him. He said that I could stay with him until we sorted something out.

It was not ideal. He lived in a bedsit containing one large room, a kitchenette hidden behind a curtain and a small bathroom. I slept on a mattress on the floor. He had offered me his pull-down bed, but I felt that it was not fair to take his bed as well as his privacy.

Some evenings we went to the pub, or he went out to meet friends. There were those times when he cooked and we stayed up talking. He was a thinking man, observant and patient. I liked it that he read books and we could spend an evening reading. I asked him why he liked living in England

'It's a moderate country. The British are well-mannered and polite. They are reserved, not easy to make friends with. But on the other hand, they live and let live.'

'That sounds good to me. Except that in order to live here I need to meet them somehow. I didn't come here to live with Israelis.'

'You will, I'm sure of it. But most people stick to their

own kind, all immigrants do.'

'You don't.'

'Be patient. You never know what life will bring, what opportunity it will put your way.'

He sounded optimistic; I was not.

Because I felt that I should leave him time to himself, some nights I carried on going out with Ella and her friends.

One evening when I was just about to go out, he said, 'Look Daniela, it isn't my business what you do. My brother is a no-good criminal. I'd stay away from that crowd if I were you.'

It was not as if I had not suspected it. There was no point in asking him what exactly his brother did. I knew he wouldn't tell me and perhaps it was best that I didn't know.

'Well Zack, when I find other crowds, I will. But for now, I love dancing.'

*

I knew that I couldn't impose on him for long, but then one day he said that he might have a solution to my situation and that he was looking into it. My hopes were raised. Maybe he would come up with something interesting for me to do. Maybe it would pay enough for me to rent a flat, even though I would have to share it, all I wanted was a room with my own door.

# Chapter 12

Zack's solution did not appeal to me. He talked about a sweet old lady who was looking for a companion. That word conjured up images from Victorian novels, of ladies traveling with big trunks and hat boxes. She was a widow of an army colonel who served in the British Army in India. She was a relative of a friend and he visited her every so often because he thought she was lonely.

I hesitated. I couldn't see myself as an obedient and subordinate person. It was not in my nature. During my National Service, I frequently got into trouble. I was often punished for arguing with my commanding officer who would say, 'Don't answer back! Do as you are told!', and confine me to barracks.

'The job comes with accommodation. Not much money, but a place to live and it's central.'

Zack must have noticed my hesitation. 'Have a trial period. I think it could work out for you. She really is sweet and kind. Give it a go.'

I felt miserable. Guillaume would be back soon and I would have to leave the basement. I had no choice but to take it.

*

We went to see her. She lived in Arlington House in St James's. A uniformed doorman opened the main glass door for us, another phoned to let her know that we had arrived. Calling us Sir and Madam he said that we could go up to see her. A man in livery took us up in the lift. I had not expected such a place, I had presumed that she lived in a house.

Mrs Birkin was ninety-six years old. She was tall and thin with sharp and pointed facial features. Her white hair was gathered into a chignon at her nape. We sat in her living room and they talked about the weather. Then she offered us tea and disappeared in the kitchen.

'What do you think?' Zack whispered.

'I don't know. What will I have to do? What sort of hours? Would she expect me to be available all day?'

'Wait to hear what she has to say. I better go and help her.'

I got up and looked around. The curtains were made with heavy brocade, and one of the windows overlooked Green Park. The Victorian furniture was highly polished. There were no books. In a corner was a pile of cardboard boxes. I felt trapped.

They came back. Zack was carrying a tray with a China tea service. We sat down.

Mrs Birkin looked at me with her beady eyes. 'Have you worked as a companion before?'

'No, I haven't.'

'Where are you from?'

'I'm from Israel.'

'Have you been here long?'

'Only a few months.'

'Zack said that you are a good and conscientious worker. I trust his judgement. Did he tell you that there is accommodation for the servants in the building?'

I didn't like her implying that I would be her servant. 'Yes, he did.'

'Would you be kind enough to pour the tea Zack?'

She looked at me long and hard. It made me feel uncomfortable. Any minute she would ask me to hold my hands out for inspection.

'Your job will be to come in the morning, not too early, and make tea. Help me in and out of the bath. Accompany me when I want to go out and help me go through those boxes.' She pointed at them. 'Do you have any questions?'

'I would like to know the hours. Would I have time off?'

Zack handed her a pretty cup and saucer.

'After lunch, at mid-day, you'll be free until four o'clock. Tea is at five and you can leave at six o'clock. You'll have Sunday off. I think that is generous.'

Not for what you pay I thought. I took my tea and sipped from the delicate China cup.

'Would you like to see the accommodation?' she asked.

'Yes please.'

She phoned the porter and asked him to come up and show it to me. I followed him through dark corridors to a flat at the back of the building on the same floor. It had a small entrance hall, a bathroom and a bedroom where high up on the wall was a small window. It was the flat that decided me. Maybe I would be able to manage Mrs Birkin, she seemed old and frail and harmless. I would be living in the centre of town with quite a bit of free time.

I found out later that the window was set up high in order to prevent the servants looking out on the gentry strolling in the garden.

*

Mrs. Birkin and I settled into a routine. In the morning, I let myself in, helped her dress and made tea and toast for breakfast. She was very fussy about tea. I had to let the tap run until the water was cold, boil the kettle, fill the tea pot with hot water to warm it up, empty the tea pot, put in the right amount of tea, pour in hot water and let it brew.

Groceries were delivered from Harrods once a week. A cleaner came in twice a week and a woman brought Mrs Birkin cooked suppers which she ate on her own.

After breakfast, Mrs. Birkin would go through one of the many boxes. They were full of papers, letters, documents and photographs. The content of the boxes encapsulated her life. I was there to listen, to be a witness to the life she had had.

Holding a photograph, she would look dreamy or smile. They were mostly small, black and white or sepia. She used a magnifying glass.

'We had a wonderful life. This is a tea party I gave in my garden.' She gave me the photograph to look at. 'The gardeners looked after it very well.'

In the picture she was wearing a long white cotton dress, standing in a garden full of roses. In the background of some of them, I saw servants and maids in uniforms who must have done everything for her and pandered to her every whim.

'Did you have a lot of servants?' I asked.

'Oh certainly. The wogs were very good. We trained them well. We, the British Empire brought them civilization.'

She was patronising, pompous, talking as if India did not have its own history, its own civilised ways and centuries of culture. I remembered reading Kahlil Gibran, looking at Indian paintings, so very colourful, and there she was dismissing it all. I thought of people I had known who went on a trail to India. They were looking for something that was missing from their lives, looking for spirituality. I looked at her and thought, how the table had turned. They would not find the India that she had left behind.

'What about their own culture?' I asked and immediately regretted it.

She looked at me as if I was mad or stupid. 'What culture? They were backwards before we came. We brought progress, refinement, we taught them to better themselves. They emulated us you know. I'm sure they appreciated it.'

She thought herself superior. But then she belonged to a bygone era and there wasn't much point in telling her how I saw her snobbism and racism, her belief in that cloak of lies, her justifications for the way she had lived. I said no more about it. It was for the best. I knew that she was not able to see it any other way and if she did, her belief in the benevolence of the British Empire that she was so proud of and held so dear, would crumble.

'Look at that one. My husband. Doesn't he look splendid in his uniform? It was taken on the day that we entertained the maharaja.'

He did look splendid in his regal dress and bejewelled turban.

Another box, another morning, I looked at Mr Birkin, wearing khaki, standing with one foot on a dead tiger, looking triumphant.

'My husband shot it. We had the head stuffed. My husband was a very good shot.'

I looked at the beautiful tiger. Its eyes were open and looking at me. He was shot for sport. I felt sorry for the tiger.

History classes had taught us events and dates, but not

what life was really like for the British or their subjects. I would have liked to know how the Indian people felt about it all at the time. But that was a question that Mrs Birkin could not have answered.

*

After five o'clock tea I helped her in and out of the bath tub. She would put drops of almond oil in the water. She said that it was good for the skin. Her body was sagging, her skin had lost its elasticity and sheen. I had never seen a body that resembled a skeleton. I thought that I would like to die young, before I looked old and ugly.

She didn't treat me badly, at least not to start with. Some days her mind was clear and sharp, at others she was muddled and irritating. One afternoon, during tea, Mrs Birkin was in a particularly good mood.

'You are a good girl. I have a present for you.'

Again, the patronising tone of voice. She took me to her bedroom and gave me a black kimono.

'Try it on.'

It was silk. It was embroidered, cranes at the back, and small birds at the front.

'It suits you. Look in the mirror.'

I did. I could not imagine why she had given it to me. It was beautiful.

'Fits you perfectly. I was your size once, a long time ago.'

I wore it in my flat. It felt soft and luxurious on my skin. I was pleased to have it, though I couldn't understand her sudden generosity. Most times she was friendly but strict and demanding. There were the occasional incidents, which occurred on her bad days. For instance, when tea was late by five minutes or her bath was not quite the right temperature, she would grumble at me, tell me off. Even though it annoyed me, I let it pass. She was an old lady, set in her ways, a relic of other times when things were done differently and I tried to make allowances. I put up with it because of the flat. It was a luxury to close the door and have time to myself. My clothes hung in the wardrobe and filled the chest of drawers. My toilette was in the bathroom and the empty red leather suitcase on top of the wardrobe.

I got in touch with Anne. We met up some evenings, had a meal or went out for a drink. It occurred to me that she was the only English friend I had. But I still couldn't bring myself to ask her about modelling jobs.

What turned out to be the highlight of my life and what gave me most pleasure was going to dance classes in Covent Garden. I had found the Dance Centre by chance one day. Inside, through the glass windows, I watched the dancers. I bought leotards, leggings, jazz shoes, and went to contemporary dance classes. It was liberating.

*

Zack came to visit every so often, and sometimes Mrs Birkin took us to have an afternoon tea at the Ritz. It felt like walking into the past, just like during our walks in Jermyn Street that felt like a step back in time.

Mrs. Birkin walked at a snail's pace, she held a handsome walking stick and stopped frequently to catch her breath. I looked at the buildings, the wooden shop fronts, the vitrine displays, the gentlemen's shops that sold traditional clothes. I was bored with the tedium of it and so I escaped into fantasy world. I imagined myself wearing crinoline made with beautiful fabrics and decorated with lace and trimmings, a pretty hat, my hair in ringlets, gliding along the street twirling a parasol.

The daily routine too was very tedious. I found her slowness of movement, of getting anything done frustrating. At her pace, she would never go through all those boxes in her life time. I did not know what it was like to be old, I didn't understand that the aim of sorting the contents was to reminisce, relive and share it with her companion, even though, in her world, a paid companion was not an equal.

It was hard enough for me to take it whenever she made snide and unpleasant comments. I knew people did that when they were in a bad mood. But one day Mrs Birkin went too far. On that particular morning I was fetching a box for her to look through. It was a very old cardboard box and no sooner I lifted it that the bottom fell open and the contents scattered.

'Look what you've done,' she shouted. 'Clumsy girl. Put it all back and in future be more careful.'

I swallowed hard and did not retort. I gathered the contents silently. I was fuming. I felt insulted.

'How many times have I told you to pay attention to what you are doing? You'd better pull up your socks or…'

I half listened to her stories and looked at the pictures with disinterest, counting the minutes till I could get out.

*

After lunch, I went to my flat and grabbed my handbag. I was meeting Anne at St James's Park. I walked there filled with anger. I didn't like the way that Mrs Birkin had told me off, particularly without good cause. On the way, my mind was filled with what I wanted to say to her. 'How dare you speak to me as if I was your servant. Not that you should talk like that to a servant, or anyone.' It must have been how she had treated her servants in India, so much for bringing civilisation to them. 'This is not India and you have no right to treat me in that way. Calling me a clumsy girl!' I couldn't stay there for much longer.

Anne was sitting on a bench by the pond bathed in the late summer sun. With difficulty I shook off my angry thoughts. I asked her about the job in Rome.

'Oh, just the usual. Work, hotel, sleep. Still, I can't complain. I want to save as much money as I can before starting university this autumn.'

'Did you always want to study law?'

'Actually yes. I believe in justice. The way to right wrongs is through the courts. It's been a dream of mine.'

The icy blond sounded passionate. Here was a side of Anne I had not seen before, a woman with a mission.

'I can just see it. One day I'll come to watch you wearing a black gown and a wig. You'll be the prettiest one in court.'

'It'll be a long time before that happens.'

'Good luck.'

'I'll need more than luck. I am a woman.'

'You certainly are,' I smiled. 'What's it got to do with it?'

She looked baffled, as if I should know.

'What do you mean? Please explain Anne.'

'It's a man's world. A closed shop. It is not easy for a woman.'

I was stunned. 'You don't mean that. Surely, not nowadays.'

Again she looked at me in bafflement. 'Aren't you aware of the discrimination against professional women?'

'No. I'm not. I didn't realise. There isn't where I come from.'

'There is here. It's extremely difficult to get a position.

Let me give you an example. When we apply for chambers tenancy, they turn us down on the excuse that they don't have separate toilet facilities.'

I was quite shocked. 'Women of my generation can pursue their chosen careers. They get their position by merit. I never felt that I was restricted in anyway just because I was a woman. That's how it should be.'

'But it isn't. We are fighting for our rights. Maybe one day…'

We were quiet for a while, enjoying the sun on our faces. My esteem for Anne rose.

'Enough about me. How is it going with the old lady?'

'Oh. It's all right. You know.' I tried to smile, but it was a feeble one.

'You don't look too happy about it. Is she difficult?'

'Sometimes. I'll find something else sooner or later. She is just a stop gap.' I could ask her now, I thought. I must. 'Anne, I enjoyed the show in Paris. I wondered, maybe… do you think I could get modelling jobs here?'

She was taking her time thinking and I feared that I might have overstepped the mark. After all, I had only known her for a short time.

Finally, she said, 'It is very competitive. It is not going to fall in your lap like Paris did. Really Daniela. I don't want to dash your hopes but… I don't mean to be unkind.'

'I could give it a try. I do have the look of the moment. That might help.'

'That you do,' she chuckled. 'The thing is, your face is too beautiful, striking even.'

'Isn't that a good point in my favour?'

'I'm afraid not. Quite the opposite. A bland face with strong bone structure is what's needed. A blank canvas that makeup artists can work with. You have a distinctive look. Sorry.'

'Never mind. It was just an idea.' I felt disappointed but tried to hide it.

'Sorry Daniela. I'm only telling you how it is.'

I watched a boy feeding the ducks, another playing with a toy boat.

'Oh, I nearly forgot,' she said. 'There is a party on Saturday. Come with me, it looks like you need cheering up.'

I didn't think that a party would cheer me up. Again, I was in a situation I needed to get out of, and again, I couldn't see how. I had hoped that Anne could help. Modelling would have been a way out.

On our walk back I said, 'I'm sorry I asked Anne. I hope that you didn't mind.'

'Not at all. I was thinking about it and I have an idea. You might be able to make money modelling your legs and hands. I'll talk to my agent.'

'Thank you. I'd like that.' I was touched. She cared, she thought of me. I felt a kind of warmth towards her. Maybe it was a beginning of a good and long-lasting friendship.

'Well then, just in case,' she smiled, 'You'd better look after your legs. Wax and moisturise them ready for inspection.'

'Yes Ma'am.'

'Please, don't raise your hopes too much Daniela. I'll do what I can.'

But I did, and since my legs were to be my source of income, I waxed and moisturised them religiously. I couldn't wait to leave Mrs Birkin but I had to bide my time. As it happened, like with Dolly, it turned out that the decision was not mine to make.

*

It was on one of those evenings when I was busy waxing my legs that Mrs Birkin knocked on my door. She had never come to see me before.

'Are you alright?' I asked at the door.

She didn't answer and walked in without being invited. She stood in my small room leaning on her walking stick and looked around and then at me. I was wearing a blouse and panties.

'Sorry,' I apologised, 'I am in the middle of waxing my legs.'

She just said haughtily, 'I'll leave you to it then.'

Slowly, tapping her walking stick she made her way out. I closed it behind her. Very odd I thought. The next morning, her door was locked from the inside and I couldn't get in. I went downstairs to see the porter.

'Good morning. I can't get into Mrs Birkin's flat. I think she left her key in the lock by mistake. Could you call her?'

'She called me this morning. I'm sorry to say, but she does not require your help anymore.'

'You must be mistaken. I saw her last night. She would have said.'

'Sorry. No mistake. She asked me to tell you that she was giving you one week to vacate the flat.'

I tried to remember if I had said something to offend her when she came to my flat. I was sure that I hadn't.

'Did she say why?' I asked.

'She didn't. She said that she wants her kimono back.'

What could I have done to bring this on? What was she so angry about to dismiss me without ceremony?

'Could you please call her. I'd like to speak to her.'

She answered.

'Why, I asked. Have I offended you in anyway?'

She spat it out. 'You had a man in your room last night.'

'But you came in,' I said astonished. 'You could see that there was no one there.'

'He was hiding under the bed.'

'No there was no one there. I swear to you,' I protested.

There was no answer. I was speaking to a dead phone. She had hung up. It was so unjust. I wanted to go up and see her, make her see that she was wrong. Even if she still didn't want me to work for her, at least she should know that I did not have a man under my bed.

I asked the doorman to call her again.

'There is no point,' he said shaking his head. 'She always does it. She dismissed at least four girls since I've been working here. She always finds something to accuse them of.'

'I see. Thank you for your help.'

'Don't take it to heart. She is very old and muddled up.'

Not that muddled I thought. I fetched the kimono and gave it to him.

*

I had wanted to quit anyway, but I thought I would have a little more time to find something else. I was beginning to see that it was not going to be easy to establish myself in England. I had no connections and no strings to pull. I didn't know how things worked and there was no one to guide me. The worst of it was that I had nothing to offer. I had no profession, no diplomas and no skills. My choices were very limited, that is, if I had any.

## Chapter 13

That night, through the high window, I watched lacy clouds moving rapidly. Behind them was a single bright star playing hide and seek. Sleep would not come. I tried to float, but this time there was no bed of leaves to cushion my fall, no safety net. I looked at the red suitcase on top of the wardrobe, it would be packed again soon. Would it ever come to rest somewhere, a place I could call home?

I sat up, held my knees and rocked backwards and forwards. I had to do something and quick. I was on the brink of finding myself on the streets. The kind porter might know of a cheap but decent hotel to recommend. I would look for a job in the newspapers. Whatever I could find, I would take. I could wash dishes, wait on tables, there must be something. I still hoped that Anne's agent would take me on, but it was not going to happen overnight.

When I finally managed to fall asleep, the dreams came. Familiar nightmares turned up mixed with one another; I was falling down chasms, my useless wings wouldn't open, I got lost in places I did not recognise. The melange of my nightmarish dreams was as incongruous as if fairy-tale characters appeared together in the same story.

When I woke up, I felt tired, my head ached and my

throat was dry. I took a hot bath, and went out. I bought the newspapers, sat at a café where over a tasteless coffee, I scoured them. I thought that I might see something that I could do and even like. I could type badly, but not in English, besides, one thing I was not prepared to do was take a secretarial job; that would be defeatist, it went together with the conventional marriage and children. I would rather have washed dishes.

Then an add caught my eyes. It said au pair. I had a vague idea what it meant but it sounded good and a possible quick solution.

I went to the red phone box and called the one that sounded the best. I would be looking after a three-year-old boy, I would have my own room, and most of all much time off. A man sounding pleasant answered and I was to go there the next day.

I rang Anne just in case she had spoken to her agent. I didn't tell her what had happened with Mrs Birkin. I was ashamed to be in dire straits and in need of help. She did have news; her agent had said that she would see me.

'I think she'll take you on, but if she does, you'll need a portfolio. That is expensive Daniela. I can talk to my photographer; he might do it for a reduced price. Think about it.'

She gave me her agent's phone number and said to ring her, but I was running out of tuppences to put in the phone box. I went back to the café, got change, then went back. There was a girl in there chatting away. I was hopping from one foot to the other impatiently, but the girl took her time. It started to drizzle. A man came and queued behind me but soon lost his patience with the girl and started banging on the phone box. She ignored him. He opened the door and told her to stop hogging the phone. She left looking angry. I told the man that I wouldn't be long and went in. My clothes and my hair were damp.

The secretary answered. I told her my name and that Anne had spoken to the agent about me and that I was phoning to make an appointment to see her. I was worried that she'd brush me off, but to my surprise she said that she was expecting my call. I walked out of the phone box with a date to see the agent and a glimmer of hope.

*

I rang the bell of the second floor flat. A burly looking man let me into a tiny entrance hall. In the living room he offered me a cup of tea and I accepted. He went to the kitchen. I expected the wife to be there, and perhaps to hear the child. The flat was too quiet. I felt uneasy.

The kettle was boiling. I could see a short corridor leading from the living room to an open door at its end. He could not see me from the kitchen. I tiptoed hurriedly down the corridor to snoop. The silence gave me a sense of foreboding, something wasn't right. There was only one other room with a large bed. There was no wife, no child and no toys. I stepped backwards, and as I did, I saw an artificial penis just under the bed, a rather large one with reddish head and leather straps attached. I was alarmed. I retreated back hurriedly, but before I could make my escape, the man came in with mugs of tea. I didn't dare run off; he was bigger than me. He motioned me to sit down and I realised that I had to keep my wits about me and think of a way to get out. In desperation I asked for a glass of water. He put the mugs on the coffee table and left the room. I only had but a minute to make my escape. I ran out and kept on running until I reached the station. Only there did I stop. I leant against a wall. My heart was pounding.

I felt scared and stupid at the same time. The man could have raped me. I remembered what had happened to Edna. I should have been more careful. My heart started thumping again when I thought that had he locked his front door, I would have been trapped. By the time I was safely back and calmer, I had come to the conclusion that while being an au pair was not a bad idea, I had not gone about it the right way. I looked in the papers again and saw that there were agencies and they vetted people.

*

The next day I walked into an au pair agency nearby. I reckoned that an agency with such a salubrious and expensive address, should attract the right sort of families.

While I was filling the form, a woman came over to the counter to fill in her own. Turning to me she said, 'Forgive me for glimpsing at your form. I was curious,' she smiled. 'I hope you don't mind.'

'Not at all.' She surely wasn't looking to be an au pair. She was not young.

'Only that I noticed that you put 'model' for a profession. Does it take a lot of your time?'

'Not really. I haven't done it for long and not in England.'

She looked at me thoughtfully. 'My husband is a musician,' she paused.

I thought it was a strange thing to mention, and waited to see where this was going.

'You see, we understand how unpredictable freelance work is.'

Was she offering me a job? I continued to wait.

She hesitated. 'I hope you won't think me too forward when I say that I think my family might suit you. I understand how irregular your work must be. I'm sure that we can accommodate it.'

She was well spoken, her clothes were dated and shapeless, she seemed kind and easy going. I thought that perhaps I would feel comfortable in a place where a musician lived. However, what choice did I have? If she was offering me a job, I would be a fool not to take it.

'What will I have to do?'

'We have two children, seven and four. It is mainly for the four-year-old that we want an au pair.'

'And the hours if I may ask?'

'We can be flexible. I suppose you are thinking of time off for modelling.'

'I was,' I smiled.

She smiled too. 'Would you like to come to us?'

'I would. Thank you.'

'Oh, good. Start as soon as you can. I'll sort it out with the agency if you like. By the way, my name is Claire.'

She offered me her hand. I took it.

'Daniela.'

They were bound to be an unconventional family and I couldn't see Claire treating me badly like Mrs Birkin. Maybe it would work out well.

*

Two days later, I was waiting for Claire in the lobby. She arrived at Arlington House in an old banger, an estate car in desperate need of a wash. It looked incredibly out of place, particularly when the immaculately uniformed doorman hurried to open the door for her. She seemed surprised. She was probably wondering what I was doing in such a place. The man who had told me that I was dismissed, carried my red suitcase to the car and put it in the already full boot. He said, 'Goodbye and good luck,' and smiled.

During the drive, I remembered that I hadn't asked Claire where she lived. I worried that it might be far from the centre of the city, that maybe I wouldn't like the family or they me. I needn't have worried.

The house in Muswell Hill was three stories with a garden. It was shabby and messy and not gleamingly clean, but it was a home. My room was on the top floor next to Jane's, with a bathroom we shared.

I put my luggage down, sat in the armchair and looked at my surroundings; a bed, a wardrobe, a chest of drawers, paintings and a bookcase crammed full of books. The room was in need of dusting. I was not complaining. Dust never bothered me. I soon learned that dust and mess did not bother Claire either, she loved reading and cooking more. I got on with unpacking and with delight put my red suitcase away on top of the wardrobe hoping not to be packing it again soon.

Rebecca was a charming and affectionate child. I liked the sweet little girl immediately. Jane was more reserved and it took me some time to win her over.

Claire's husband Alan was a freelance violinist. When he had work, he was hardly home. Claire busied herself with chores in the house. Even though it was not expected of me, I helped her. There was no method or routine in the way she went about it. She had many projects on the go; unfinished clothes for the children sat in a pile by the sewing machine, there was a basket full of mending, curtains hung with their hems unfinished. I liked helping her. She treated me with kindness and as a friend.

Every day, Rebecca wanted to go to the playground. She climbed on everything and laughed with that pure, carefree joy of children. Her favourite record was *Chitty Chitty Bang Bang* and she would listen to it ad nauseam. In the evening, I would give her a bath, put her to bed and read her a story. Sometimes Jane joined us. For me it was an introduction to English children's books. I had grown up mostly on European ones. Now I met Christopher Robin, Wendy, Pan, Toad and his friends, Peter Rabbit and many more. Rebecca would suck her thumb and listen with eyes full of wonder. Spellbound she entered the world of magic as only children can, as I had done a long time ago.

Claire and Alan had fights. They fought behind closed doors in their bedroom below me. I could hear him, sounding angry, raising his voice but I could not hear what he said nor could I hear Claire's answers. The next day she would launch into a flurry of activities, cleaning and tidying. She never mentioned the fights. She must have known that I heard them. I hoped that the children didn't. My parents fighting, also behind closed doors, had cast a strained atmosphere in my home. In the silences that had followed, we had walked on shaky ground that threatened to erupt into another fight.

*

With a place to stay and a telephone number I went to see Anne's agent. She took me on, and asked for photographs. The photographer did a good job, not as good as Benyamin though. It was strange to be photographed by someone else. It ate most of my savings but I hoped it would pay off.

After the session, walking back to the underground, I

saw a painting in the window of a gallery in Cork Street. It was a large rectangular painting of a reclining female nude. I walked into the gallery and looked at the paintings on display. A woman came out from behind a desk and asked if anything in particular appealed to me. I told her that I liked the one in the window. 'It is by Lucien Freud,' she said. I had never heard of him. Without thinking I asked for the price. 'Three hundred pounds,' she said. I smiled sadly, thanked her and left. Outside I looked at the painting again. I dreamt of a place of my own, filled with books, a wall big enough to hang it on.

My first job went well. The agent's secretary phoned to say that the cheque was in the post. When it arrived, I looked at it for a long time. I felt optimistic. It was a small step forward to my independence.

*

One night Claire and Alan had a terrible row. Rebecca came to my room and cuddled up to me in bed. She looked upset and confused. I held her stroking her hair until she fell asleep. I heard somebody coming up the stairs. It was Claire. She was shaking and sobbing, her face was wet with tears. She collapsed in the armchair. I got up and gave her my glass of water, crouched on the floor beside her, held her hand and let her cry.

'I'm sorry we woke you up,' she whispered.

'I was not asleep,' I whispered back.

She sat silent for a while staring into space.

'He loses his temper sometimes. It'll pass. It'll be fine.'

I thought that she was saying it to convince herself rather than me.

'Does he hit you?' I don't know why I asked. I regretted it immediately.

She didn't answer for a while. Then she looked at me. 'He is not a bad man. He is good and kind. He loses his temper, and rarely, very rarely… yes, he hits me. Not hard. He doesn't mean to. Really, he doesn't. He always regrets it. It hurts him that he hurts me.'

I was horrified and without thinking asked, 'Why do you stay with him?'

She looked surprised. 'I love him. I can't imagine life without him. He doesn't mean to. Really.'

We looked at Rebecca sleeping. Her thumb was in her mouth.

'Thank you for looking after her. I'll go back. He'll be asleep now.'

I got into bed carefully trying not to wake Rebecca. I would not stay with a man if he hit me, not for one minute, however much I loved him. Poor Claire. The house revolved around Alan, he came first; his work, his time, his needs.

And then for the first time, I realised that my life with Benyamin had revolved around him. I never questioned it or was even aware of it. But I was happy.

Rebecca moved and sighed. I envied her innocence. Tomorrow she would forget all about the night row.

# CHAPTER 14

It was Gina who suggested that I go to the auditions. I had met her at dance class. She was half English and half Italian, good looking with olive-coloured skin, long black hair and dark brown eyes. We sometimes went to have a coffee after class.

It was at the café, on a winter's day that she talked excitedly about the auditions for a musical going to Germany.

'Everyone is going,' she said. 'Are you?'

My first reaction was to laugh. The thought that I could go on stage and perform seemed ridiculous.

'You know that I am not a dancer, nor is it an ambition of mine. I just love dancing Gina. But thank you for thinking of me.'

She insisted that I stood a chance. The pay was good, hotel and transport and laundry paid, and there would be a generous living allowance.

Out of politeness I said, 'I'll think about it.'

*

At supper I told Claire and Alan. I thought they would be amused. To my surprise, both thought that I should go for it.

Claire said, 'It'll be far more exciting than staying with us. It is an opportunity for you to do something interesting. I don't see you staying an au pair for long.'

Alan said, 'First let's see if you can sing.'

'I sang in the school choir,' I chuckled. 'But, Alan, I really think it's a bad idea. I don't stand a chance. I'll just make a fool of myself.'

Alan said, 'Well, let's find out.'

He played the piano and I sung. They both decided that I should go for it. Alan offered to prep me. He told me to go and buy the sheet music for a song called '*Love Hurts*'. On the tube I read the lyrics. *Love hurts… love scars… love wounds… Love is just a lie…* How strange that he chose that song.

I reflected on how kind they were to me, encouraging me even though it meant that they might lose their au pair. What was I thinking of? Modelling is one thing, but to go on stage and perform, was quite another. On the other hand, I loved dancing. Gina thought that I could do it, Claire and Alan thought so too and he, I felt, should know what he was talking about.

*

In a West End Theatre, Gina and I sat on the floor outside the auditorium with our backs against the wall. We watched dancers in leotards and leg warmers doing warm up exercises. A woman came out and called out a list of names. Ten people followed her into the auditorium. Shortly after we heard the choreographer's instructions, the piano playing and dancers' feet on the stage floor. Then they came out. Some of them picked up their bags and left. I was called in with the next batch.

I walked onto the stage and the choreographer told us to

line up. Out there, in the semi darkness, sat the people who were holding our fate in their hands; they were watching, deciding, looking for something in us that would inspire them.

We followed the routine, marking it first and the choreographer said, 'from the top.' He signed to the pianist to start playing, then said loudly, 'Five six seven eight.' We danced. I was relieved that I could follow. It was within my ability. Then he left the stage to join the people who were sitting in the auditorium. We could hear their voices, not what they were saying. They were discussing us. When the choreographer returned, he chose six people and asked them to move aside. I wasn't one of them. I was sure that I was left standing with those who failed. I was not surprised.

He turned to those he had called. 'Thank you very much for coming. Better luck next time.' They started leaving. He turned to the rest of us and told us to wait outside.

I joined Gina. Soon it was her turn. when she came out, she picked up her bag. She hadn't passed. I looked at her in disbelief. She smiled sadly and wished me luck.

It was a long wait and I was beginning to lose my nerve. Once the selection for dancers was over. We were called in individually to sing. From inside the auditorium, I could hear people singing beautifully. What chance did I have? Maybe I should leave. But I felt that I owed it to Alan, who gave me his time, and transposed the music to a key that suited me. At least, I would be able to tell him that I tried.

I was called in. I climbed on to the stage and handed the pianist my music sheet. He scanned it. I stood alone under the spot light feeling lost in the big stage. My legs felt unsteady. Cigarette smoke was rising from the semi darkness bellow, where those who would decide were watching me.

'Ready?'

I managed to nod my head. He played the intro. I opened my mouth. Nothing came out. He stopped playing. I wanted to run away.

'We'll start again. Forget about them down there. Sing it to me. I like this song. Now, look at me. I'll cue you in.'

I nodded at him and he played the intro and cued me in. I sang. After the first refrain, a voice came from the dark auditorium. 'Thank you.' The pianist stopped and so did I. 'We'll let you know.'

I thanked the pianist. If it wasn't for him, I would have probably run away.

*

To my utter surprise, the phone call came, I had passed. I was going to Germany. I was stunned, I couldn't believe it. I thought it was madness. I knew nothing about performing. But I did feel a little excited about going.

I brought the red suitcase down from on top of the wardrobe and dusted it. As I was packing, I thought, if all I had to offer was my body, then maybe I was fortunate to have an asset that I could capitalise on.

*

We rehearsed in Essen in a large stadium that usually held sports events and horse shows. The stage was built meters high above the ground with three different levels. The cast was half German and half English. I particularly liked the choreographer; Black American, big Afro hair, tall, muscular and full of inspiring enthusiasm and energy. He was always stoned. It didn't seem to affect his choreographing or his fabulous turns and leaps.

Rehearsals were gruelling. We were told often enough to give it all we've got, to try and do better, to put life into it, to smile. I heard the lead singers rehearsing. I heard them every day trying to project feelings and emotions that they had dug from deep inside themselves. And when it worked, I could hear it resonating in their singing voices. I was a part of it, and though often exhausted, it felt good and satisfying.

We had a technical rehearsal, and a dress rehearsal, the pre-run came and went. The reviews were not good. We were called to an emergency rehearsal the next day. Tempers were running high; the director barked at us, the producer told us that we could do better, and the conductor screamed at the orchestra, banging his baton impatiently on his music stand. The costume designer was hysterical, but the choreographer, as always was stoned and calm. The show was tweaked in the hope of improvement. The feeling among stage crew and performers was that the changes only made it worse. They whispered it in corridors, in dressing rooms, even in asides as they stood on stage.

\*

We performed for a month in Essen, then in Cologne, then in Dusseldorf. After that we moved to Berlin where we were given a few days off. Since I was there with time on my hands, I called Herr Wagner. He was delighted to hear from me and took me out to dinner. We ate, we drank wine, we chatted.

Half way through the meal he said, 'You're looking great. I wish I could have you modelling for me.'

'Why don't you?' I teased him.

'You know why. It's Dolly. You know what she's like. She's still angry with you.'

'She. Angry with me? I don't see what she's got to be angry about. It's me who should be angry. She left me in Amsterdam. But you know all about it.'

'She says that you are ungrateful.'

'Oh, well. She can say what she likes. By the way, thank you for Geneva. It was kind of you to help me. How is Herr Schafferman.'

'He's all right. I think he was very sad to lose you. Why don't you go and see him?'

'I'd like that. I'll call him.'

'I'd stay away from Dolly if I were you.'

'I have no intention of seeing her.'

\*

The next day I took the train to Frankfurt to see Herr Schafferman. He was so excited to see me that he could hardly speak. We sat in his office for a while. He kept smiling at me, his head lolling, his arms flapping. Once he recovered, we chatted for a while and I told him about the show. I asked him to come and see it, but I knew he wouldn't. He just smiled sadly.

He pointed at my old coat. 'Schmatte,' he nodded his head disapprovingly.

'Dolly didn't bring all my clothes to Amsterdam. I meant to ask if you still got them.'

'She got rid of them. I couldn't stop her,' he sighed. 'I wanted to send them to you but she wouldn't let me. I'm sorry.'

'It doesn't matter. Really. I can always buy more clothes. I'm just sad about the fur coat that you gave me.'

'I have something for you.' He smiled conspiratorially, tapping his nose with his forefinger. He went to the rail and pulled out a silver fox, full length.

'For you,' he said laughing. 'Schöne? Ja?' He had a huge smile full of delight and naughtiness. He was getting one over Dolly.

'Ja. Sehr schöne.'

I put it on and twirled for him. I hugged and kissed him. He laughed heartily.

I was fond of Herr Schafferman. I admired him for his courage, for surviving, for building a life despite the horror he had lived through. I should learn from him, I thought, after all, what I had to face was nothing in comparison. And I loved my fur coat. And I got one over Dolly, not that she'd ever know.

*

In Berlin everyone was nervous. The reviews and the audience response in that city could make or break the show. We rehearsed days and long into the nights. We were shouted at, cajoled, and drilled mercilessly. We were exhausted. I wanted the show to succeed because of all the effort and hard work we had put into it.

On opening night, a hush fell as the house lights went out. In the semi darkness, we took our places. The stage lights came on. The orchestra played. We sang and danced in our lavish costumes. We got a polite applause, no shouts of bravo.

The reviews were lukewarm. We huddled together and our dialogue coach translated for us. Only the costumes and the choreography were highly praised. I was disappointed, but not surprised.

*

One night after the show, a group of us went out to a discotheque. The scene that met my eyes brought to mind scenes from paintings by Bruegel the Elder. The place was heaving, the music loud and we were bathed in a moving psychedelic light show. Men and women with long flowing hair or big afros, wearing caftans, embroidered jeans, headbands and beads, were dancing, flailing their arms, laughing, or sitting on the floor floating in their own world.

In dark alcoves strewn with cushions, I saw couples kissing, some were half-undressed. In one of the alcoves, a couple was having sex. His trousers were wrapped around his ankles, her yellow caftan was raised up to her waist, they took no notice of the people who stopped to watch. I felt revulsion and quickly moved on.

We found a place to sit near the bar. I sipped my drink and smoked the passing joints. The music was too loud for talking. I was still reeling from what I had seen. Was this the face of my generation? The face of sexual liberation? Did it boil down to copulating in public? I hoped not. I felt angry. I was all for breaking the conventions that had no reasoning behind them, but we should not abandon decorum and decency. We should not, as the English say, 'throw the baby out with the bath water.' If that was what we presented to the world, no one would take us seriously.

*

The show went on and wasn't a big success. The rumours were that it would fold. But then when Easter came, we were given time off and I witnessed something quite extraordinary. For the first time since the dividing wall had been built, West Berliners were allowed to visit East Berlin. The production company managed to get us visitor permits.

At Checkpoint Charlie, the sight of armed soldiers scared me. There was barbed wire and above us a watchtower with soldiers holding guns. I, who came from a country at war, who had been a soldier and who knew war first hand, felt a familiar fear. I couldn't stop the images from coming; blackouts in the cities, skies lit up with approaching bombs, dead soldiers. The sound of guns and rockets rang in my ears. One night during the war, I had been in a bunker in the Sinai Desert when the bombardment started. I went out to watch. The explosions were deafening. The sky was lit up with fiery colours. A gigantic moon hung in the sky. I stood and watched entranced. Someone came and pulled me back into the bunker. I was told off.

I handed over my passport and permit to the soldier at the gate. I tried to keep my hands from shaking and my face expressionless. My legs felt unsteady. Once through the checkpoint, my body stopped obeying me and I stumbled; my legs felt week and I had to lean against a wall. I must get hold of myself, I thought instinctively, I must not attract attention. We strolled along *Friedrichstrasse*. There were soldiers everywhere.

The next day the papers were full of sad and harrowing stories about families who had met again for the first time in years, about successful and unsuccessful escapes. One story that touched me the most, told of a West Berliner who had smuggled her sister's baby, strapped to her belly, pretending to be pregnant.

*

Just after a month in Berlin, the show folded. The goodbye party was sad and emotional. People drank too much, hugged and kissed in a flamboyant manner, promised to keep in touch in that exaggerated way they have in the theatre. We probably would not see each other again and we all knew it, but it didn't stop the extravagant show of emotions. The good thing was that I had somewhere to go back to. Claire had written that I could have my room and that the children missed me. I missed them too and was looking forward to seeing them all.

In one of the bad reviews was a fabulous picture of me, standing on top of the stage next to the lead singer. I looked fabulous.

# CHAPTER 15

Eight young men were sitting at the kitchen table having supper with the family. Alan had joined a rock band. The members were a mixture of rock and classical musicians from different countries and were in London recording an album.

I often caught Robert, the English keyboard player, looking at me. His eyes were small, hazel in colour and warm. He was slightly taller than me, big, but not fat. His mousy coloured hair receded from his high forehead and the small red lips were surrounded by a well-trimmed goatee. He was neither handsome nor ugly.

One afternoon he came round with the excuse that he wanted to practise the piano as it was much better than his own. Claire gave me a meaningful look and made herself scarce. We sat in the music room and he played. Rebecca sat on my lap sucking her thumb. Robert played something soft and gentle, sometimes it sounded like water bubbling, at others, a tinkling of raindrops on puddles. I looked out of the French windows, Claire was pottering in the garden, above were patches of blue spring sky and small, fluffy white clouds that hardly moved. In my head I went where sometimes music took me, into a kind of a dreamy spell.

At the end of the piece, he turned round and said, 'I am not needed in the studio tomorrow. There is a place that I'd like to take you to. Will you come? Are you free?' He was twiddling with the gold signet ring on his little finger. His voice was deep, warm and mellifluous.

'Can I come too?' Rebecca asked perking up.

He smiled at her. 'Not this time Rebecca.' He looked back at me. 'It's a magical place. I think you'd like it. How about it?'

I nodded my head.

*

Robert came the next afternoon and drove me to Highgate. I was taken aback when we entered a cemetery. I looked at him perplexed. 'Wait,' he said. 'Wait till you see it.'

We meandered amongst graves with elaborate headstones in silence, not wanting to disturb the enchanted world. It was so very peaceful, there was no one around, no traffic noise, and the birds were singing and fluttering about. We passed classical statues, sculptures of winged angels, large follies and mausoleums, walked through arches, all pitted and greyed, mellowed by time. Majestic trees rose above us. Shrubs covered the ground. Ivy was taking over, rampaging, threatening to swallow it all up.

I felt Robert's presence close to me as we walked silently in the unreal world.

Some angels held musical instruments. I imagined that at night, when no one was there, they came alive and played. I thought I felt the spirits whispering gently in the breeze, in the rustling of the leaves. The space belonged to them. I knew they were there.

Robert pointed out graves of famous people. One of my

favourite writers was in residence, George Eliot. She was in good company.

We sat on a bench. 'It's wonderful. Thank you,' I whispered.

'I thought you might like it.' He too whispered.

He took my hand in both of his and played with my fingers. He was not looking at me. His hands were warm, smooth and soft, the hands that had played the piano for me. His bear-like body was next to mine and I wanted him to cuddle me. I suspected that I had been feeling lonely. I squeezed his hand. He turned round to look at me and we smiled. We stayed there for a while listening to the birds and the whispering leaves, holding hands. It had been a long time since anyone touched me, showed affection. I had forgotten what it felt like.

We were silent during the drive back. Something had happened between us and it was there in the air, unsaid. He stopped outside Claire's house. He turned to look at me. We kissed. His lips were warm and soft. His neat beard brushed my face.

In my room, I sunk into the armchair. I thought of the man who had played the piano for me, had taken me to a magical place, held my hand and tenderly kissed me. I had no idea how I felt about him. But something in me was awakened, it felt like being alive.

*

Robert came to the house often. We would go to the park with Rebecca. She adored him. She demanded he push her on the swing, and when he did, she would scream at the top of her voice. 'Higher, higher!' On the walk back she would hold our hands and we would swing her up and down.

Claire said, 'He's fallen for you, hook line and sinker.'

'What do you mean?'

'It's a saying, it's to do with catching a fish on a hook. You caught a fish and he is completely hooked. Don't tell me you haven't noticed.' She looked at me. 'You're blushing.'

I smiled. 'I don't know that I want a fish. I'd rather have a tiger.'

Claire laughed, 'Don't we all?'

I felt comfortable with him. I enjoyed his attentiveness. I liked his calmness. When we met, his eyes lit up with a big smile. When we parted, he always made sure that we agreed on the next time we would meet. An uncomplicated relationship I thought.

*

One evening after we've been out with his friends, all musicians who talked only about music, Robert stopped the car outside his house. I hadn't been there before.

'Shall we go in?' he asked.

I knew what he was asking. It would be love making, only without love on my part. We got on well together and I was prepared to settle for it. I didn't think that it was wrong. I nodded my head and got out of the car. He came round, put his arm round my shoulders and we walked the tiled path to the front door.

Robert shared the house with two other guys. They were playing chess in the living room. He stuck his head inside to say hello. A dog came out. Robert stroked its head. He then took my hand and led me up the stairs. The dog followed.

'Out,' he told the dog and closed the door of his bedroom. He turned on the standard lamp then threw some clothes out of an armchair for me to sit on. He took off his corduroy jacket, sat at a small table strewn with sheets of music and rolled a joint. The room was messy, clothes on chairs, books on the floor, a pile of washing by the wardrobe, but it was cosy.

'Play something for me,' I said.

He smiled, lit the joint and went and sat on a stool for two by the upright piano. 'Come and sit next to me.'

I sat beside him and he gave me the joint to hold. I took a puff and handed it to him. He didn't take it.

'I'll play and you feed me smoke.'

He started playing. I held the joint to his mouth and then to mine. When it was finished, I went and lay on the bed, resting my head against the headboard. He played a classical piece that I didn't recognise. He later told me that it was written by Schumann for his beloved Clara.

When he finished playing, he threw a shirt over the standard lamp, the only light in the room. He came to the bed, kissed me, took my blouse off, and then his shirt. He caressed my body with one hand and struggled to take my trousers off with the other. I helped him. He wriggled out of his trousers and lay on top of me. There was urgency in his manner. He made love to me. It didn't take him long to come. He was very upset. His face was red with embarrassment. He apologised. He said it was because he wanted me so badly and for such a long time that he was too excited. I said I understood, and hugged him.

I lay awake next to his warm body. He was asleep with his arm across my chest. I listened to his soft breathing. He was neither a fish nor a tiger, he was a cuddly bear. I didn't want him to love me. Maybe a little would be all right. I could not return his love. It hadn't been that long since Benyamin had left me. I still had hope for us even though it was fading away.

I was lying next to one man and thinking of another. Maybe there were different kinds of love. There were no other words for love, I couldn't think of one, I couldn't find any in the dictionary. Why were there no variations like, 'I sort of love you'? Or a measurement like 'I seventy percent love you'? I could not find the word for what I felt for him.

Late morning when I opened my eyes, he was looking at me. He smiled and kissed my forehead. He seemed happy. 'You are lovely. I do love you.'

I closed my eyes. I couldn't say it back to him. It would have been a lie. I opened my eyes, smiled and said, 'You are lovely too.'

He kissed me and went downstairs to make us a cup of tea.

I sat up in bed. I hadn't realised that he loved me deeply. I remembered the afternoon when we had sat in the park watching Rebecca playing. 'Do you want children?' he asked. I evaded the question. Maybe watching the child playing brought it on, or maybe he was envisaging us having a future together.

I thought that maybe I should stop seeing him before it gets too serious. But I didn't want to. He was a part of what made me feel safe and secure; my room, the family that made me feel at home, my modelling work and Robert's love. It was selfish of me and I felt a little guilty. But he was happy, I gave him what I was capable of giving, and if he was satisfied with that, then it was alright.

He came back with tea and got back into bed. He looked happy.

*

Summer turned to autumn and winter was soon upon us. Claire and Robert had taught me to drive and I bought a second-hand Vauxhall Viva. I loved the independence driving gave me. I could go anywhere, anytime I wanted. There was to be no more standing at bus stops, no more walking to the underground or running to catch the last train. And best of all the car had a heater. My modelling jobs, even though I didn't get that many, paid well. I felt that I was able to pay rent. Claire objected when I offered, but I insisted. It made me feel good to do so.

It was during that time that I met Poppy Lovett. She had come in to the studio one evening after dance class. I noticed her when she went to talk to Gina and because of her looks. She was petite in stature, with very white skin and had wavy, shiny red hair that amply fell to her shoulders. I intended to leave them to talk when Gina called me over and introduced us. Poppy Lovett was Gina's agent.

Poppy smiled. She had lively brown eyes. She said that she was impressed with my dancing. 'Come and see me. I can put work your way.'

I smiled politely and told her that I wasn't a professional dancer.

There was a hint of amusement in her eyes. 'I watched you dance. You are underestimating yourself. You should be on the stage. You dance well and look good.' She said it with conviction and gave me her card.

'And Poppy should know. She is a performer herself,' Gina said. 'She is a jazz singer.'

I must have looked surprised.

'Singing jazz does not pay the rent. I run an agency for performers. I can get you work as a dancer. If you are interested of course.'

'That's very kind of you.'

'Nothing to do with kindness. I take ten percent commission. Look, I can see that you are not sure about it. Here is my card. Call me if you change your mind.'

I thought it odd that I kept coming across people who wanted to put me on the stage. I took Poppy's card out of politeness. I didn't take her offer seriously any more than I had when in Berlin, in the restaurant, Herr Wagner had told me that I had the making of a model. He had got me onto the catwalk, Gina had got me to sing and dance in Germany, and Poppy's card, as it turned out, had come at the right time.

*

On a calm but very cold January day, Robert and I went for a walk to Alexandra Palace, as we often did. We sat on a bench looking at the panoramic view of London. I enjoyed us sitting close together in a comfortable silence, just being.

Out of the blue, he said looking straight ahead of him, 'I have to leave you.'

I was sure I had misunderstood or misheard. Maybe he was going to play somewhere for a while. But there was something in the tone of his voice, a combination of sadness and determination.

'I love you to distraction. I can't think, I can't work Daniela. My infatuation with you is all consuming. You bewitch me.'

I felt the cold seeping into my bones.

'You have no idea what a devastating effect you have on me. All you have to do is look at me with those beautiful eyes of yours, I lose myself… I…'

The sentence hung in the air. He was still not looking at me.

We sat in tense silence. I stared at his signet ring. He was twiddling with it.

'I feel that you are holding back. Sometimes you seem remote, elusive, I feel left out. It confuses me. It unsettles me. I can't handle it, Daniela. I love you too much.'

What the hell was I supposed to say to this? Love me less? I never was the begging kind, too proud for that. I wasn't about to try and hold him against his will. My mind scrambled but I couldn't find anything to say. We were sitting so very close that I could smell his familiar odour, the one that was left on his pillow, the one I smelt when he held my head against his chest. I hugged myself into my fur coat looking for warmth, but it could not warm the icy wind I felt inside me. I shivered. The sun was setting. It was getting dark. He stood up. His face contorted in pain. I wasn't going to kneel down, clasp his knees and beg him to stay.

He said, 'Sorry', turned and walked away.

I watched him go down the hill until he disappeared around the corner. I felt alone. I didn't want him to go. I got up and walked to the house and up to my room where I slumped in the armchair. I couldn't believe that he had left me. I knew that I would miss his company, his warmth and even his love that I had not returned, that I wished I could.

*

My eyes were red when I went down stairs the next morning. Claire surely noticed but said nothing. When Rebecca asked if Robert was coming, she would hug and distract her.

During the following days I was hurting deeply. I couldn't blame him. I had not returned his love. Still, it hurt. It hurt more than I expected it to. I didn't want to feel that way. At night I snuggled in the armchair trying to make sense of what had happened, to put my thoughts and feelings in order.

I remembered a conversation that my mother had had with her Gypsy friend. I had used to listen in as they dished out their wisdom over a cup of Turkish coffee.

My mother said that a woman needed to please her man if she wanted to keep him. 'The way to a man's heart is through his stomach.'

Even if it were true, I could not cook. What was true was that I couldn't keep my men.

The Gypsy said, 'They are all like children. They need to be amused. Make them laugh.'

Mother added, 'Be what they want you to be.'

I wanted to be loved for who I was. What they were advocating was deceitful.

The Gypsy said, 'In the kitchen, a cook. In bed, a whore.' They both cracked up laughing.

I was not sure that my mother really knew how to be a whore, but I didn't want to think about it and have that picture in my head. I had been called frigid. I was sure that I was not a nymphomaniac. Perhaps it meant being somewhere in between.

I had thought that what we had together was good, calm and solid. It had suited me, but it was not enough for him. I had been selfish. Still, it hurt. I thought that it showed a strength of character to love me very deeply, yet be able to leave me. I was sure that he was hurting. I wondered if the strength of pain that people inflicted on each other was in direct ratio to how much they cared and how deeply they felt. I found it strange that red was the colour for love and also for alarm and danger.

I saw myself as a seed blowing in the wind, looking for fertile ground where I could thrive. Robert was not the answer.

What I yearned for was a place of my own. I had dreamt it so often that I could see it clearly. The sun would stream through the large windows into spacious rooms filled with old furniture and rugs. There would be bookcases and paintings. I would be lying on the sofa reading and listening to classical music, and the sheer, white cotton curtains would be bellowing in a light breeze. I had to achieve this on my own.

And Robert? My life had not and should not revolve around him, or any man come to that, he would become a memory, a cherished one.

Then one day I woke up feeling different, stronger, determined. I knew that my mind often worked things up while I was asleep. I put on my dancing clothes and went to a morning class. I enjoyed it, and as I danced, I decided that as my best assets were my beauty and my dancing skills, then I would use them.

Back in the house, I found Poppy Lovett's card and phoned her. She was pleased to hear from me and made me an offer to join a revue that was going to Portugal. It took me by surprise. Portugal? I sort of expected her to offer me something in London. I couldn't think straight.

'Don't take too long to think about it. You will be replacing a dancer who had to leave. The rehearsals have already started and you'll be leaving in ten days' time. In case you're interested, you need to show up for rehearsals tomorrow morning. Could you let me know within the next few hours? I am sorry that it's such a short notice.'

I replaced the receiver and sat at the kitchen table. Claire put a cup of coffee in my hands. I told her about the job.

'It's the best thing for you right now. It would help you get over Robert. What the eye don't see…'

# Chapter 16

In the nightclub, the pianist was tickling the ivories. The performers were sitting together around small tables. I approached them and said 'Hello.' They looked at me then turned away and carried on smoking and chatting, ignoring me. I went and sat on the edge of the empty low stage.

I was about to leave when a dancer got up and looked at me. 'What now?' I thought. Tall and graceful she walked towards me, smiled and joined me.

'My name is Helen.' Her lips were heart shaped and her blue eyes looked at me from under a light brown straight fringe. I saw a gentle face with high cheekbones and a long neck.

'Daniela,' I said.

'Don't take any notice of them,' she said nodding her head discreetly towards the dancers. 'They have already decided that they don't like you. None of them are good dancers and, how shall I say it, not the brightest buttons. They see you as a threat because you are beautiful and they are jealous.'

'Thank you for the compliment. They really have nothing to fear from me. But under the circumstances, I am not going to stay.'

'I'll be honest with you; I'd like you to stay. Do the rehearsals and we'll go for a coffee after and talk about it. Yes?'

I saw the dancers lifting their heads to look at us. 'You'll get into trouble for befriending me.'

'I couldn't care less. So yes? You'll stay?' there was a naughty twinkle in her eyes.

I nodded.

The choreographer, Tomas, sauntered in, clapped his hands and everybody went on stage. He asked for my name and said in a Spanish accent, 'Welcome, try to catch up.' The pianist played and the gutsy singer sang *'Come on baby light my fire'.* The dance routine was simple and easy. I soon caught up with the others. Tomas smiled at me in approval. He then told me and one of the dancers to swap places thus putting me in the front and her in the back. As she passed me, she whispered, 'Bloody bitch'. When rehearsals finished, the singer bumped into me on purpose. 'Don't get too comfortable,' she hissed. She's the leader of the pack, I thought. I got off the stage, took my bag and marched out.

Helen ran after me and grabbed my arm. 'Come, we'll go for a coffee.'

Over coffee, Helen persuaded me to stay. 'Please,' she said. 'I don't like them, but I get on with them. I'd rather you were there with me. I really do.  I promise you'll be alright. We'll stick together. Please stay.'

I liked her, I wouldn't be alone with them in Portugal and I did want to go away.

I never understood why many times I had a sense that certain women took an immediate dislike to me. I never felt comfortable with them, nor was I accepted into their circle. They had an understanding amongst themselves that

I didn't share. I did not think that it was all down to my beauty, more than that, I clearly lacked something, perhaps social skills. I was not good at small talk, I found it difficult to find anything to say.

I had always been nervous walking into a room full of strangers. I was shy but I learned to hide it. I suppose people sensed something and misinterpreted it, taking me to be closed and aloof.

*

When the ship we travelled on arrived in Bilbao, I was refused entry; I did not have a visa for Spain. I was sent back to England immediately. While I was waiting for the ship to leave, Helen took me for a short walk on the dock and rolled a joint. I was sad to part with her and she promised to call me on her return. I reboarded the same boat that we had come on and sat at the bar resting my head on my hands. The same barman, taking pity on me, laced my tea with brandy. To my surprise, no sooner had I arrived in London, than I was sent to Portugal by air, thus avoiding going through Spain.

Helen and I rented a small house for the month. We went out shopping for food and wine. Helen stopped at a pharmacy where she produced a list of drugs that she could buy over the counter in Portugal; Quaaludes, Mandrax, Valium, uppers and downers. When we came out, she laughed, 'We are well stocked up now.'

And that was the beginning of my drug education.

Each night after we had performed two shows, we had to stay and sit in the club looking decorative until four in the morning. There was no way out of it, it was stipulated in our contract. Punters bought us drinks. They were older men with lustful eyes. Those men, sometimes would put their hands on our shoulders or try to give us a hug. I would remove their hands in disgust. I would say to them the only sentence in Portuguese we had been taught: Naoe me toque. It meant: Don't touch me.

What I enjoyed the most was the time I spent with Helen at our little house. When we came back from the casino, we would sit at the kitchen table talking until dawn, recounting our lives to each other. I found it easy to talk to her and we found that we had a lot in common.

Helen was born in Ceylon where her father managed a tea plantation. Her face lit up when she talked about her happy childhood there and her ayah that she loved. I thought of Mrs Birkin and her stories about her life in India.

'They sent me to England, to the cold and dump country on my own, to a prison called Boarding School. The only good thing about it was going to ballet classes.'

I wondered what she was doing in a revue dancing in nightclubs and cassinos. She must have read my mind.

She laughed. 'You are wondering what I am doing here. I am too tall to dance ballet. Not the regulation 5'5,' she chuckled. 'But I can still do the splits.'

At dawn we would take a downer and go to bed. In the afternoon we got up, took an upper and went to the casino where we did dance exercises. The first time we showed up, we went on stage wearing our exercise clothes and followed a warm-up routine that we both contributed to. The staff were busy cleaning and setting up for the night. They stopped working and watched us amazed; a man leant on his broom, a woman held a tablecloth ready to be spread, another clutched her duster, the man that was moving chairs, stopped and sat down. They were smiling. I suppose that no other dancers had ever done that. A manager came in and told them to go back to work. They did, but kept on looking. At the end, Helen smiled and did the splits for them. They clapped her. Helen bowed. They bowed back. Helen and I burst out laughing and the staff joined us. I could see that it gave her pleasure to give them a little fun. People responded to her kindness; it was a gift she had. I envied her.

\*

A letter waited for Helen on her dressing table. The room was small, had no windows, was airless and smelled stale. She opened the letter. She looked distressed as she read it.

'What's the matter?' I asked.

'My father is coming back to England,' her lips were pursed.

We were putting on our makeup. I had difficulties putting on the false eyelashes, they wouldn't stick. I swore. She passed me her glue. Her face looked strained.

'You look upset about it.'

'Of course I'm upset. I don't want to see him.'

'You don't? I would have thought…'

She broke in. 'He sent me away to England. I've hardly seen him in years. Yes, he wrote, letters full of excuses about why he can't come. Why I can't visit. I missed my ayah.' She was holding her lipstick open about to apply it, but stopped in mid-air. 'It broke my heart when they sent me away. She was always there for me.'

I didn't know what to say. I thought it was cruel to send a child away to another country on her own. Was it a punishment? Did she misbehave? I couldn't see sweet-natured Helen being an obstreperous child. I saw Helen's face in the mirror. Her eyes were dreamy, in her mind she was probably in Ceylon.

'Are you angry with your parents because they sent you away?'

She looked puzzled. 'Not with my mother. With him.'

'But you must have loved him Helen. Can't you let it go?'

She paused, then with a wry smile, 'I didn't just love him. I adored him. But after what he did to my mother…' She broke off again.

Helen took a joint out of her bag and lit it.

'Helen, you know that we are not allowed to smoke in the dressing room. You'll get caught and not just for a cigarette but for dope. Put it out.'

'Sod them.' She took her chair and put it against the closed door and sat on it. She took a deep puff of the joint.

There was a knock on the door. 'Ten minutes.'

We jumped to our feet. Helen put out the joint. We dressed and ran to the stage.

*

At our house, we sat at the kitchen table. Helen was obviously shaken by the letter. It hurt me to watch her pain. I wished I could do something to alleviate it. I poured us wine; she rolled a joint.

'I was never aware of the troubles between my parents,' she said as if continuing a conversation. 'When I was ten, mother came to live in England. I presumed my father would soon follow. He never did.'

She drank her wine, rolled another joint, and I waited.

'One day I found Mother in tears. She had a letter in her hand. I recognised Father's hand writing. I was fourteen then. I shouted at her. I accused her of keeping my father away from me. That made her cry even more. It was then that she told me how she had put up with his infidelities and philandering all through their married life.'

'Well, why did she put up with it?'

'She said that she loved him, that she had been prepared to put up with whatever he did as long as he was discreet. She didn't want to lose him.' Helen paused, then in a softer voice she said, 'Mother says that she still loves him. That he is the love of her life and there will never be another.'

After a while, I asked, 'Helen, why didn't she tell you earlier? I think that she should have.'

'I know. I did ask. She said that it was because through all those years, she was hoping that he'd come back to her and everything would be all right. They're divorced now.'

I put my hand on hers wanting to comfort her.

'Oh, but that's not all,' she went on as if she had never stopped. 'It gets worse. He'd taken a mistress. He set her up in a house and spent most of his free time there. Everyone knew. He didn't even attempt to hide it. Can you imagine how much my mother suffered?'

'How cruel. Is that why she divorced him?'

Helen laughed sarcastically. 'She didn't want a divorce. He demanded it. He threatened her, saying that he'd bring me back to Ceylon to live with him and his mistress and she would not see me again.'

'She could have fought him in court. They normally award the child to the mother.'

'My mother? Fight? You have no idea; My mother wouldn't say boo to a goose.'

'What? What goose?'

Helen smiled indulgently. 'It's a saying. It means someone timid, compliant; she couldn't stand up for herself. That's my mother.'

We sat in silence for a while. Helen was absorbed in thoughts, in memories.

'I can't forgive him,' she continuing her thoughts out loud. 'No. I can't. He married that woman you know. I don't want to meet her. I don't think that I could be nice to her, not after what they did. They ruined my mother's life. No, I can't forgive him. Mother didn't deserve his cruelty. The way he treated her…'

She burst into tears. I was lost for words to console her. I got up and hugged her. When her sobs subsided. She looked up at me with eyes full of sorrow.

We took a downer and went to bed.

# CHAPTER 17

By the time we moved to the casino in Figueira da Foz, I knew I was pregnant. I tried to remember whether I had taken the pill when I was with Robert. I couldn't. Sometimes I did forget to take them. I was scared, I didn't know what to do. I didn't think about it all the time, but when I did, I felt trapped and scared.

There too we rented a house for the month. A few days after our arrival, a small dog started following us, or rather Helen. He took to sitting outside the house waiting for her. On the third day she took him in.

'Not a good idea,' I said. 'He might have rabies. You shouldn't bring him in.'

There was no stopping her. After she washed and fed him, he looked really pretty and appeared very well behaved. We decided that he had come from a good home and somehow got lost. Helen named him Dog.

The next stray Helen brought back was a teenage boy that she found sitting on a street corner, looking in need. After he had a wash and food, he still looked in a bad state. Helen told him that he could stay the night on the sofa. I hid my passport and money. Not a bad idea as it turned out. When we got up the next day, Helen's blouse and my trousers were missing from the washing line and he had taken the money from Helen's purse. We found him in town, slumped on a bench wearing our clothes. He looked at us with glazed eyes. I became aware that the two soldiers standing nearby were looking at us with interest. We left him where he was.

That night, when we arrived at the casino, we were summoned to the manager's office.

'The police were here.' He looked and sounded annoyed. 'They told me that you took this boy to your house. Do you realise that the boy is a heroin addict? Do you want to get into trouble with the Guardia Civil?'

'I don't see the problem,' Helen said softly. 'He looked hungry and homeless. No harm done.'

'No harm done? You have no idea. I had to promise the police that it would not happen again. You two work for the casino. Do you understand? I expect you to behave and not cause trouble. It is not a good idea to be noticed by the police and the Guardia Civil. This is not England.'

'Oops,' Helen said after we left his office. 'He was pissed off.'

'We must be careful Helen. There are police everywhere. We don't want to get into trouble. Do we?'

'No. of course not,' she smiled mischievously. 'But Dog stays. He didn't say anything about Dog.'

*

To finish my drug education. Helen wanted us to take a trip together. I was scared. I didn't like not being in control of myself. I had heard of trips that went bad, about people who during it thought they could fly and took off from high places only to plunge to their death.

'You'll be all right with me. It is an amazing experience. Really it is. There is no way of describing it. Come on Daniela. Don't be a scaredy cat. We will only take half a tab each, and I'll be with you all the way through. There is nothing to be afraid of.'

The next night, after we left the casino, we shared a tab of LSD. We walked up the hill and sat down. It was the blue hour. Translucent Red, yellow, orange and blue spread over the horizon. The world was calm. Then strong, vibrant colours started moving and breaking into patterns like a kaleidoscope. Into it rose a ball of fire. It was surrounded by swirling patterns and colourful flames, like the ones I watched in Mina's fireplace. It was the most spectacular sunrise I had ever seen. I could physically feel the enchantment of a newly-born world, the magic of the hour was tangible. I felt a part of it. I looked at Helen. I saw a benevolent angel with wings looking at me smiling. She spread her wings and hugged me. I felt safe.

When we got back. Helen went to the kitchen to get water, and for some reason or other, I sat on the stool in front of my dressing table. In the mirror I saw my face, I looked beautiful. Then it started changing. Lines appeared, they deepened. Wrinkles formed around my eyes. I watched in horror as the face distorted beyond recognition. An old woman with hollowed out eyes was staring at me from a skeletal face that I knew was mine. I started screaming. I couldn't take my eyes off of the mirror. Helen came and pulled me away. She put me to bed, gave me water to drink and lay by my side holding my hand. She kept reassuring me that everything was fine and all would be all right.

The room was moving, the furniture distorting and elongating like in a Salvador Dali painting. I was floating or rather a part of me was. I was watching the transparent me rolling in mid-air, moving to music that I could hear. Slowly, the image faded.

It seemed ages before I came to myself. I felt very tired and fell asleep.

When I woke up, Helen was sleeping next to me. She was still holding my hand. The acid trip had been beautiful in parts, but I did not like the fact that I lost control. That woman in the mirror reminded me of Mrs Birkin, only I looked worse, almost a skull with big holes for eyes.

Of course I knew that one day I would die. Sometime, when I had wished that I were dead, I always saw myself wearing a long gown and looking beautiful. The trip had shown me the truth. In it I saw what would really happen; that if I would live long enough to die old, that would be what I would look like. My beauty would be gone, there would be a skeleton in a flowing gown. No one can share dying. In my image there was no one sitting beside me holding my hand.

*

During our last week at the casino, I couldn't stop thinking about being pregnant, that it was not going to go away and I would have to face it when I was back in London. But at least I had somewhere to get back to. I smiled when I found a letter from Claire on my dressing room table. Seeing it made me feel a connection and a sense of belonging somewhere, even if it was ever so slight. I opened it with happy anticipation.

It fell from my hands. I dropped my face into my hands and a cry of anguish escaped me. 'Oh no, no. It can't be.'

'Daniela? What's the matter? Are you alright?'

I couldn't speak.

'Hang on. Hang on. Here. Have a glass of water. Take a deep breath. Now tell me.'

'Sorry Helen. I didn't mean to… There's been a crash, a car crash. It's too awful. They must be devastated.'

'Who?'

'Alan's sister and her husband died in a car crash.'

Helen put her hand over her mouth, her eyes were wide open. We stared at each other in silent understanding.

It was later, in the house that I told her about the rest of the letter.

'They took the daughter in. She has my room. Claire says she is sorry, very sorry. I understand, of course I do. But I have nowhere to go back to. I feel selfish worrying about myself now.'

She looked at me thoughtfully. 'Right. When we get back, you'll stay with me until we sort something out.'

'No Helen. I can't let you do that. I… I can't impose on you. It is not your problem.'

'It'll be fine. You will stay with me and that's that.'

People say things like that on the spur of the moment, like all those who had given me their phone number and had said to call them when I came to England. But Helen meant it.

A need to tell her everything came over me and so I blurted it out. 'I am pregnant.'

'Bloody hell Daniela. Are you sure?'

'I'm sure.'

'Robert's?'

'Yes.'

'Perhaps you should tell him. He might be glad of it.'

'No.'

'Why? He loves you. You told me so. This changes everything. If you tell him…'

I didn't let her finish. 'I don't want him to be with me because I carry his child. He made it clear that he doesn't want me. I will not force him into that.'

I was certain that if I told Robert, he would do the right thing. I didn't want that. It wasn't his fault that I had failed to take the pills regularly.

'All right, if that's how you feel. So what? Are going to have the child? On your own?'

'The last thing I need is a baby. I'll have to have an abortion.'

I had been carrying this horror and fear inside of me in silence. I hadn't thought of what to do about it. It had sat at the back of my mind, waiting, then coming to the fore and I would push it back. But now that I said it, I knew that I had no other option.

Helen came, stood in front of me and put her hands on my shoulders.

'It's a big decision Daniela. You might regret it one day. Are you certain that it is what you want?'

There was no doubt in my mind. 'Yes Helen, I really do.'

I watched her. She was genuinely concerned for me. I knew no one who would have taken in an abandoned dog and a stray boy, and now it was me. In all this darkness that I swam in, she was the only light.

*

Dog ran after our taxi when we left the town. Helen cried watching him losing the race. I looked at the arid and barren countryside. Time to face the pregnancy was getting nearer. I had a sinking feeling and wondered at what I was going back to.

# CHAPTER 18

I went to see doctor Jacob in the hope that he would agree to an abortion. I was scared that he might refuse. I had to have an abortion. I wouldn't be a good mother, one that would be prepared to commit herself to years of looking after a vulnerable human being. I could barely look after myself, let alone a child.

With a shaky voice I explained my situation. I could not have a child on my own with no secure income and no fixed abode. It was unthinkable.

He looked at me as if weighing me up. 'And the father? Have you spoken to him? Maybe...'

I broke in, 'No. Sorry doctor Jacob, it is out of the question. I can't speak to him.'

He thought for a while and I held my breath. 'Did you not take the contraceptive pills I prescribed for you?'

I had to admit it. He would probably find me stupid. 'I forgot sometimes. Sorry.'

'You needn't say sorry to me. I am not the one who got pregnant.'

Was he telling me off? No, he wasn't, he was smiling kindly. After he established that the pregnancy was less than three months he said, 'I'll book you for an abortion at the

Whittington Hospital.'

I was relieved and grateful that he didn't try to make me change my mind.

*

I walked to Claire's to collect my car and belongings. Her face was drawn, she looked tired. The effect of the accident was felt in the house, in the subdued atmosphere, in the silence that did not feel peaceful. It was as if all joy and happiness had been taken away. Alan was not in. Claire told me about the death of Alan's sister and her husband in the car accident, how painful it was for all of them and especially seeing the daughter's unbearable grief. 'It was one phone call,' she said. 'Just one, unexpected call, out of the blue, and in a few seconds our lives were changed.'

I tried to tell her how sorry I was, but there was not much I could say except to hug her and thus try to convey my feelings.

As I was loading my car, Rebecca and her sister came back from the park. Rebecca clung to me, she offered me her bedroom, it nearly brought me to tears.

I was sad as I drove away. It was an end to a period in my life when I lived with Claire's family.

*

At Helen's one-bedroom flat in West Hampstead I tried not to be in the way. I slept on the sofa in the living room and the red suitcase lived in the boot of my car. During the day I went out for long walks and sat in the park watching the children play. Sometimes I took Helen and her boyfriend's dog with me. In the evenings, I hid in their bedroom waiting for guests to leave.

When the time came, I spent a fretful night alone in the hotel I had booked, and the next day I walked to the hospital.

I woke up from the sedation alone in a crisp, white room, the colour of purity. Rays of sunlight streamed through the dirty windows. It felt surreal, dreamlike, and in it I lay feeling light and without substance. I had killed my child. There was nothing pure about it, it was bloody. But I felt nothing. I was numb. All I wanted was to get to the hotel room and be alone.

A nurse in a starched uniform came in to check on me. She took my pulse and my temperature and kept saying, 'Good'.

They released me that afternoon. Helen had said that she would come to the hotel, but it would probably be late. She was rehearsing for a West End show. I walked to the hotel, stopping to rest every so often. I was very tired. In the bedroom I closed the curtains, got into bed with my clothes on, curled up, and pulled the blankets over my head. There was an emptiness, a hollow inside me. I killed a child, a child that had been conceived and could have grown and could have had a life. What had I done? I felt miserable and guilty. My eyes were dry.

I tried to sleep. I couldn't. I said aloud to the darkness under the blanket, 'I had no choice. I had to do it.' I said it as if I was giving an explanation for my crime; but to whom? To myself? To the unborn child?

I tried to empty my mind, but thoughts kept coming. I uncovered my head and through the gloom, I made out the ugly shape of the ceiling light. I had made a mess of my life, I thought. I remembered the social worker at high school. She had called me out in the middle of a class. It was shortly after my parents divorced. 'Children need a stable home,' she had told me in her room. 'They need love, they need to be nourished, they need to feel safe. Children from broken homes are damaged forever, I'm afraid.'

As she spoke those hateful words I stared at the plant on her windowsill, a cactus of some sort. I thought that it was almost impossible to kill a cactus by not giving it water. I had expected her to be understanding, sympathetic and compassionate. I couldn't understand why she was so heartless. From what she was saying I took it that I was doomed, and doomed forever. I came out of her room and sat on a bench in the corridor. I began to feel angry. I believed that people dealt differently with given situations. I thought that a weak person would be damaged, but a strong person could overcome. I was determined to prove her wrong. But it looked like she was right.

Most people wanted marriage and children to fulfil their lives. My life would have been simpler had I wanted the same. I only knew that I didn't, but I couldn't understand why.

I had no idea how long I was lying there before Helen came. She turned on the lights, kissed my forehead and produced food.

'Soup. Good bread and butter. And chocolate! Come on, sit up.'

'I'm not hungry.'

'I don't care. You need to eat. Sit up Daniela, I made soup. Vichyssoise. It's really good even if I say so,' she smiled.

I sat up and tried to eat.

She searched my face. 'Daniela, does it hurt? How are you feeling?'

I couldn't answer. The tears that had not come before,

now came. Helen took the bowl out of my hand and got a box of tissues. She sat on the bed next to me, put her arm around my shoulder and let me cry. She dabbed my eyes with the tissues.

'The best thing for you is to get a goodnight sleep. We'll have a joint, I'll give you a sleeping pill and we'll go to sleep.'

'We?'

'You didn't think that I was going to leave you alone tonight. Get into your P.Js.'

Her kindness released another round of tears.

*

I didn't wake up till mid-morning. My face in the bathroom mirror was covered with tears' runs, streaks of makeup and mascara. My eyes were red and puffed. Helen was already up and had packed my overnight bag. She ordered a coffee and phoned the club to say that she was ill and wouldn't be there for rehearsals. We checked out, leaving a pile of tissues on the floor by the bed.

Helen drove. We were silent in the car and then I remembered.

'How was your visit to your father?' She had gone to see him on the night I had spent alone in the hotel bedroom.

'It was awkward. We were ever so polite. He controls his wife just like he had controlled my mother.'

'What's she like?'

'She's all right really. Nothing special. Plain and simple but she obviously loves him.'

She was quiet for a while. I waited.

She winced. 'I can't forgive him. I tried.'

'Will you see him again?'

'I suppose I'll have to.'

'What about your mother? Does she mind?'

'I haven't told her yet. I'm dreading it. It will hurt her.'

I looked at my friend, her face was contorted with so much pain that I felt it too. Helen was not all right and there was nothing I could do to help her, nor had I been able to do anything for Claire. I felt useless.

*

For the next few days, I had no energy. In the mornings Helen brought me a cup of tea before she left for rehearsals. I lay on the sofa for hours intending to get up. I tried to read, but I couldn't concentrate. I knew I had to find a place to live but I wasn't able to think straight. Somehow, I had to find my will and my courage, without them I'd be lost. I remembered the Chinese proverb that had influenced my decision to leave home. "Pearls don't lie on the seashore. If you want one you must dive for it." It had been a long time ago, that strong and full of hope I had crossed the sea, plunged into its dark and mysterious floor to search for pearls.

*

It was Helen who helped me find a place to live. One night when I was in the bedroom, she said that there was someone that she wanted me to meet. I stood at the bedroom door for a moment reluctant to enter the living room. There were a few people there passing the time, drinking and smoking. A big man with long hair that fell over his face was sitting on the sofa. Helen introduced us. He lifted his head, smiled and shifted to make room for me.

'Helen tells me that you need a place to stay.'

'Yes,' I said simply.

He brushed his hair off of his face and tucked it behind his ears. Every part of his face was big too. 'Where are you staying at the moment?'

'Here.'

'Where?'

'You're sitting on it. This is my bed.'

'What? You crash here?'

'Yes.' Why was he asking me all this questions? I wished he'd go away. I stared at the big silver rings on his fingers.

The Big Man smiled. 'I can sort you out. Easy.'

I was surprised at that. Maybe he was having a laugh, or worse, he was about to offer to share his bed with me. But then why did Helen want me to meet him?

'Honestly, I can fix you up with a squat. Tomorrow if you like.'

'What's a squat?'

'An empty property that we take possession of and move in. There is a very nice flat nearby. I can get you in there tomorrow.'

'What do you mean? What about the owners? Don't they object?' It all sounded very peculiar and suspicious.

'Once you're in, you will have squatters' rights. It will give you time with a roof over your head. Well, do you want me to fix you up then?'

It worried me. 'It sounds like breaking the law. The owner will come and throw me out. He will want to rent it. Won't he?'

'No, he won't rent it out because he doesn't want to end up with sitting tenants, and he can't throw you out without a court order to evict you. That takes about six months. How about it? Better then Helen's busy living room.'

I felt sorry for the landlord, but anything was better. 'Yes please.'

'Good. I'll come for you tomorrow around mid-day.'

*

I waited for him, and waited and waited some more. When I was just about to give up, the Big Man arrived with two young men in scruffy jeans. He took me to a terraced house in a nearby street and we walked through the swinging door of the main entrance. The lobby looked tidy. The young men got busy breaking the lock of the ground floor flat. I worried that the other occupants would call the police.

It didn't take them long and the Big Man and I walked into the flat's square entrance hall. There were three open doors and a corridor.

'Choose a room,' he smiled.

I looked at him in disbelief. 'Go on. You get first choice.'

'How do you mean?'

'The other two rooms are for other squatters.'

'What?!'

'You didn't think that you get the place all to yourself, did you?' he chuckled.

Actually, I did.

'Don't worry. I'll make sure that they are nice,' he smiled.

I walked through the flat, the rooms were empty, all they needed was a good clean. I chose the room at the back with its window overlooking an unkempt garden. The Big Man and his helpers turned on the gas, electricity and water, also illegally. He said that he would come the next day with his van to take me shopping to second hand shops to buy furniture.

He gave me the keys and said, 'These places stand empty while people haven't got anywhere to live. I'm sure that you will look after the place.'

'Of course. Thank you.'

*

After he left, I looked at the keys in my hand in disbelief. I walked around the flat and tried everything; The loo flushed, the taps ran, the fridge hummed, the electric cooker worked and there was even an electric boiler to heat the water. There was something calming in the constant humming of the fridge.

I sat at the top of the metal steps that led down from the kitchen to the garden. The spring sunshine was warm, the surrounding gardens were full of flowers, the tree at the bottom of the garden had fresh leaves that danced in the light breeze. A Jasmin in flower was climbing up the metal railings. Wafts of sweet smell reached me. It evoked memories of summer evenings when we sat in my grandfather's garden, where flowering Jasmin perfumed the air. I looked down the squat's garden and saw roses poking their heads through the tall weeds. There must have been a garden there once, I thought. I listened to the birds singing and the faraway hum of traffic. I felt at peace.

I stayed. I slept on the carpeted floor wrapped in my fur coat. In the morning, the Big Man and his helpers took me out to second hand shops to buy furniture. After they left, I cleaned. I didn't like cleaning, but I was taking possession, making the space mine. I sat on a chair and leant on the small table that I had placed by the window. I looked around me with satisfaction. My clothes were in the old mahogany chest of drawers and hanging in the wardrobe that had a full-length mirror. I looked at the red leather suitcase on top of it and hoped that it would stay there for a long time. From the beautiful old brass bed with mother of pearl inlay on its headboard, lying on white crisp cotton bedding, I could look out of the window. It was the first bed I had ever owned. On the table was a pile of books waiting to be read, a vase full of flowers that Helen had brought, and my new transistor radio. I turned it on. The sound of string quartet filled the room.

## Chapter 19

Poppy's top floor flat was near Marylebone High Street. She sat me in her office told me that she needed to finish what she was doing and asked if I wouldn't mind waiting and answering the phone so that she could get on without interruptions. I said that I would be happy to help.

The woman on the phone asked me to tell Poppy that she couldn't dance that night. I said I would. But then she started pouring her heart out.

'You see, my boyfriend left me. I can't cope. I'm in bits. Will you tell Poppy?' she said in a shaky voice full of tears.

'Of course.' I felt sorry for her and intuitively I asked, 'What happened?'

She launched into a sobbing monologue about her boyfriend leaving her and how cut up she was. I kept saying, 'I know, I know. Poor you.' Her pain was not unfamiliar to me.

All I could see of Poppy was her red hair. She raised her head and then her eyebrows. I put my hand on the speaker and said, 'Jody. She can't dance tonight. Boyfriend problems.'

Poppy made circles with her hand as if to say carry on. Meanwhile Jody was still pouring her heart out sobbing and snuffling.

When she eased up, I said, 'Look, it is none of my business, but I do understand. You see, my boyfriend left me not that long ago. I really do know how painful it is.'

Her sobs were choking her. Mine had too. I could feel her pain inside of me. I wanted to help her, but at the same time, for Poppy's sake, I wanted to get her to perform that night.

'I really do know your pain. I felt just like you do. You mustn't let it take over your life. The best decision I had made was to go on performing.' I lied, but the lie was well intended and I had a purpose. Another sob. 'I'll tell you something. It was the best thing I could have done. It took my mind of off things and I felt better for doing something instead of moping around. You must be strong.'

'How can I. What if I cry on stage? How am I supposed to smile eh? Look happy? No. I can't do it. I can't bear it,' she whimpered.

'You are a performer. Don't you forget everything when you are on stage?'

'Well. Yes, I do.'

'Well then, don't let him win. Go and dance. It'll take your mind of off it. I promise you, really I do. You will feel better for it.'

It was a good advice. I had let a man debilitate me and I didn't want to see it happening to her. I wanted her to overcome her grief, and despite of the pain get on with her life. It wouldn't be easy.

She sounded taken aback and stopped sobbing. 'Let him win? How do you mean?'

'He had inflicted unbearable pain, he left you to suffer, and if you don't dance, you might lose your job. Is he really worth it?'

She didn't say a word but kept on sobbing.

'You have a career. Are you going to let him ruin it too?'

I waited to see if she would take the bait. I hoped she would. I felt a little guilty for lying to her, but for some reason or other it was important to me to make her find strength in herself. I did know how hard it would be.

Her sobs turned into soft snivels. 'No. My career is my life.'

'Well then.'

Silence. I waited. I could feel that familiar pain rising within me. It was not as if it had gone away. I pushed it down. I hoped that she would do the show instead of staying in and wallowing in her agony that would grow until it would take her over and debilitate her.

She snuffled, sounding like a child that had been mollified. 'Yes, You're right. I shouldn't let him ruin my career.'

'That's the spirit. Good on you. So, you'll dance? With a smile?'

'Yes. I will. Thank you. You are very kind.' She swallowed and sniffled, but more subdued this time.

'You're welcome.'

I put the phone down pleased with the outcome. Poppy was looking at me.

'She'll dance,' I said.

'Well done. I am nearly finished.'

Shortly after, Poppy put her pen down. 'Thank you for sorting Jody out. I thought you handled her very well.'

Over a cup of tea, Poppy talked about an engagement that she had in mind for me and outlined her terms and how much commission she would take.

*

The next night a taxi took us to an exclusive nightclub in Regent Street. They were looking for dancers for their new show. Sitting at the club, in semidarkness, in a red velvet booth, drinking champagne and waiting for the show to start, Poppy told me what was on her mind.

'You were very good handling Jody yesterday. Thank you. I thought that you might like to give me a hand sometimes. I'd like you to.'

I didn't expect this. I stared at her speechless.

'Think about it. I'll pay you of course.'

She was serious. 'Kind of you to think of me. I know nothing about working in an agency. I can't see how I'll be any use to you.'

'Let me be the judge of that. If you can handle my other prima donnas like you did Jody, then believe me, you'll be extremely useful to me. think about it.'

*

The show started. It was indeed fabulous. The theme was Music of the Caribbean. A small orchestra accompanied the four singers who flanked the stage. On a lavish set, dancers in beautiful and imaginative costumes danced. Tall showgirls were gliding around with their breasts on display.

Shortly after the show ended, an icy blond in a long slinky black dress, came and sat at our table. Poppy introduced her as the club's owner. She asked about my experience, asked me to stand up, then to turn around slowly. She looked me up and down. I didn't like it, but my looks were what I was selling. At least it was an appreciative look. She asked me to come and audition for the new show.

*

Mid-morning, I arrived at the club. The house lights were on, dancers in leotards and leggings were slumped on red and gold chairs chatting and smoking. They all turned to look at me. They smiled and waved. The choreographer called me up to the stage. The dancers shouted, 'Good luck.' What a relief, a friendly bunch, I thought.

He gave me a few dance routines to follow and then said, 'Welcome'. He clapped his hands and the dancers came on to the stage. The dancing was more sophisticated than in the Portuguese revue and the dancers were professional, good and able.

It was called 'The London Show.' By the end of rehearsals, I knew songs like *My Old Man's a Dust Man, Doing the Lambeth Walk, Daisy, Daisy, London Pride,* and the like. It was another introduction to English culture just like when I had read the children stories to Rebecca. I did recognise one of the songs, *Knees up Mother Brown.* I had learnt it from Rebecca, only her lyrics were different: *Knees up Mother Brown, get your knickers down, Under the table you must go, Ee-aye, Ee-aye, Ee-aye-oh.*

I was back in sequins, chiffons and elaborate head-dresses. The club's regime was very strict. We had to clock in and out. When not on stage, we sat in a room upstairs under the supervision of a middle-aged lady wearing a thick pair of glasses. She knitted incessantly with a cigarette dangling out of her mouth. We were to wear long dresses when we walked through the club but I didn't have to sit there being bothered by the punters.

Every so often the phone would ring and the knitter would send one of them down to the club. I did not know what it was about, but I soon found out. Not long after the show opened, the knitter called me over. I sat at her desk and she asked me if I wanted to sit with the punters. I looked at her surprised and with apprehension.

'Oh,' she said, 'has no one explained this to you?' I shook my head. 'Clients ask for a particular girl to join them at their table. You get paid for this service of course. I've had quite a few requests for you but we thought it better to let you settle in first.'

She looked for my reaction. I said nothing. I didn't like the sound of this. It was not in my contract.

'When you are sitting with a client,' she continued. 'You have to order food even if you don't eat it, let them buy you cigarettes and flowers, but most importantly get them to buy you a bottle of champagne. The bigger the better.'

'Do I have to?' I asked through clenched teeth. I hadn't bargained for that and if it turned out to be part of the job, I would not stay.

'No, you don't. But it would be silly not to. The punters pay handsomely if they enjoy your company. Most of the girls do it and the club would like you to. We do not like to disappoint the punters.'

Without hesitation I said, 'I'd rather not. I hope that's all right.'

'Of course. Let me know if you change your mind.'

So that was where they were going, dressed in sexy long dresses that showed lots of cleavage. The show, I thought, is like a vitrine, the merchandise put on display for the delectation of the clients. As far as I was concerned, they could look, I would not come out of the glass case.

The women were of different nationalities. In the rest room, they retouched their makeups, filed their nails and chatted in English with strong accents. I listened to talks about fashion, gossip from women's magazines but also to my surprise politics and money. They exchanged advice on where to save and get the best interest. They talked about the recession, the oil crisis, inflation. I was not aware of any of it. I didn't read the newspapers nor was I interested in politics then.

One night the German dancer asked me, 'Do you go case?'

I looked at her perplexed. 'Sorry. What?'

'Oh, nothing. Not important.' She exchanged a meaningful look with the English rose.

I was intrigued and wondered what she could have meant.

*

I had accepted Poppy's offer, and started working for her once the show went into its run. I worked a few afternoons a week. I answered the phone, took messages, organised the bookings and made tea. Most of the time the performers wanted to chat and talk about their personal life and their careers. I was a listening ear at the end of a phone, not quite an agony aunt. I found it all interesting and enjoyed the work. Maybe it was the start I had been looking for. It suited me well, and I was good at it.

I asked Poppy what the German dancer had meant by 'going case'.

'It means going with the punters. You know?'

'You mean when they go downstairs to sit at their tables? Our carer asked me if I would. I said no. Is that what it means?'

'Well, not quite. The thing is that officially the girls are not supposed to meet with the punters outside the club. But they do. Not all of them. The club knows of course.'

I stared at her in disbelief. 'They are prostitutes?!'

'Sometimes Daniela, you do surprise me. You are so naïve. What did you think they were doing? Let me shock you even more. The reason she asked you if you go case, is that sometimes the punters ask her to bring another girl with her.'

I was shocked. I stared at Poppy. 'She thought that I am a prostitute? I can't believe it.'

'Why not Daniela. Do they look like prostitutes to you? Do they have a scarlet mark on their forehead?' She sounded a little reproachful.

I didn't answer. I was confused. To be thought a prostitute was insulting to me. 'Don't think too badly of them. They are women, just like you and me. Some have families to support. You didn't think badly of them before you knew, did you?'

'No. I didn't.'

I began to feel ashamed. I was being too quick to judge. I remembered the women who lined the streets in Frankfurt, out in the freezing cold, scantily dressed, running to Dolly. I had thought badly of them. I had never wondered what misfortune had brought them to the streets near Schafferman's warehouse. I remembered the young girl that I had given the fur jacket to, the look of fear and plea for help in her pale blue eyes before she got into the punter's car, had stayed with me. The women working in the club, in the warmth, well fed, well dressed and well off, were more fortunate than her. I had no right to judge any of them. I didn't know their stories. Maybe it was the only choice that was left to them in order to survive and feed their children, their last resort, and they took it. Poppy was right.

## Chapter 20

The club closed for two days due to an electrical failure. At Helen's flat, before going to the Roundhouse to see a rock band she knew, the rest of the party smoked joints and took speed to get their heads in the right frame of mind. I didn't. At the gig, my companions would not stay in one place but moved around chain smoking and chatting incessantly. I gave up trying to keep up with them and went to sit with the sound man. From there, I looked down at the excited crowd and saw the guy that everybody called Jesus. I had seen him at gigs before. He always wore a striped caftan and danced and jumped wildly and at some point, he would strip naked, which is what he was doing as I watched from my vantage point.

The band came on stage and started playing. They had a solid rhythm section and a good singer. They were cooking and the sound man and I banged our heads in unison. When the two guitarists had a guitar conversation, we smiled at each other appreciatively.

After the show we hooked up with the band in their dressing room. The windowless room soon filled up with smoke and the smell of marihuana filled the air. I was beginning to feel nauseated, when a young man with long, silky, straight brown hair, came and stood next to me. I recognised the bass player.

'You're not enjoying this mad house.'

I smiled. 'Not really.'

'I'm hungry. Always am after gigs. Let's go eat.'

I wasn't sure why I said yes. Maybe because I wanted to get out of there and away from the speed mad people who were chain smoking and talking ten to the dozen.

I followed the bass player up the stairs. He wore very tight trousers which showed his small and shapely behind. In the nearby Indian restaurant, we had a bit of a laugh and talked about music we liked. He was easy-going, uncomplicated and I liked the fact that he was not one of those who felt they had to impress me. When we got into a taxi, he gave his address, then looked at me to see if I objected. I didn't. There was something about him that attracted me. Perhaps that night, I wanted to feel a body next to mine, to feel wanted.

In a flat somewhere near the Portobello Road, I curled up in a comfortable sofa. He chose an album, put it on the record player, came and sat on the floor by my feet and rolled a joint.

'Who is it?' I asked.

'The band is called, It's a Beautiful Day.

I closed my eyes and listened.

*White bird in a golden cage, on a winter's day in the rain*
*White bird in a golden cage alone.*

We didn't speak. We smoked and listened. I heard the most beautiful violin solo soaring high. I lay my head back and let the music take me over. When the song finished, he turned on a reel-to-reel tape recorder. The rhythmic rock music, the driving beat made me want to dance.

He took my hand, pulled me up, led me to the bedroom,

and gently laid me on the bed. I watched him undress in the dim light. He came and slowly took my clothes off. His hands explored my body, he kissed and caressed me all over. At times his eyes held mine intently, watching, looking, reading me, seeing if I liked what he was doing. I did. I liked being caressed. It felt nice. He was focused and absorbed in one thing only; arousing me. It was that same focus that I had seen in his eyes when he had played his bass guitar.

I felt his hands on me, his lips on my skin, his tongue was warm as he drank my wetness. Something more than my usual response to sex was happening. I felt desire, a craving, urges like I had never had before. I began to breath heavily. He smiled. His touching and kissing became less gentle, harder, demanding. I found myself responding. He held my eyes when he penetrated. I shuddered. We fell into a rhythmical, silent and physical conversation. My inhibitions were gone. I was taking part. He moved with the music and I with him. A dance, an erotic pas de deux.

*

Daylight was filtering through the closed curtains when I woke up. I rested my head on my elbow and watched him sleep. He was relaxed, and I saw the sweet child that he must have been. That was a revelation, I reflected, a wonderful one. It had taken that one man to open my eyes. I felt a deep gratitude to him. I kissed his forehead, whispered 'thank you,' dressed and tiptoed out. I didn't know his name. I didn't think that I'd see him again.

I walked down Ladbroke Grove. I remembered his eyes seeking mine, above all his sense of rhythm, after all he was a base player. I smiled to myself.

I reached the Portobello Road, stopped and bought

vegetables from a stall and then took a bus to my squat.

*

I sat on the metal stairs. In the pale blue sky small clouds were changing shapes. One of them, passing slowly over the sun, looked like a man in a flowing robe, his head outlined in bright gold like a halo.

I reflected on my sex life, how it had been. I had heard sayings and words bandied around like finding one's sexuality, hang-ups, libido, but they were abstract and meaningless to me. I realised that it was inhibition that kept me shy about exposing my body. When Benyamin had touched my breasts as he passed me in the house, I recoiled. I had thought it a rude gesture. I felt uncomfortable being naked in front of him, I didn't like it when he walked in while I was having a bath, I did not want the light on when we made love. This had stemmed from being brought up in a house where nakedness was frowned upon as if it was something to be ashamed of. I had even heard my father telling my mother off for walking around the apartment wearing a see-through negligee.

I thought of my sex experiences with Benyamin, Robert, Chris the ski instructor and the few one-night stands. I realised that what I had been doing was what the English call, 'lie back and think of England.' No wonder the French pilot had called me frigid.

The old man was no longer floating in the sky, he had taken the form of a strange animal with horns. The leaves on the tree fluttered in the summer breeze. A flock of sparrows took off. A dog barked, another joined it.

I had expected men to know the mechanics of sex, relying on them to teach me. It occurred to me that they were not all good at it. I had been told that men had urges they had to relieve. I could see now that sex was not just a solo act for men. Up until then, no one had taken time to arouse me. They would have been well-rewarded. But then, perhaps it wasn't their fault, perhaps no one had instructed them either.

It was near dusk and I went in to get ready for my outing with Helen. It was my last night off and we were going out to the disco. I rummaged through my wardrobe and chose a salmon, see-through beaded, midi dress from the thirties. Its skirt would twirl around me when I danced, and the beads would twinkle as they caught the light.

# CHAPTER 21

My new room was large, north facing and looking onto the road. There was a bay window that did not flood the room with light. I was sitting on the floor playing with my dog. I had been sad to leave my peaceful abode, but the landlord had come and asked us to vacate it. Myself and the two young men that the Big Man had brought to share the flat with me, felt that it was the right thing to do. The Big Man said that we shouldn't had, but rehoused me in another squat nearby.

The first thing that had hit me as I entered the ground floor flat was the smell of joss sticks. After that it was the noise. There were people lounging in the living room where the smell of cannabis competed with the joss sticks. Music was playing and people were sitting around chatting.

I was to share it with a couple who were living the hippie life, Jimmy and Marie. He fancied himself a keyboard player. He was full of himself, opinionated and irritating. She was a home maker who cooked macrobiotic food, brown in colour and tasteless. There was no peace and quiet in that squat, people were coming and going all day and night, taking drugs, playing music and putting the world to right.

*

I had ended up with the dog when I visited Helen. She was holding it in her arms when she opened the door.

'Isn't she lovely?' she said in the living room and left to make tea.

The dog wanted to play. I obliged. She was cute. Her hair was light cream in colour and she had rings of ochre around her expressive eyes. I sat on the floor and she jumped onto my lap and stared at me. I stroked her. Helen came back with tea.

'She likes you. Pretty, isn't she? I think you should have her. She's taken to you.'

'You're joking.'

'No. I'm not. Look how she looks at you. She chose you. Come on Daniela, how can you resist?'

'She is yours, isn't she? Besides, I have no idea how to look after a dog. I never had one.'

'We can't keep her. Our dog does not like competition.'

The dog looked at me and I looked at her. She turned over in my lap to lay on her back.

'She wants a tummy rub.'

I went back to the squat with a dog on a lead walking next to me. Had I lost my mind? I could hardly look after myself, let alone a dog. I had no idea what to do with her. She was very cuddly and warm, and looked at me with big brown trusting eyes.

I needn't have worried about Lilydog, she became the darling of the household and the constant visitors. There were those who advocated rigorous training. Others, the free-loving spirits, said that I should let her do her own thing. Lilydog learned to please very fast. When told to sit, jump, or stand up on two legs, she did, and expected her reward to be put in her mouth promptly.

Marie fed Lilydog with cooked meat and vegetables. Everyone was told not to let her out and not to leave the front door open. I even put a large notice in big letters on the inside of the front door.

I asked Poppy about Lilydog. 'I have a dog. She really is sweet and obedient. You won't notice her. She…'

'Stop. Stop. I love dogs. Of course you can bring her.'

Lilydog grew to reveal a calm, obedient and amiable nature, and she was clever. I loved her. She came with me everywhere except to the club and the odd modelling jobs. She charmed everyone who met her. Her good nature and friendliness to all were winning. She slept in my bed, got me up in the mornings and took me for walks in the park. We were inseparable.

*

I met Tom at the squat. He was a drug dealer who imported cocaine from Colombia. In those days, smuggling drugs was done on a friendly basis. It was in the days when the Flower Power movement was putting flowers in the barrels of guns. It was later that drug dealers would replace the flowers with bullets.

I didn't make friends with the people who came to the squat. In this transient society friendship often came and went. Even so, Tom and I became friends. I liked it that he was not a great talker but more of a listener. He was generous with the white powder. He did not cut it with speed or talcum powder or anything else. The first time that I snorted his cocaine I realized how impure was the cocaine I had sampled previously. His had a different effect, it made me float pleasantly and at the same time heightened my awareness and brought sharpness and clarity to my mind.

Tom was thin and had a strange-looking face. His eyes, as blue and clear as the sky in summer, were small and close together. He had a long thin nose and wide but narrow lips. What with a tall forehead and a square face, the overall impression was inharmonious. His unruly, frizzy, dark blond long hair was gathered with an elastic band at his nape. It looked as if he never combed it.

I always knew when Tom was doing a deal, he would be quieter than usual. I could see that he was on edge, worrying should it go wrong, should the shipment get stopped, the drugs confiscated and people arrested. His poker face did not show any of it, but I could tell.

I often visited Tom in the cottage he rented in Muswell Hill. It was in a large garden behind one of the few detached houses that had not been sold to developers. On warm days, Lilydog and I would sit in the secluded calm garden where I could escape the madhouse that I was living in. Sometimes, I stayed the night in the spare room. We would get a takeaway and watch television.

*

It was on the day that I went for an appointment with a photographer in Mayfair that I met Sebastian. Tom had said that he could meet me afterwards in a house nearby and he would drive me back.

A pretty young woman in a flowing kaftan let me into the house in Marble Arch. I asked for Tom and she told me that he was somewhere around. I followed her up a staircase to the first floor and into a large bedroom. 'He'll show up soon,' she said and jumped on the enormous bed where a few people were lounging or sitting in the lotus position.

Others were occupying chairs and the floor. Someone kindly vacated a chair for me. No one asked me who I was, nor what I was doing there. A man with afro hair was sitting by the window rolling joints nonstop. Tom had told me that the people living there were a famous rock band, only I had never heard of them.

In an armchair directly in my line of vision, sat a handsome young man, his long legs crossed, one foot swinging back and forth. From the window behind him, sunrays highlighted a red hue in his straight, luxuriant brown hair that fell in its fullness to below his shoulders. Unlike many who thought that scruffy was the look of the time, his hair was well kept, and he wore a bottle green velvet suit with a crisp white shirt. The jacket was well made and sat perfectly on his slightly wide shoulders.

I stole glances at the man in the green velvet, averting my eyes when his gaze fell on me. I pretended to listen to the silly conversations of people who were out of their heads. When his eyes caught mine, I saw slate blue, slightly narrow, inquisitive eyes that looked at me with intensity. Our eyes locked for a few seconds. I looked away. In that short instant, there had been recognition, I have no other word for it, it disturbed me.

A guy picked up a guitar that was leaning on the wall next to him, stuck his cigarette in the end of its neck and played. Everyone fell silent. He was an extremely good player. Some people banged their heads to the rhythm, others drummed on their knees.

The joint roller stopped rolling and pulled a mirror from under his seat. From his jacket pocket he pulled a bag of white powder. Using a razor blade, he drew white lines on a mirror. I returned to look at the handsome man, he caught my eyes and smiled. I smiled shyly back. I felt uncomfortable, I wanted to get out of there, but if I stood up, they would all look at me. I wished that Tom would come.

The mirror started making the rounds. When it was passed to me, I was stupidly embarrassed not to snort a line, so I chose the shortest one. When the mirror got back to the man who rolled joints, he asked, 'Who took the Horse?' I had no idea what he was talking about. Soon I began to feel out of sorts. It got worse. I knew that I was sitting on a chair but it felt like I was sliding of off it. I found myself on the floor seeing stars, feeling disconnected and sick. I heard someone saying, 'She took the Horse,' another, 'Who is she?'

The man in the velvet suit was lifting me up and I floated downstairs feeling nauseated and helpless. I do not remember the drive back. I do not remember being put to bed. I was conscious but not conscious. I was sinking into darkness.

I must have fallen asleep. When I woke up, I wasn't sure where I was. I was slow to regain a sense of being. Marie came in.

'Oh good. You're awake.' She sat on the bed next to me stroking Lilydog. 'How are you feeling? You look pale.'

'I feel awful. I don't think I can get up.'

'I'm not surprised. Stay in bed. I'll make you a cup of tea with lots of sugar. You need to drink.'

'What do you mean you are not surprised? What happened?'

'You took the Horse you fool.'

'What is that damn Horse?'

'Heroin.'

'What? I thought it was cocaine.'

'Well, it wasn't and it wasn't meant for you. The band is on heroin.'

'Damn. It looked the same, a line of white powder on a mirror. How was I to know? Will I be alright? Will I get addicted?'

She laughed. 'Not by taking one line. I believe that this will put you off Heroin for good.'

Heroin had not been included in the drug education Helen had given me in Portugal.

'You are not kidding. Why would anyone take to it when it makes you feel so awful?'

*

I was in the kitchen when Tom called by with the man in the green velvet suit, only this time he was wearing a maroon-coloured corduroy one. His name was Sebastian. He asked how I was feeling and I thanked him for looking after me. Then Tom discreetly left us alone.

His slate blue eyes held mine for longer than a heartbeat. He narrowed them and asked, 'Shall we go for a walk?'

I nodded my head.

Lilydog happily jumped into the back of his old Daimler and he drove us to Hampstead Heath. It was unseasonably warm. The sun sporadically appeared through hazy clouds. We walked, played with Lilydog who bounded along and made us laugh at her antics.

'Tom tells me that you dance in a nightclub. Are you a dancer?'

'Yes and no.'

'An intriguing answer. Would you care to elaborate?'

'Well, I can dance. It's a way for me to earn money. That's about it.'

'I see. I'll come and see you dance.'

'Please don't.'

Lilydog ran back to us and Sebastian threw her a stick.

'I've seen you once before.'

I stopped to look at him.

'I did. At the Speakeasy. You walked in with a group of people. I thought you looked stunning. I watched you until you left. I thought that I'd like to know you.'

I did a quick calculation. I must have been with the Abbey Road crowd, that was more than two years ago.

'But you didn't talk to me.'

'No.'

'Why?'

He looked uncomfortable. 'You looked aloof, remote; I didn't dare.'

I wished he had done.

We stared at each other and then burst out laughing. Lilydog ran around us wanting to join in.

We were still laughing when he said. 'You made it easy for me. You walked into that bedroom, you fainted, all I had to do was to scoop you up.'

The thought that it was brought about by a white line on a mirror taken by mistake, amused me.

By the pond, we sat on a bench. Sebastian put his arm around my shoulder. The afternoon in the hazy sun had the quality of a dream. Even Lilydog who had settled by our feet, had a faraway look in her eyes. Before we got up to leave, we exchanged a smile in which we told each other that we were happy to be there togcther.

A shadow of a cloud crossed the grass in front of our feet. I hoped that I would see him again.

# Chapter 22

Quite often, at two in the morning, when I left the club, I would find Sebastian outside sitting in his car reading spy novels or science fiction. He once gave me a book to read. It was called *Fear and Loathing in Las Vegas*. We had a good laugh talking about it. Sebastian, reminded me how starved I was of serious and interesting conversations. He was knowledgeable and had a sensible and logical way of looking at the topics we discussed. My brain was challenged and it was good to feel it working.

When with him, I reminded myself to keep my guard up, but I didn't find it easy.

Sometimes we would go to a café nearby and have breakfast, or at others we walked in Soho aimlessly, our heels echoing in the empty cobbled streets.

Once when we were at a cafe having breakfast, I asked him where he went to school.

'Boarding school when I was six. The usual, you know?'

'No, I don't know. The best schools in Israel are the state schools. Tearaways and Juvenile delinquents are sent to boarding schools.'

'That would have been fun I would have thought.'

We chuckled.

'Did you miss your parents?' I asked.

He didn't answer immediately. I had a feeling that he didn't want to talk about it.

'To begin with a little. I missed my home more.'

'But later, did you like it?'

'It was all right.'

His curt answer sounded like he wanted to end the subject. We ate our English breakfast for a while. I remembered that Anne had called boarding school a prison, a cold and harsh place.

'Where is your home?'

'Somewhere in Kent, in the middle of the countryside.'

'Sounds lovely.'

'Indeed. it is rather.'

I broke the yolk and dipped a piece of bread in it.

'How about university? Where did you go?' I asked.

'Cambridge.'

'Did you enjoy it?'

'As a matter of fact, I did. It was fun.'

'Fun?'

'Yes, well,' he grinned. 'We got up to all sorts of shenanigans.'

'Like what?'

He thought for a minute. 'We had a dare once, who could climb all the way up the church steeple.'

'That's dangerous.' I visualised a tall and tapering steeple and gasped.

He smiled indulgently. 'I dare say. It had to take place late at night of course. Unfortunately, we got caught and I nearly got expelled.'

'And did you get to the top?'

'Oh yes. I won. I didn't have to buy drinks at the pub for

a whole month.' He smiled mischievously. 'Then, there were the wild parties. We drank a lot, swung from chandeliers and got up to all sorts.'

'It doesn't sound like you did much learning.'

'I'm a quick learner.'

'Where you ever caned?'

'Ah, well,' he smiled. 'As it happens, several times.'

'How awful. So cruel. Teachers are not permitted to hit pupils in Israel.'

He grinned. 'It might have done you some good, don't you think?'

I slapped his face lightly.

*

In one of those nights, near the Windmill theatre he said, 'You are very sweet.'

'I can be sour and bad tempered too.'

He stopped walking, turned me around to face him, kissed one cheek and said, 'For sweet,' kissed the other and said, 'For sour.' He then put his palm on the back of my head and kissed my lips passionately. His silky hair fell over my head, His lips were soft and his breath warm. When our lips parted, we looked into each other's eyes. We lingered there, aware of something between us.

We took to going to my room after the show. I would get into bed and he would lie on the blanket beside me. We would talk about books, art, music, our travels, our thoughts and observations, but never about deep and personal feelings, and I never told him about Benyamin. We kissed a lot, touched and caressed each other but did not make love. It was as if we had an unspoken agreement to wait. When I got sleepy, he would tuck me in, kiss my forehead, say 'Good night,' then leave. l would fall asleep feeling his warmth and smelling his aftershave.

*

My contract at the club came to an end and to celebrate my first free night, Sebastian took me to Mr Chow Chinese restaurant in Knightsbridge.

Afterwards, in the car, he asked, 'Shall we go to mine? It's nearer.'

I had never been to his place. I knew what he had in mind but I wasn't going to make it easy for him. 'Only because it's nearer?'

He smiled peevishly. 'Well yes. Why else?'

'I can't imagine.'

'I... I..' He stuttered. 'You haven't seen my house. I thought…' He faltered.

I looked at him, challenging him to say it. He looked very uncomfortable and I took pity on him.

'Is it because you are planning to seduce me?'

He looked as if he was caught doing something he shouldn't. I smiled at him.  His face relaxed.

'You do make me laugh Daniela. Straight to the point, no mincing your words. Say I was planning to seduce you, would you object?'

'Mmm. Let me think about it.'

He folded his arms as if to say he was waiting.

'I've no objection Sebastian.'

There was glee in his eyes. He started the car and raced down to a mews near the Kings Road.

*

I had an inkling that making love with Sebastian would be a

199

pleasure for both of us. Perhaps it was because of the nights we had spent kissing, the gentle and passionate way he had caressed me, his being sensitive to my reactions, finding out where I liked to be touched. He even discovered that I liked the inside of my arms stroked gently.

He was forceful but at the same time gentle. We seemed to know each other's wishes instinctively, our rhythm flowed seamlessly as if we knew each other's bodies intimately, as if we had made love before.

In the middle of it, I said, 'I'm on the Pill.'

'Thank goodness for that,' he smiled wickedly.

I stuck my tongue out at him.

He kissed me.

We climaxed together; I now knew the word for it. As we lay next to each other sweating, panting and smiling, I wondered where it was that he had learned the skill of making love.

We woke up at mid-day. Sebastian went to make us coffee. While he was gone, I looked around me. The room was on the first floor. It was very tidy. I could tell that every piece of furniture had been carefully chosen and placed. It was all old and made of dark oak. His clothes from the night before were neatly put on a chair. Mine were strewn on the floor.

We stayed in bed. He had his arm around me and my head was resting on his shoulders.

'Did you have many love affairs? Liaisons?' I asked. I felt him stiffen. 'Sorry. I shouldn't pry.' But I did want to. I wanted to know him better.

He relaxed a little. 'Have you?'

'I asked first.'

'All right. Have it your way.'

'I will. Have you?' I wasn't looking at him.

'A few. I had girlfriends. You can tell I am not a virgin.'

'Ha, ha. Anyone in particular? Someone more than… A serious one?'

He stiffened again. I had touched on something. I waited. Then I thought that perhaps it was better to leave it. Before I did, he answered.

'I was deeply in love with a woman. She was much older than me.'

I wanted to know more. It was probably with her that he learned how to pleasure a woman. I was glad of it but unreasonably felt a little jealous.

'Was she pretty? How did you meet her? When was it?'

'All these questions. Well, she was not pretty. She looked attractive in a quiet sort of way. She worked at the university in the Biology Research Department. I was a student then.'

'And?'

'What do you mean by 'And?' We met, we loved, she left me. What do you want? Chapter and verse?' He sounded irritated.

I propped myself up leaning on my elbow and looked at him. 'Don't be cross. I am just curious. You don't have to tell me anything if you don't want to. I didn't mean to upset you.'

'It is not easy for me to talk about her. I thought that she was the love of my life. But then she said that it was time for me to leave the nest.' His slate blue eyes looked sad.

'Do you still see her?'

'No. she didn't think it would be a good idea. It's over.'

'It is never over.'

'How do you mean?'

'There will always be a box in your heart where your love for her will live.'

'You do come up with the strangest notions. Are you speaking from experience? Have you such a box?'

I put my head back on his shoulder. 'Yes, only it is not closed.'

'You still love him?'

'I don't know. I wish I knew. I haven't thought of him for a while now.'

Immediately I said it I knew that I shouldn't have. 'I'll make us coffee.' I said and went downstairs.

In the kitchen, I put the kettle on and looked out of the window at the cobblestones, the pot plants, the grey skies and the pretty mews houses. I had not wanted to tell him about Benyamin, it was as if I wanted to keep them apart. But I had stupidly done so. He was probably wondering what I was doing with him if I loved someone else. We both had a box and I was not convinced that his was closed either.

I took the coffee upstairs. Our conversation was still hanging in the air between us. Maybe he was ready to ask me to leave. I searched his face. He searched mine. I put the coffee down and stood there unsure that I was welcomed back in his bed.

'Come here,' he said as if answering me. He opened his arms and gathered me to him. 'Perhaps we should leave the past where it is?'

'Yes,' I said to his shoulder.

*

But the past has a way of ambushing us. It was on a Sunday afternoon that we bumped into his. We got up late and went to buy the papers and to have brunch at a café on the Kings Road. The sunny autumn day had brought the strollers out. On our walk back I saw a striking looking couple walking towards us. They were both tall. He wore flared jeans, a flowery shirt and Cuban heeled boots. A red headband held back his long blond hair. On his fingers were large silver rings and from his neck fell many beaded necklaces. A long Afghan overcoat was slung around his shoulders. The woman in a flowing blue silk maxi dress, wearing masses of jewellery, looked like the super model Veruschka. Her brown hair was long, wild and voluminous. She held an Afghan dog on a lead. I was just about to point them out to Sebastian when the woman noticed us and they approached.

'Sebastian.' She looked at him meaningfully. 'It's been a while.'

'Cecilia,' he said acknowledging her. He didn't smile, he just nodded his head. I noticed his body stiffening.

Their polite, short conversation was strained. Instinctively I took a step back, so did her companion. We both had sensed the tension, the awkwardness between them. When they left, Sebastian's face was a mask. He didn't offer an explanation and I didn't ask.

At the mews house, he put Schubert's '*Going to Sleep*' on the record player, a sad and beautiful song. He settled on the sofa and read the papers. He hardly said a word to me. I thought it was best to leave him alone. I took the weekend section and sat in the armchair with Lilydog at my feet. It was in there that I saw an article about Titian's painting *Bacchus and Ariadne*. It was in the National Gallery.

I showed it to Sebastian and said that I wanted to go. He said that he was not in the mood. I said that I would go on my own. 'All right,' he said without lifting his head from the paper. I was peeved.

'Very beautiful,' I remarked as I left. 'An old flame?'

*

I sat on a bench in front of the painting. It was the real thing, not a copy in a book. There was Ariadne being abandoned by her lover Theseus, she was watching him sailing away from her, leaving her behind on the shore.

I looked at the painting, then at the people that were silently looking at it. Maybe they saw it in a different way. Did they feel her pain, her desperation, the tearing in her heart as she watched him sail away? I did.

I was sure that Sebastian and the beautiful woman had been together. It was in the way she had looked at him, a knowing look, in the way he stood stiff and rigid, in his curt, polite answers. There is so much that I didn't know about him. But then, I never talked to him about my love life either.

Lilydog was waiting for me in the car. I didn't go back to the mews house. At the squat they were having a rowdy party. I went to my room and closed the door. I started sorting out my clothes, making a pile to go to the laundrette. I began to feel angry. I didn't care about the beautiful woman or that he didn't want to talk about her. I did care that he had shut me out and hardly said a word to me, behaving as if I wasn't there.

There was a knock on the door. 'Yes,' I yelled. Tom stuck his head in, looked at me gingerly, waiting for an invitation to come in. I started stripping the bed. He came in, sat on the chair and calmly watched me.

'Don't take it out on the bed,' he said,' It's done nothing wrong.'

I ignored him. He came and gave me a hand.

'Shall we go out to eat. Indian at the Bullock Cart?' he asked.

I looked at him, he was smiling. My anger began to ebb.

'And then we go dancing,' I said.

'You know I can't dance.'

'You can watch me.'

'Always a pleasure Daniela.' He started laughing.

*

Three days had passed and Sebastian had not called. I was not going to call him. I had a lot of work keeping me busy, but every time the phone rang, I hoped it was him. I went out every night with Tom or with Helen. After four days I began to fret. Maybe he would never call. I was getting anxious.

'Is anything the matter Daniela?' Poppy asked. 'You seem distracted.'

'No, nothing's the matter.'

'Boyfriend's problem?'

Was it that obvious? 'I'm fine. Really.'

But I was not fine. I was beginning to think that maybe I should call him. At least I'd know where I stood, it would be better than not knowing. But before I did, one evening he showed up at Poppy's. Lilydog ran to greet him. I nodded but did not smile. He sat in the armchair stroking Lilydog's head. Poppy carried on working at her desk and I at mine.

When I was ready, Sebastian and I walked downstairs in silence. We stood on the pavement facing each other. Lilydog sat between us looking from one to the other.

'Shall we go in my car?' he asked.

Now that he had come, I was relieved and felt more confident. I wasn't going to brush the incident away. I thought we should talk about it.

'I was going to go to dance class,' I lied. The Dance

Centre had been closed. Gina and I were going to The Place for Dance, also in Covent Garden.

'Do you have to? I made supper.'

Was it an olive branch? It was not good enough. I wasn't going to let it go. I didn't answer.

'You are angry with me and rightly so. I'm sorry.'

A channel was opened, 'I take it you were upset, but it was not my fault.'

'No, certainly not. I did behave badly, sorry.'

'Why?'

He didn't answer immediately. 'Do you expect me to always be in a good mood? Things happen.'

Not a good enough excuse, I thought. 'You didn't have to take it out on me. Have you any idea how hurtful it was?'

'I said I'm sorry. You're right and I can only apologise. I've been wretched in the last few days. I thought you wouldn't want to see me again.'

He had just given me a little power over him, but instead of using it, I simply melted. My anger ebbed away and I was overcome with the wish to comfort him, to reassure him.

'What did you cook for supper?' was my way of saying that all was forgiven.

He beamed at me. He looked so very pleased and relieved. I wished that we could avoid causing each other pain.

In the kitchen I helped him make a salad. He gave me chores to do, chopping, washing up and setting the table.

'You took your time coming to see me. I suppose you had better things to do,' I said as I was trying to slice carrots evenly.

'Well, it takes time to build up the courage to walk into a lion's den,' he giggled.

'A lioness if you don't mind.'

During supper, he asked if I wanted to go out later. I said I didn't and remembered to ask him.

'Do you like the theatre?'

'Yes? Why? Would you like to go?'

'Poppy said that she can get free tickets. British theatre is the best in the world. I've never been. Would you come with me?'

'Definitely. Any particular play?'

*The Deep Blue Sea.*

'Rattigan. That should be good.'

I loved the theatre but it was too expensive. To be able to go for free would be a wonderful perk of the job. It was the first time that Poppy offered and I hoped there'll be more.

After supper, he put a Moody Blues record on and we got comfortable on the sofa. He rolled a joint. We smoked, closed our eyes and listened. I lay my head on his shoulder. Words were unnecessary. Those were the times that I cherished the most, our closeness in a timeless time when everything felt right and in its place.

The song '*Nights in white satin*' came on'. I went and stood at the window. The light of the moon reflected in the wet cobblestones. I wrapped my arms around me and swayed to the music.

Sebastian came and held me from behind. I rested my head on his shoulder and we swayed together.

*Cause I love you*
*Yes I love you*
*Oh how I love you*'

'Are you going to stay in England?' he asked softly into my hair.

'How do you mean?'

'Well, I don't know. You might be just passing through.

You could take off at any day now.'

'I want to stay. I'd like to.'

*'and I love you, oh how I love you.'*

He turned me round. 'I wish you would.' He squinted, his eyes intense as if he was conveying something to me and at the same time looking for an answer. I smiled at him and put my lips to his. It was my answer. I turned back to look out of the window at the dark clear skies. He stayed behind me and held me tight against him.

We were back to how it had been before his moodiness, before his past popped up in front of him in the shape of a beautiful woman.

In his arms, I felt the quiet sort of strength he had; not showy, not displayed. It was in his manners, in his posture, confident yet relaxed. He was in command of himself and he could master his emotions. He was not going to fall helplessly in love with me like Robert. I was glad for that. But on that day in the Kings Road, I saw his vulnerability.

# CHAPTER 23

It was Christmas, and with Lilydog on the back seat we drove to his parents' house. What appeared at the end of a long, meandering drive was a stately home. Not what I expected. He had not warned me, nor told me about his family. We drove past the grand front entrance and along its towering facade, gargoyles looked down at us from their high perches. He parked the car in a cobbled yard. I was feeling nervous. We entered the house through a side door and climbed the well-trodden stone steps. I followed him down a long gallery with beautiful chairs and large, blue and white vases placed along its walls.

Sebastian opened a door and I followed him into a large room. The panelling and the floorboards were dark oak and so was the carved furniture. Big paintings, so dirty that you could hardly see the details, hung on the walls. On the floor was a large old faded rug. The piece de resistance was a four-poster bed, its carved posts supporting an elaborate canopy draped with red velvet curtains. The crisp white bed linen stood out in contrast to the dark oak and the red velvet.

I had always wanted to sleep in a four-poster bed. I dropped my suitcase and vanity case and jumped on it. Lilydog followed and seemed very happy and comfortable.

Sebastian laughed, put his suitcase down and turned to leave.

'Don't leave me,' I said.

'Don't worry. You'll be fine. My parents are not frightening, just a little mad. I won't be long. The bathroom is two doors down the Blue Gallery on the right.' He came over and brushed my hair from my face, cupped it in his hands and kissed me. It was a reassuring gesture and I loved it when he did that.

I stretched on the bed. Lilydog was asleep.

I remembered that Jimmy had scathingly said to me that Sebastian was a toff. I had asked Tom why Jimmy disliked Sebastian even though he hardly knew him. Tom said, 'It's because Sebastian is upper class and Jimmy is middle class with issues.' I had to have him explain this to me. He tried. It sounded complicated. This class system that I was beginning to be aware of was a mystery to me. It seemed that people could tell a lot about a person just by their accent, and the words they used.

*

Sebastian came to get me. I was to meet his parents. We walked down another gallery and entered an enormous room with tall gothic windows. The large fireplace, almost big enough to stand in, was flanked by two stone lions. In front of it were sofas and armchairs covered with beautiful faded fabrics. The ceiling was high above us.

A man and a woman rose to greet me. He was tall and had Sebastian's eyes. His suit was charcoal in colour, old fashioned in style and adorned with a fob watch. She was wearing a plaid skirt, a cardigan and pearls. I thought her clothes were dowdy. She was plump with rounded pleasant face. I didn't see a resemblance to Sebastian.

We shook hands. 'How do you do?' I said politely.

They nodded and immediately lavished attention on Lilydog. The Father patted her head. Lilydog offered him her paw. He shook it.

'Please take a seat,' the Mother said.

We all sat down. Lilydog went to her and she bent to stroke her head. 'Pretty dog. Not a breed I take it.'

Was that bad, or was she a snob? 'No, she's a mutt.' I was sitting up straight. I didn't know how to make small talk, particularly not to those two who were probably forming an opinion of me.

She spoke to Lilydog in that tone of voice people talked to children. 'Aren't you pretty. Yes, you are. Good dog.'

Two dogs ran in wagging their tails, sniffed Lilydog and the three of them ran off together. The parents smiled. I suppose I looked worried.

'She is in g... good company,' the Father said. 'She'll be all r…right.' He stuttered.

I felt awkward. I didn't know what to say to them.

'Not bad weather for this time of year,' the Father said looking at the windows.

'I guess not,' I said.

'Is this your first winter here?' she asked.

'Not the first. It's not as cold as Switzerland though.'

'Oh, it could very well be.' He turned to the mother. 'Remember 1946?'

I looked to Sebastian for help. He was staring at the fireplace.

'I sure do.' She turned to me, 'Do you find it terribly cold? Coming from a hot country that is.'

She knew where I came from. What else did she know? They were both sitting upright. Their faces did not betray their thoughts, or I didn't know how to read them.

'I find that a fur coat helps,' I smiled slightly.

Sebastian said, 'I'd better take Daniela to see the house and go up to the roof before it gets too cold even for a fur coat.'

I was relieved, the conversation had been stilted. I had found them cold and remote. Sebastian's demeanour when with them, seemed so too.

'Sebastian. We'll be gathering here at around seven for drinks before dinner,' the Mother said. 'Please don't be late.'

\*

We went to fetch our coats. I wondered what they thought of me. I didn't think I was the sort of woman they expected their son to bring home. I was a foreigner, not a Christian, and not one of them. Maybe there was one advantage to being a foreigner, people could not pigeonhole me.

We walked down long galleries and entered rooms that led from one to another. There were many four-poster beds and antique furniture from different periods. I admired the sumptuous fabrics, the highly polished wood; all pristine, preserved and cordoned off. The library had wall to wall bookcases filled with old books judging by their faded spines. There was a distinct musty smell in the room. Sebastian opened drawers and showed me collections of stones, shells and corals. I recoiled seeing dead butterflies and moths pinned to boards. It somehow felt wrong, cruel even.

We climbed the spiralling stone steps that led to the roof. On the way up, I saw a room with a huge telescope and brass instruments. 'Father gazes at the stars,' Sebastian told me.

We entered the roof. A low stone wall surrounded its edge and we walked along it. The cold, bitter wind nearly blew me away. The landscape stretched out for miles. A veil of suffused pink and purple haze spread across the horizon. Sebastian put his hand on my shoulder and silently we stood and watched the daylight fade away.

'Let me tell you a family story,' Sebastian said looking into the distance. 'I'm not sure that it's true though. In Victorian times, here lived a very unhappy young lady who was in love with an unsuitable young man. There was no hope for the lovers. One day, in her despair, she decided that life without him was not worth living. She threw herself off of this roof.'

I looked down. 'What an awful way to die.'

'She didn't die. Her huge crinoline acted as a parachute, or so they say.'

I laughed. 'I'm glad to hear it. Even if not true, it's a good story, plausible. Was there a happy ending? Did she marry her beau and lived happily ever after?'

'I very much doubt it. Sadly, life is not a fairy tale.'

*

Dinner was to be a black-tie affair. I watched Sebastian dress. He looked dashing and very handsome. I told him that he looked like a penguin. He flapped his arms. For the occasion, not that I expected it to be so grand, I had bought a long and flowing silk dress the colour of indigo. Sebastian had not warned me how cold the stone house would be but I was determined to wear it.

There were about twenty people drinking and chatting around the fireplace. My courage left me and I felt shy and nervous. My face did not betray me, it had turned into a mask for me to hide behind. I wished that Sebastian would hold my hand. As if he heard me, he put his hand on the small of my back and steered me towards the gathering. They all turned to look at me. Sebastian did the introductions. I heard names, shook hands, received polite smiles and nods. Sebastian's sister seemed stiff and reserved. She shook my hand hardly touching it, and turned back towards the man she had been talking to. I thought her rude.

The Father offered us drinks. 'Sherry? Or would you prefer Madeira?' He didn't stutter this time.

I sipped the Madeira. The cold seeped into my bones. I noticed that the women were dressed more sensibly and were wrapped in shawls. I started shivering. Sebastian must have noticed and led me to stand near the fire. I began to warm up, one side only.

'I won't be a minute,' Sebastian said and left.

He went and talked to his mother and then left the room.

There was a huge Christmas tree at the far end corner with presents piled underneath it. Sebastian came back and put a black woollen shawl around me.

'Mother's.'

I was glad it was black. It didn't clash with my indigo dress. I tugged Sebastian's sleeve and whispered, 'I didn't bring presents!'

'Don't worry. I did, for both of us.'

'I didn't get you one.'

'You did. You are my present. We are going in. Come.'

# Chapter 24

At the end of the Great Hall, two doors opened onto the ornate dining room which was eighteenth century in style, mahogany rather than oak. The room was lit by two large crystal chandeliers and the silver candelabras on the table. On the walls hung large mirrors in gilded frames. There were large paintings of women in flounced dresses adorned with flowers and ribbons, and men in silk and lace. The long, long mahogany table, highly polished, was adorned with small vases that held flowers and greenery, bowls on stems were filled with sweets and glazed fruit, delicate glasses and place settings of beautiful bone china. I had seen similar scenes in paintings and movies. It looked opulent and festive. I had never thought that I would be dining in one.

Sebastian guided me to my seat holding my elbow. I saw my name written on a nameplate. He walked away to take his place far away from me, leaving me between two strangers. I stood behind my chair like everyone else until the Mother sat down. The thin man on my left pulled out my chair for me.

'Jolly good weather we're having, don't you think?' he said once we were all seated.

The weather again. 'So it is,' I offered for something to say.

'Cold but dry,' said the man with the chubby face on my right.

I tried to think of something to say. 'Very pretty village. It looks very old.'

'Indeed. Medieval, you know. Not a jot been changed. Just as it was for hundreds of years.'

'You'll see the church tonight. I take it you are coming,' said the thin one.

I had not an inkling as to what he was talking about, but I said yes and smiled. Sitting there in the beautiful setting, I felt like a voyeur.

'What a dreadful year,' the thin man commented. 'Let's hope next year will be better. What with the strikes and the inflation? The country is on its knees.'

He should be discussing this with the ladies in the club in Regent Street. They could tell him a thing or two, I thought amused.

'Rather. Not forgetting the troubles in Ireland. The bombs in London. It doesn't bode well, does it?' He looked at me including me in the conversation.

I was at a loss for something to say. I was vaguely aware of all this, but only because of the petrol shortage. I had paid very little attention to the news, but I didn't want to show my ignorance.

I was glad that the doors opened and young women and men came in carrying soup tureens, and I didn't have to struggle with having a conversation.

'They are from the village,' the chubby man said. 'The cooks are very good I gather.'

People started talking across the table and there was no need for me to join in. A woman opposite us was talking about someone who had accused her children of stealing from her.

'Very unlikely,' said the thin man.

'Poppy cock,' said a woman at the far end of the table.

'What do you expect?' asked another. 'She has bats in her belfry.'

Everyone laughed. Strange expression. No need for explanation, but I did wonder how it came about.

The food was delicious. Roast turkey, ham, beef with all the trimmings, and the Christmas puddings came in alight. By then, some men's cheeks were turning red, people spoke louder and laughed harder. A truckle of stilton was served with biscuits, accompanied by decanters of port.

*

After dinner, we gathered at the Great Hall. Sebastian came to stand by me.

'All right? Are you enjoying yourself? Not too much for you I hope.'

'Not at all. It's lovely. Really.' And it was the truth. Now, after I had wine and port, I relaxed somewhat and felt assured that no one would bite me. I was enjoying being there, in the most amazing settings, having a look into a kind of life I had only read about in books.

'It's not over yet,' Sebastian smiled.

I could see that he was taking pleasure in introducing me to this side of his life, sharing it with me. It told me that he had strong feelings for me. An inner warmth rose within me.

An old woman went and sat at the grand piano and played a few chords loudly. Everyone fell silent.

The Mother clapped her hands. 'Come everybody. Carols.'

We gathered around the piano. Sebastian stood next to me. He had a pleasant voice. His face told me that he was enjoying the singing. I could see that he belonged to this place, it was a part of him. I could not join in, I didn't know the songs, Christmas was not a part of my tradition.

After the singing we danced quadrilles and Scottish Reels. I picked it up as I went along. It got wild; couples galloped like horses under the arches we made with our arms held high. I laughed with everybody and galloped too. Afterwards we collapsed for a while in front of the fire with drinks.

'Time to go,' his mother said standing up.

'Where are we going Sebastian?' I whispered.

'Church. Midnight mass. Oh, sorry. Do you want to go? You don't have to. It might not be your sort of thing. Religion I mean.'

'I am not at all religious, but it shouldn't stop me coming, should it?' I wanted to see his world where he looked comfortable, at home and in his element.

'Put your coat on. It's even colder in the church if you can believe it.'

We walked to the village. The sky was clear and full of stars. Some of the guests held torches to light our way.

'I went to midnight mass once,' I told Sebastian on the way there. 'In Bethlehem. It was magical. The processions, priests in elaborate regalia, and the singing… soaring up to heaven. Beautiful.'

'The perfect place to hear it. Why would you go if you are not religious?'

'It's famous. I heard a lot about it. Afterwards we stayed to watch the sun rising from behind the Judean Hills. It was an amazing night. I'll never forget it.'

*

The church, decorated with evergreen leaves and berries,

was small but beautiful. Mass took forever, there was a lot of standing up and sitting down. I shivered in my fur coat.

On the walk back I asked, 'Are you religious? Do you believe in God?'

He didn't answer immediately. I couldn't see his face in the darkness. 'I am not sure how to answer. It's not as simple as a yes or a no.' He paused.

We were bringing up the rear. I could hear chatter and laughter ahead of us.

'I'll try to explain. The church played a big part in my life, here, at school.' Another pause. 'I don't quite know that I believe in God as such. I don't think that it matters. It's a way of life, do you see?'

'I don't think I do.'

He was struggling. 'All right then. Take this village for example. The church is the centre of the community, it brings people together. Tradition is what matters to me. It's an anchor. Sorry, I find it hard to explain. It's not as if I've ever thought about it. It is just how I feel. And you?'

I laughed. 'Well, as for God, Nietzsche said that God was dead. That implies that he believed that once there was a God. I think God was invented by humans to fulfil a need because they were scared of the thought that life on earth is all there is. There is nothing wrong with that if it helps them.'

'"Religion is the opium of the people"'

'Karl Marx. Yes. But it is the people who preside over religion who anger me. Religion should be a force for good. Can you honestly say that it is?'

'I'm not saying that the church hasn't got a lot to answer for. But if you take God out of the equation, then you are left with tradition, the glue that binds people together. At least I believe it does, and mostly for the good.'

'Yes, I agree with you there. Tradition is important.'

I thought of my family's traditions, the gatherings, the merriment, the joy and the good food. Those times when they forgot their petty squabbles and enjoyed one another. I felt nostalgic, but then I remembered how badly they had treated me and felt bitter.

We walked in silence for a while, each to our own thoughts, following the light from the torches.

Watching my breath freeze as I exhaled, I said, 'After finishing high school where we had studied the bible and translations to the bible as part of the curriculum, I picked it up and read it as a book, as an epic novel if you like. It has every plot and every story that could be written about: love, hate, envy, betrayal, murder, poetry and more. It is all there.'

'And politics, and wars, customs and rites. Not forgetting sex.'

'Mustn't forget sex.'

Our giggles rang out in the crisp icy air.

*

'It's time,' the Mother said to the Father as we all stood around the fire.

Sebastian and his father left the room. Time for what? I wondered. What is she going to make us do now?

'To the cloisters everybody,' the Mother commanded.

We followed her through the Blue Gallery and down two flights of the stone stairs and entered the cloisters.

Sebastian and his father were standing by the entrance. The Father gave us a long torch each and Sebastian lit them for us from the flame that was burning in his own. I held mine and waited with everyone not knowing what to expect.

Once all the torches were burning, the Mother started running around the cloisters holding her torch high above her. Every one followed and so did I. It was so strange. They were all hooting and laughing, running like children in a playground. The Mother led us to the middle of the cloisters. We formed a circle around a huge, black cauldron. Sebastian and his father gave their torches to people to hold and helped the mother climb into the cauldron. She disappeared inside it. Her voice came loud, echoing all around us, she was singing Jerusalem. They all joined her. I had heard that beautiful song before but didn't know it well enough to sing, so I sort of hummed along.

Something powerful was happening, intangible, a ritual, they had done this before. I looked at the faces of the people. They were full of joy and were totally absorbed in the moment. Yes, tradition was good.

After that we dispersed. Some people drove away and the house guests went to bed. Sebastian and I walked to our bedroom through the empty and silent gallery where the only sound was our shoes on the stone floor. We fell asleep almost immediately.

# CHAPTER 25

I woke up to Sebastian gently kissing my face. I stretched but did not open my eyes. I caressed his body, silky and hairless to the touch. I arched my long neck and he kissed the hollow between my shoulder blades. There was something dreamlike in our love making, long and leisurely. I didn't want it to end.

'You look beautiful when you come,' he said stroking my hair.

Thank you, bass player, I thought.

We lay quietly side by side. A dim light filtered through the drawn curtains. I looked at Sebastian and a deep, long forgotten feeling came over me. I took his hand and squeezed it. He lifted mine to his lips.

Sebastian shook himself and sat up. 'Time to get up darling.'

It was the first time he had called me that. It felt nice. It ratified something. Perhaps building a relationship slowly was a good thing. I could not follow this line of thought because Sebastian flung the blankets of off me, and laughing pushed me out of the bed.

'Come on lazy bug. There is a schedule to follow.'

As I was getting dressed, I asked, 'Your parents don't mind us sleeping in the same room? After all they are religious.'

'They don't like it but know perfectly well that I wouldn't come if they objected. As it happens, mother suggested that we have two bedrooms with a connecting door. What the eye doesn't see…'

What a hypocrite, I thought. I noticed Lilydog's absence. 'Have you seen Lilydog? Where is she?'

'I let her out earlier. She'd be playing with the other dogs. Don't worry, she'll show up sooner or later.'

\*

There was breakfast, then a walk, for which I had to borrow a coat and wellies from the boot room. We had lunch and then opened presents. I opened Sebastian's present discreetly. In a red velvet box was a gold chain with a cameo that could also be worn as a brooch. He was looking at me. I smiled and put it away. It was private, not to be shared.

'Back here at five for tea,' the Mother announced. 'We are expecting the vicar.'

Until then we had time to ourselves and went for a short walk in the woods. Its floor was covered in small, white flowers that were poking their nodding heads through the thin layer of snow.

'Pretty flowers,' I said.

'They are called snowdrops. They are very early this year.'

We stopped by the stream. The water gurgled and sang as it flowed and lapped around the boulders. The bare trees were asleep. The world was standing still, a place in a dream. If I believed in anything, it was in nature. It had a rhythm all of its own that never stopped. There was beauty in it that no designer could match; beautiful flowers, the intricate symmetrical patterns on butterflies' wings, and the carpet of delicate snowdrops nodding at my feet. I too am a part of nature, symmetrical.

In the charmed surroundings, I looked at Sebastian's profile. He was deep in thought. Tender feelings welled up in me again. I reached for his gloved hand.

'You are deep in thoughts,' I said.

'I was thinking of how much I love it here.'

'It is a wonderful place. It really is. You are very fortunate.'

'By birth, not by choice.' There was a hint of irony in his voice.

A strange remark I thought. I could probe. But maybe it was not the right time. I did not want to spoil the moment.

On our way back I asked, 'Sebastian, why does the National Trust own your home?'

'Well, the family had huge debts after the war, particularly because of the new taxes that came into force. There was not enough money to pay and no money for the upkeep.'

'But you still live here.'

'They own it, but the family has the right to live here in perpetuity.'

'How sad. It must have been quite a blow.'

'There was no other choice. The house is always in need of repairs; leaking rooves, crumbling masonry, the ground's upkeep. Then there are the taxes, death duty… They had to make that deal. Maybe it was a good thing.'

'Why do you say that?'

'Running it is a fulltime job and financially ruinous, let alone the stress and the worries.'

I wondered what it was like to live in a house where curious strangers paid to walk between the fancy, restricting, crimson ropes.

'Do you mind the hordes of people traipsing through the house? Does it not bother you, even a little bit?'

'You get used to it. The house is a national treasure, it's only right for the nation to own it.'

\*

When we got back, Sebastian went to help his parents. Despite the cold, wrapped up in my fur, I went to the cloisters. I walked around slowly. It was a place for contemplation, for musing. I sat on a stone bench. It would be lovely to sit in its coolness during the heat of summer, read, weave dreams, meet a lover secretly.

A strange half thought half feeling came to me; I was slowly coming back to myself. It was as if the essence of me, old and new, was emerging. Maybe it was because I wasn't in a state of panic anymore about finding a place to live and a job. Now that I began to see that I could have a future in England and felt more settled, there was room in my life to think and grow. My relationship with Sebastian, where we were able to be individuals together, allowed me to breathe, to pursue my own development. For the first time since I had arrived in London, I felt content.

Lilydog appeared. I hugged her and then we ran around the cloisters, me laughing and laughing and she panting and panting at my heels. That was a moment of happiness I thought as we climbed the stone stairs.

\*

We gathered in the Great Hall for tea. I sat by the fire thinking that I shouldn't be hogging it. The conversation with the vicar turned to church matters and village affairs. I sat straight, holding my cup and saucer, stroking Lilidog's head and pretending to be interested.

I was getting too hot on one side so I got up and walked

to the tall, gothic windows and looked out. The light was fading, the magnificent cedar of Lebanon was becoming a silhouette against the darkening sky. There was a sound of fluttering to my left. I looked and to my amazement I saw butterflies hibernating in the folds of the heavy, long drapery. I walked back, but my seat by the fire had been taken.

My mind had wondered off. I was thinking about butterflies. I didn't know that they hibernated, it didn't tally with them having a very short life span, about two weeks I seemed to remember. I was not listening to the conversation as such but kept it in the background of my thoughts just in case anyone addressed me. My ears pricked when I heard the Mother say, 'Give a dog a bone.' Since Lilydog was the only dog in the room, I thought she was talking to me. I looked at her, she was looking in my direction but not directly at me.

When we were alone, I asked Sebastian. 'Your mother said 'Give a dog a bone.' Did she want me to give Lilydog a bone?'

He couldn't stop laughing.

'Stop laughing. What's so funny?'

'It's a saying,' he chortled. 'It means, give someone what they want. But depends how you say it, it could mean, what do you expect if you give a dog a bone. Or you could say, he is like a dog with a bone, meaning, someone who doggedly pursue something and doesn't give up. Or, throw me a bone, meaning, give me a clue, or a little help. Would you like more expressions with dogs Daniela? There are plenty.'

'Don't be pedantic. I think I've had enough.'

*

On our way to dinner, we stopped to look at a painting. His sister came towards us. She nodded her head politely. I gave her a big smile on purpose to see what she would do. I suspected that she had been avoiding me. She stretched her mouth reluctantly and walked on.

'Your sister doesn't like me.'

'She doesn't like anybody. I wouldn't take her too seriously if I were you. She is a sourpuss.'

'You are not close?'

He looked at me as if I asked a strange or unusual question. He didn't answer. I just could not understand this family. I could not read them. Possibly because I was not familiar with the characters that made up the English nation. I still wanted to know more about his growing up in this house.

'You don't seem to have a room, Sebastian? The room you had when you grew up?'

'I don't use it anymore. It's in the family apartment in the east wing.'

'Can I see it?'

'No point really. All my stuff is in London or in one of the attics.'

Had I brought him home with me, my mother would have brought out the family albums and he would have seen me from being a baby and all through my growing up years. She would have told him many stories about me. But we had agreed to leave our pasts alone. I thought that meant we wouldn't talk about hurtful episodes to do with the heart. I had expected his memories to pop up as we walked through the house and for him to share them with me. Maybe his relationship to the place was more complex than it seemed.

*

Boxing Day was the day of the hunt. We walked to the medieval village to watch it set off. The hounds were impatient to go and the horses restlessly stomped their feet, steam pouring from their noses and rising from their dung. The riders sported their red jackets which were called pink. Sebastian's mother sat on a white horse which they called grey. After drinking a glass of sherry, the horn sounded and off they rode looking magnificent.

It was the most beautiful sunny winter's day, so fresh that I wanted to fill my lungs with air. I watched the hunt gallop away. I imagined myself on a white horse, wearing a tight-fitting riding jacket and an old-fashioned riding skirt that draped over the horse's rump.

'We are going beagling,' Sebastian announced.

'We are? What's that?'

'Hunting on foot.'

'Really? Fat chance of catching anything. I'd rather be on a horse.'

'Can you ride?'

'No.'

'Well then. On foot it is.'

We ran round and round in the fields chasing after a hare we never caught sight of. Sebastian was a fast runner. I could hardly keep up with him.

'Where is the hare?' I asked when I caught up with him.

'I've no idea. We hardly ever catch one. Just follow the dogs.' He looked fresh, his face was flushed and he was breathing deeply.

'Even when they go into a ditch? or the stream?'

'Stop being awkward Daniela. If you keep on talking, you will run out of breath. Onwards and upwards. Stick with me. If you are lucky, I'll carry you over the stream.'

When it was over and we were catching our breath he said, 'You look lovely, radiant, your cheeks are red and your eyes are shining, good enough to eat.'

*

At the bottom of the stone stairs, we said our goodbyes. Sebastian's parents patted Lilydog and told her that she was a good dog. They showed her more affection than they showed their son. The sister did not come out.

Sebastian shook his father's hand, said 'Mother' and bowed his head slightly. I wondered if this family ever hugged. I shook their hands and thanked them for having me.

Lilydog promptly went to sleep on the back seat. She was exhausted but happy.

'Did you enjoy the visit?' he asked in the car.

'Very much. Thank you.'

'My pleasure. We'll be back in the summer for the celebrations of the house's seven hundred and fiftieth anniversary.'

In that sentence, he said "We". In that sentence he told me that he envisaged us still being together in the summer. His words cemented something between us. It made me happy. I leaned over and kissed him.

'What's that for?'

'Oh, I just felt like it. Any objections?'

'Certainly not. Do it again.'

I did. 'I must remember to send your parents a thank you card.'

'Yes. Good idea. They'll appreciate it.'

We drove in silence for a while. Lilydog poked her head between us, had a look and went back to sleep.

'Sebastian,' I said. 'I'd like to ask you something.'

'Ask away.'

'You don't work.' He sharply turned his head to look at me. 'I don't mean anything by it. I know that you are not poor. I just wanted to ask if there was…'

'Something I'd like to do instead of loafing around?' he sneered.

It was obviously a touchy subject.

'No. No, no. I didn't mean it like that. You can loaf around as much as you like as far as I'm concerned. It's your life. But I only wanted to know if there was something that you would like to do. That's all. And you don't have to tell me.'

He didn't answer.

I looked out of the window. The undulating countryside with the bare trees and the smattering of snow was very beautiful.

'Sorry. I didn't mean to snap at you,' he said.

'That's alright. I only asked.'

After a pause he said, 'As a matter of fact, there is something. I want to open a designer furniture shop with a friend of mine. His designs are inspiring, tasteful and practical.' His face lit up. 'I'll show them to you when we get back.'

He was animated and full of enthusiasm as he told me about the plans and his vision.

'Have you a place in mind?'

He laughed. 'It won't happen for quite some time yet. Indeed not. There's no hurry.' There was a wicked, naughty expression on his face. 'It's the loafing thing you know, good old loafing.'

'To be young and in London. Lucky you.' There was a

hint of resentment in my voice. I didn't mean it to sound like that.

'I see. What you're trying to say is that I am fortunate, that I can afford it, and that I don't have to work for a living. Well, yes, I am. What's more, I can and I do indulge in being "young and in London", as you put it. I was born to it. It was not my choice as I've told you before.'

We drove in silence for a while. I knew he was thinking.

'I don't feel guilty about it. I'm not ready to get serious about life just yet.' He paused and grinned wickedly, 'We can do it together. We are young, it is our time to drink life to its full.'

I smiled. 'So we are. I sometimes forget.'

He took his eyes off the road for a second and looked at me puzzled. I just smiled.

\*

We had left the tranquil countryside behind us and were crawling through an ugly suburb of London. After the silence of the land, the traffic noise seemed louder than I remembered, the smells of fumes more pungent, the pavements were covered with slushy, dirty snow and people were huddled in their coats, heads bowed against the cold wind.

## Chapter 26

I hadn't meant to bring the subject up with Sebastian that evening, although I intended to talk to him about it when the time was right. Unfortunately, I said it without thinking and it didn't go down well.

Sebastian had come to collect me. We were to meet some of his friends for a drink. He sat on the chair and watched me packing my vanity case with clothes for work. I would be spending the night at his place. I always did when we went out.

'I bought you a toothbrush,' he announced looking pleased with himself.

'You bought me a toothbrush.'

'Yes. A rather good one, I might add.'

'Why?'

'Don't you think that it makes sense for you to have one at mine?'

'As long as you don't let other women use it.' I have no idea why I said it, it just came out.

There was a look of incomprehension on his face. 'What? What other women? What are you on about? Pray tell me.'

'You never know. You might wish to spend the night with someone else.' Now that I brought it up, I was resolved to continue. 'I'm not objecting. You are free to do whatever you want,' I added hastily.

My back was turned to him. I was moving hangers in the wardrobe, choosing an outfit for the evening. I turned to face him. His eyes were fixed on me.

'And you wouldn't mind?' His tone was cold.

We stared at each other.

'That's not the point.'

'What is your point? Do enlighten me,' he sounded vexed.

I started undressing. I tried to find the right words. 'You wouldn't want to eat bacon and eggs every day. You'd get bored with it.'

'So now you compare yourself to bacon and eggs.'

'Don't be obtuse.'

Part of me wished that I had never said it. Did I expect him to like the idea? Wouldn't most men welcome it? But it was what I believed in and so I tried to explain.

'I believe in freedom. Freedom of the individual to pursue their own life even in a relationship.'

'How noble of you. Does that apply to you too?' he said in an even, biting tone.

'Yes. But…' I faltered.

'But?' He started laughing.

It angered me. I stamped my foot. 'I am serious Sebastian.'

He was still laughing when he said, 'Clearly. But you can't expect me to take you seriously standing there in your G-string.'

I turned my back to him and faced the wardrobe long mirror. I slipped on a green mini dress and slung a wide leather belt on my hips.

Into the awkward silence he said, 'Are we going to have

a fight over this? What is your point? Do you want me to sleep with other women? Do you want to sleep with other men? Is that it?'

'No, definitely not. What I am trying to say is, that it is not unlikely that one of a couple would meet someone and there would be a physical attraction between them. If they do sleep together, they mostly do it behind their partners' back.'

I stopped and put on my blue platform shoes. 'It's deceitful, it is cheating,' I continued. 'But, if they had agreed to give each other the freedom to have sex with other people, then it is not a betrayal. That's all I'm saying.'

He looked at me thoughtfully. He rubbed his chin. 'I suspect it was that man that you said you keep in a box. I strongly resent the fact that you judge me by his actions.'

It was the truth. His insight surprised me. 'We learn from our experiences, don't we?' I offered.

He looked at me with an indulgent smile. It infuriated me. 'Look here Daniela. The past has a hand in defining us but we shouldn't let it control us or cloud our judgement. I'll say it again, I am not him.'

'Emotions, feelings, they do not always follow logic.'

'The problem with you Daniela, is that you are driven by your emotions.'

'And you bury them,' I spat.

We glared at each other.

He broke the silence. His gaze was steady, his voice calm. 'People deal with their feelings in different ways, and just because I don't let them rule me, it does not necessarily mean that I don't feel. What is it that you want Daniela?'

'I do not want to find out about you and another woman from someone else. I would rather you tell me.'

He got up and came to stand in front of me. 'And you wouldn't mind?'

'I would,' I mumbled.

'Then why Daniela? What good would it do?'

'I want us to be honest and truthful with each other. I think that it is a reasonable request.'

'And it applies to you too, I take it.'

'Yes.'

He took a step back. 'I would mind.'

'Mind what?'

'You know perfectly well what. Sometimes Daniela…' He stopped. 'And all this because of a toothbrush. I hate to think what you would have said had I bought you a hairbrush.'

'I am very particular about my hairbrush. You now know that if you told me, however painful I would find it, it would not break us up.'

I turned to the mirror and started pinning up my hair.

'So, there is an "us," he smiled wryly in the mirror. 'It's good to know.' He turned me around, cupped and lifted my face and looking serious said, 'I don't wish to hurt you, Daniela. I can't do anything about your past, it is up to you how you deal with it.'

I envied him his ability to control his emotions.

'Come here,' he said and drew me to him. 'I've heard you. Shall we leave it at that?'

I nodded.

'Please let your hair down.

'I like it like that.'

'For me?'

He started pulling the hairpins off. I let him.

*

We didn't speak in the car. I guessed that we were both digesting what had passed between us. He was right of course. It all came about because of what had happened with Benyamin. I remembered the day I had found out that he had sex with someone else. A friend of his who had once grabbed me and tried to kiss me, told me about it, he was a man spurned. When I confronted Benyamin, he said what all cheaters say, 'She didn't mean anything to me.' How banal. We had a fight. I exploded, there were accusations, tears and hurt and then I stormed out. I went to stay at my mother's. When I got in, she saw my face and immediately hugged me. I shrugged her off, went to my room and closed the door. A little later, she knocked on the door and came in holding a steaming mug. She put it down on my bedside table. She looked at me and said softly, 'I know you don't want to hear it. You are better off without him. He is egocentric.'

I was surprised that she knew that word. I stared at her, then turned to face the wall.

Benyamin came by the next morning, told me that he loved me very much, and pleaded with me to come back. I eventually relented and went back with him.

Sometime later, he told me that he hadn't managed to have sex with her. He had tried, he even pretended to himself that it was me. 'She probably thinks that I am impotent,' he said looking very sad.

I believed him when he promised that it would not happen again. I abhorred the jealousy I had felt. I didn't want the same thing to happen with Sebastian.

Sebastian voice broke through my thoughts. 'We're all right now, aren't we?'

'Yes,' I said.

## Chapter 27

The sight of the Orchard along the road was breath taking; the floating delicate clouds of pink and white flowers looked ethereal. They swayed in the breeze and their sweet scent wafted through the open car windows. The perfumed wind brushed my face and blew my hair back. I had the same carefree feeling when I had been driven in an open Jeep through the Sinai Desert, along the golden dunes. But there, the wind was hot.

Sebastian had gone home because his father was ill. Before he left, he had offered me the key to his house.

'No,' I had said curtly. It was an involuntary reaction.

'Suit yourself,' he answered looking peeved. He gave me a peck on my cheek and left. I felt bad about it.

*

The Saturday after Sebastian had left, Tom who was back from Colombia had suggested a drive to Brighton. It was a beautiful sunny day. I had squeezed into a Mini with Lilydog and three other guys. They all wore scruffy jeans and unpolished shoes. The other car was a Triumph.

I had not been to the sea for a long time. Sage green and patches of deep blue rippled gently, a light breeze stroked my face and the faint smell of the sea held memories of a long time ago; times when I had sat on the sandy beach in Tel Aviv listening to the angry waves loudly attacking the sea shore, and dreamt of escaping.

I walked to the edge of the water, pebbles shifting under my feet, my light, summer dress bellowing behind me in the light breeze. Lilydog shot into the sea and swam happily, I didn't know she could. I took my shoes off and stood where the waves, depleted of their vigour, licked my feet. But here, even in summer, the water was cold. Gulls looked menacing as they circled above, screeching and swooping down suddenly. There had been no gulls on the beach of Tel-Aviv. It had been a few years now since I stood on its golden sand. It had been a long and arduous journey. But now, I was working, I was earning, I was independent and I had my precious liberty. My life had changed for the better. Yet, standing by the water, I felt a little melancholy.

Tom called me to come back. At the pub, he raised his pint and challenged the drivers to a race back to London. It was madness. They drove fast and at the many roundabouts along the way the cars forked, one to the left, the other to the right. We were in high spirits and laughed all the way. Just before we got to London, we heard the siren. We stopped. Two policemen approached. I could tell that they were stifling their laughs. They said that they had followed us all the way from Brighton and gave the drivers speeding tickets.

\*

That night we went to a party in a farm somewhere in the countryside. Tom drove my car with me sitting next to him and three of his friends sat in the back with Lilydog. On the way there, we were in a party mood, laughing and joking. But after what had happened during the drive, I was angry with Tom.

We had been stopped by the police. They checked Tom and my driving licenses and ordered all of us to get out of the car. They searched it. Then they asked us to empty our pockets and looked in my handbag. They found nothing and let us go. The three at the back of the car burst out laughing.

'Where did you put it?'

'What did you do with it?' asked another.

When they managed to stop laughing, one guy said, 'When I got out of the car, I dropped it and kicked it under it.' He held up a large bag of cocaine which he then stuffed into the front of his trousers. He was obviously the mule; Tom knew better than to carry himself.

'Right on man,' one of them said.

'Groovy,' said another.

'Fuck me, man.'

I winced, but then some people laced their sentences with 'fuck' all the time.

The three caried on chatting and laughing. Tom was quiet as usual. No one noticed my anger.

'Tom,' I said,' when we got out of the car. 'A word please.' I was shaking with anger.

He turned to look at me surprised.

'You should have told me. You should have asked my permission. It is my car! It is in my name! Do you realise that you have put me in danger? If I got caught with drugs in my car, I would have been deported, and would have had a criminal record.'

He stood in silence waiting for me to finish. His face fell. He looked as if I slapped him.

'Daniela. I am so sorry. You're right. I didn't think. I

would never do anything to hurt you. Please, believe me. I am so sorry.'

I didn't answer. I stared at him. He looked sad and worried.

'I'm sorry Daniela. You have every right to be angry. I promise you, it will never happen again.'

He looked like a child who was being told off. I did not make friends easily and there was a man who wanted to be my friend. I saw that I mattered to him more than I had realised. He had made a mistake; he admitted it and took responsibility for it. Perhaps I had been too harsh. It was time for forgiveness. I took his hand in mine.

'Are we alright now?'

'Yes Tom,' I smiled. 'Just this once.'

A little smile of relief lit his face. 'Thank you. I've given you a promise and I shall keep it.'

'You'd better.'

He kept my hand in his as we walked to the barn, it felt cosy and safe. Lilydog trotted along.

In the barn, a hog was roasting on a spit, drinks and drugs were in abundance, people were dancing wildly to rock music that was blaring from huge speakers. Some of them looked like they were tripping.

I had a drink, smoked joints, and maybe be it was hypocritical of me, but I had a snort of Tom's high-quality cocaine. Deep Purple's *Smoke on the Water* rocked the place. I grabbed Tom and we danced. He didn't like dancing and soon left me to it. Blind Faith *Can't Find my Way Home* was followed by Led Zeppelin *Whole Lotta Love,* and I danced, losing myself in the music.

We ate hog roast and potatoes from the fire. I gave some to Lilydog, who then disappeared somewhere. The chocolate cakes were cut into very small portions. I thought that it was because there weren't enough cakes to go round. The effect did not hit me till a while later. I asked Tom what was in the cakes and he told me it was cannabis oil. I noticed that people were giggling, sitting or lying on the floor rolling in fits of laughter over nothing. Some were dancing, others curled in corners dozing off.

The party dwindled. Outside they were fetching kindling, logs and branches and making a bonfire. We sat around it. Lilydog reappeared and lay beside me. The music from the speakers was turned off and the guitars came out of their cases. I listened to the strumming and to people singing. It was lovely. The smell of woodsmoke reminded me of outings with the scouts, of sitting around the campfire singing Kumbaya.

I wished Sebastian was with me. We would have sat back-to-back, watched the fire, listened to the music and felt close to each other. I had not heard from him.

I looked at the dancing flames. I regretted my reaction to Sebastian's offer. When he had said it, an image flushed across my mind of opening Benyamin's front door with my own key. The association made me react the way I did. Looking at the fire blazing I thought that Sebastian probably did not have an ulterior motive in offering me his keys. I had upset him. I was reacting like a turtle, at the slightest sign of danger, retreating into its shell.

\*

It was near dawn when we arrived back at the squat. Tom came in with me, we were going to have a coffee before he went home. All the lights were on. Jimmy and Marie called me from the living room. We went in.

'We've been burgled,' Jimmy said.

I hadn't noticed before, but now I could see that the stereo was missing.

'They've been to your room too,' Marie said.

Tom and I went to my room. Lilydog started sniffing around. The drawers from the chest were on the floor, their contents scattered, and the wardrobe doors were open.

'Bloody hell,' Tom said.

I looked under the bed. My vanity case was still there where I had hid in. I went to the wardrobe.

'They took my fur coat.'

'I'm so sorry Daniela. What a mess. I don't think that you should stay here tonight. Come to mine.'

The room felt sullied. I took my vanity case and we left. There had been strangers in my room, in my private space. They had touched my things. They had taken my fur coat. I would be cold in the coming winter I thought sadly.

# Chapter 28

On the Monday, to my relief, Sebastian phoned me at Poppy's. I hardly let him say a word, I blurted out what I had rehearsed.

'I'm sorry Sebastian. I reacted badly, unjustifiably so. I am really sorry.'

'All right, all right, but what brought it on? What was it about? Had I said something to offend you?'

'No.' I couldn't explain.

'I thought you might enjoy some peace and quiet away from the squat. That was all,' he chuckled. 'You didn't think that I was inviting you to move in, did you?'

'Of course not,' I forced a laughed.

And to my relief, that was that. He told me that his father was better and therefor he was coming back.

When he arrived at the squat and walked into my room, he was holding a bunch of flowers. I felt happy to see him. I had missed him more than I realised. We held each other tight.

'Did you miss me? A little?' he whispered into my hair.

'Yes.' I didn't dare ask him.

'I missed you too.'

'A little?' I asked.

He lifted my chin, 'More than a little, Daniela.'

We held each other's gaze for a long moment. His eyes were expressive, telling me something, or maybe asking. The word love hovered in the air unspoken.

'Soon it'll be the seven hundred and fiftieth anniversary of the estate. There's going to be a big celebration. Would you like to come? I'd like you to.'

'Yes please. I'd love to.'

I felt happy. He was back. I reached and stroked his face. He smiled.

*

At the mews house, Sebastian went upstairs to unpack his suitcase. I stayed in the living room. I put Blind Faith on the record player, took two cushions from the sofa and lay on the rug. He came and lay beside me. He closed his eyes. He looked peaceful. I wanted him, all of him. It was the first time in my life that I instigated sex. I rolled over him. He opened his eyes surprised, then smiled wickedly. I kissed his lips, his eyes, the crook of his neck. I could feel his manhood waking. He moaned gently. I smiled.

'You are full of surprises Daniela,' he grinned.

We made love. *Can't find my way home* flowed from the speakers. Our movements synced with the music. Sebastian had a sense of rhythm but he wouldn't dance with me at the discotheques, he would watch me and smile appreciatively when I happened to look at him.

We rolled over, he was now on top of me, his eyes shut tight, his face contorted. His movements became forceful. He must have felt my gaze, he opened his eyes and looked directly into mine. He put his hands on my shoulders and pressed me down. His movements intensified, became a little rough. He closed his eyes again. I closed mine too. Afterwards, when we lay exhausted side by side, he reached for my hand.

*

It was the height of summer when we drove to the estate. As it transpired, it was the last time that I would stay there with Sebastian. We arrived the day before the celebrations. There was a hive of activities, little panics and last-minute changes of plans. We helped with the preparations. The Mother oversaw the operation in a military fashion. The father took a step back. It seemed to be what he always did.

*

I woke up in the morning to a warm sunny day, there was not a cloud in the sky. I put on a, flowing white cotton dress and a long, thin, sleeveless, blue velvet coat with a hood, it had a medieval look, suitable for the occasion. In the grounds were stalls selling food and bric-a-brac. A folk band played, Morris dancers danced, jugglers juggled and people on stilts towered over us. Sebastian and I were in charge of the house stall. It was very popular. People hoped that they would find a bargain amongst the stuff that had come out of the attics. Lilydog, tied to the back of my chair, behaved beautifully. She would stand up and greet everyone that came.

Later, Sebastian's sister came to relieve us. We strolled through the fayre with Lilydog on a leash. We stopped to watch the archery for a little while and then crossed the main avenue and into a field below the Ha-ha where a few men were shooting clay pigeons.

I watched Sebastian's father. He was a good shot, didn't

miss, not even once. Others took their turn. I had a strong urge to have a go. Eventually I gathered up my courage and whispered it to Sebastian. He repeated it out loud. They all looked at me. For a flicker of a second their faces betrayed their thought that I wouldn't know one end of a shotgun from another. It was quickly covered with a forced, indulgent smile, more like stretching the mouth slightly.

Sebastian whispered, 'Can you shoot?'

'Yes. To target. Never clay pigeons, but I'd like to try.'

A discussion followed as to which gun would suit me.

I handed Lilydog's leash to Sebastian. 'May I choose please?'

Again, that veiled look. They watched bemused as I carefully chose a four ten shotgun. It was the right weight for me and had a smooth, beautiful wood.

'Good choice,' Sebastian said. 'It was my grandmother's.'

I took my position, loaded the gun, planted my feet firmly on the ground, raised it, looked along the barrel, aligned it, shouted 'Pull!', held my breath, aimed at the clay, fired and missed.

Again, I shouted, 'Pull!', aimed, fired and missed.

By now, they must have realized that I could use a gun.

Sebastian came and stood by me. 'Have another go,' he said and handed me two cartridges. 'Follow the clay pigeon, feel its speed, travel with it and then pull the trigger.'

I loaded the gun, planted my feet firmly on the ground, raised the gun and shouted, 'Pull!' I fired and missed.

I had one more cartridge, one more go. I raised the gun and shouted, 'Pull!' I concentrated, followed the clay, felt the speed it was traveling at, matched it fired and hit it.

Sebastian came, hugged me and gave me two more cartridges. I had it now, I understood how it worked. I hit the clay pigeons both times. I felt triumphant.

I turned to smile at Sebastian and saw a little look of appreciation hovering on his father's face.

Sebastian was standing by his mother who was holding Lilydog. I went and joined them. He beamed at me. 'Well done you.'

The Mother was watching me with curiosity. 'Where did you learn to shoot?'

'In the army.' I saw a flicker of a shock in her expression before she rearranged her face. I was pleased to catch her off guard.

'The army? You were in the army?' She looked at Sebastian as if to say, you didn't tell me. And to me, 'Were you a soldier? What did you do in the army?'

'I'm sorry, all I can tell you is that I served in the Air Force. The greyish-blue uniform suited me well.' I smiled politely but relished the intrigue.

The Father who was standing nearby said, 'Well, I... I say.'

The Mother smiled forcibly and handed me Lilydog.

'Time to go,' Sebastian said. 'Duty calls.'

*

I left Sebastian at the stall with Lilydog and went to buy food for our lunch. When I came back, he suggested that I take a break. I took my food to the cloisters. We sat in the coolness, away from the heat of the sun. Lilydog looked up at me, sniffing, eyeing my hot dog, I gave it to her, I didn't like it.

For some reason, I thought of that night in my flat at Mrs Birkin. That night when I had been desperate and lonely, prepared to take a washing up job and live in a cheap hotel. It seemed such a long time ago.

I leaned back and closed my eyes. I felt the cold stones on my back, I heard the noise of the fayre in the distance. This was Sebastian's world, kept apart from his life in London. I had relaxed, I had let my feelings grow and I had begun to trust him. I had let him in and I was no longer scared.

I thought of Benyamin. I said his name out loud. Tears did not prick my eyes and the lump did not rise. I opened my eyes and sighed. Lilydog's ears shot up, her head tilted to one side, she looked worried. 'Nothing to worry about,' I told her. She lay down and flipped over for a tummy rub. I obliged.

It was peaceful in the cloisters. I banished all thoughts and closed my eyes again. A little later, I heard Lilydog thumping the stone floor with her tail. 'We're alright now, aren't we?' I said softly. She thumped faster.

Walking towards our stall, I watched Sebastian talking to an old couple, smiling, animated. Strong emotions that I couldn't quite define, rose within me. He saw me, waved and smiled happy to see me. I went to him.

## CHAPTER 29

It was the end of summer, and after a brief fine spell the weather changed. Dark and gloomy days followed accompanied with oppressive lowering skies. The sun did not come out to light the darkness. Then good news, the female voice on the weather forecast announced: "Tomorrow it will be a lighter shade of grey".

When I woke up to the promised lighter shade of grey, I decided to take Lilydog for a long walk. I got dressed, washed my face, brushed my teeth and I was ready. But where was Lilydog? Probably in the living room being fussed over by her admirers. I heard a car come to a screeching halt, then a scream followed by complete silence. A sense of foreboding instantly came over me. I ran. I heard shouting. I ran faster. I burst through the open front door. I stopped to look. A few people were standing near the front of a blue car that had halted slap bang in the middle of the road a little further up. They were looking down at something I couldn't see.

I ran towards them. I saw a blond young woman. She was standing by the car's open door, holding her head in her hand and saying repeatedly: 'He ran in front of me. I couldn't stop. I couldn't stop.'

I kept on running. Those seconds felt like an eternity.

I was closer. I could see a cream-coloured tail. I pushed through two people and immediately collapsed on the floor. Lilydog was lying motionless on her side. She didn't lift her head to greet me. I touched her. She was warm.

'Get an ambulance,' I shouted repeatedly. I stroked Lilydog's head. 'An ambulance. Someone. Please.'

Marie came and crouched next to me. 'Daniela. She is dead. I'm so sorry.'

I picked Lilydog up. People moved out of my way.

Marie followed me. she said, 'Someone left the door open'.

I walked on. A guy came and stretched out his hands to take her, to help me carry her. I pulled her closer to my chest.

In my room, I sat on my bed cradling her, rocking back and forth. 'Wake up. Please wake up. You can't die,' I told her over and over, wetting her with my tears. She felt warm in my arms. Marie had said that she was dead, yet it didn't feel real. She looked asleep, any moment she would lift her head and look at me with her beautiful expressive eyes. But she didn't.

There was a sense of unreality, as if the world had stopped, and Lilydog and I were inside an opaque glass bubble. I don't know how long it was before Sebastian came. I don't know who had called him. He tried to take her from my arms. I wouldn't let him. He sat beside me, held me and silently rocked with us.

I had no sense of time. Sebastian did not say anything. He just held me in the silence of the room. I don't know how long we rocked before Sebastian prised her gently from my arms. I held my head in my hands and sobbed. He laid her on the large cushion by the window, came and squeezed me to him. I cried into his shoulder. I tried to say something but my sobs chocked me.

'Hush… shush.' He held the back of my head with his hand and said in a soft voice, 'There, there. There, there.'

He did not leave me alone for one minute. He brought me water and made me drink. He dried my eyes when I cried, he kissed me gently, he stroked my head and held me tight as if to squeeze out my pain. And all the time, Lilydog lay on the cushion. She looked asleep.

Helen came and she and Sebastian took turns holding me. I had no sense of time. In the evening they put me to bed and Helen gave me a sleeping pill.

When I woke up in the morning, my pillow was wet. For a few seconds I forgot and expected Lilydog to jump on the bed. Then I remembered. I disentangled myself from Sebastian and went to her. Maybe it was a mistake. Maybe she was breathing. I put my hand on her heart. It was silent. She felt cold to the touch. I collapsed next to her sobbing. Sebastian picked me up and walked me back to bed. He let me cry.

It was Sebastian who took her away. It was him who had her cremated. It was him who brought me her ashes.

The next few days were unbearable. When I saw her food in the kitchen, I would think, I must feed her. Then I cry. The food disappeared and so did her lead. I think it was Marie who removed them. The nights were the worst. I would wake up periodically expecting her to be sleeping at my feet. But she wasn't there.

Helen came when she could. Sebastian stayed. His eyes were full of sadness. He kept calm and did not try to allay my pain, letting me be but staying close. I was grateful for that. After a few days I insisted on going to work. I forced myself to function. I painted my face. My eyes were red. I put in eyedrops that made them white. I dressed carefully, took my vanity case and my handbag and got in the car. Lilydog's rug was on the back seat, a painful reminder. I couldn't find it in me to remove it. I sat unmoving for a while.

The palm like leaves on the London plane trees were losing their colour but still hanging on. Autumn had always felt sad to me, moody in its filtered opaque light. It echoed my mood. I was dead inside.

## CHAPTER 30

Sebastian and I went out a lot. I think he was trying to distract me. But the loss of Lilydog had lodged itself inside me. We went, to rock concerts, to the theatre, to clubs and restaurants. Then a few weeks later we went to a house party in Cambridge. It was sometime after midnight that we decided to go for a stroll by the river. We were walking on the grass when I heard the explosion. I fell to the ground. Sebastian crouched down beside me.

'What's the matter? Are you feeling ill?'

'No, I thought it was a bomb.'

'You thought it was a bomb? Here? It's fireworks.'

'I know. Just for a second…'

'The war?'

'Yes.'

'Do you want to tell me about it?'

'I will, but not tonight.'

Sebastian lay down leaning on his elbow, resting his head in the palm of his hand. We watched the firework. A beautiful multicoloured flare shot up and opened to an umbrella from which pretty teardrops fell down. There was a lull.

'Do you want to tell me about that man?'

'What man?'

'Don't be cute. You know who.'

I watched another flare spreading in the sky.

I thought for a while. 'I can do a Sebastian. We met, we loved, he left me.'

We burst out laughing.

'Will you ever?'

'Yes, but not tonight.'

*

On a dark and miserable day, Tom came to the squat to see me. I was in the kitchen with my back to him putting the kettle on. The rain was pelting down, I could hardly see through the window.

'Tea? Kettle's on.'

He didn't answer. I turned and looked at him. His face was drawn, he looked troubled and in pain.

'What's the matter?' I asked. 'Sit down. You look dreadful. Are you ill?'

He sat at the kitchen table and put down a newspaper. He didn't speak. I made tea and joined him. We sat facing each other nursing our mugs. He was very quiet. I searched his face. He held my eyes with intensity. I could see that he was trying to say something but couldn't get the words out.

'What is it?' I asked. 'What's the matter?'

He swallowed, reached across the table and took my hands in his, 'Sebastian is dead.'

The words hung in the air without meaning. Tom held my eyes and tightened his grip on my hands as if to stop me from falling. The words took shape, I felt my blood draining away from my veins, there was a roaring noise in my ears, my head exploded.

When I came to, I was in bed. Tom was sitting on the chair next to me, holding my hand. The gas fire was on but I felt cold and shivery under the blankets.

The newspaper was on my bedside table opened. I glimpsed at it. The print jumped out: "Lord and Lady…… their son Sebastian…" There was a pressure in my head as if my mind was trying to detach itself from me.

Tom squeezed my hand hard as if to steady me, to keep me conscious. 'Breathe,' he said.

I sat up. Nothing seemed real, I wasn't real. Tom looked in pain, he kept hold of my hand and every so often said, 'Daniela, Oh Daniela.' I don't know how long we sat there like that. I felt frozen, empty, lifeless, but the odd thing was, that at the same time, I was holding fast, as if waiting for the blow to come, the one that was going to destroy me.

'Do you want me to tell you what happened?'

I nodded.

'Sebastian was at the house in Marble Arch. There was building work going on. The builders had taken the handrail off of the staircase and left the spindles standing.' His voice broke. He swallowed. 'Sebastian had been binging on drugs and alcohol.' He stopped unable to continue.

My head started pounding again. I was hardly breathing. My eyes, unblinking, felt dry.

'Sebastian tripped and fell down the stairs. He hit his head on a pole.' He stopped. 'Oh. Daniela. I'm not sure that I should tell you more. It's too awful.'

'Please,' my voice was almost inaudible.

Tom's face contorted as if the words were struggling to come out. I could see that he was close to tears, but managing to hold them back. 'He bled to death at the foot of the stairs, while above him…' his voice trembled, 'in the bedroom, the crowd continued drinking and taking drugs.' Suspended tears fell slowly and silently down his cheeks.

The words took shape. I saw Sebastian in his green velvet suit, lying at the bottom of the stairs. There was blood on his white shirt.

'Oh, no!' I cry out in anguish. 'Oh no, no, no! Tom, they could have saved him. They could have… '.

Tom let me sob. He held my hands and waited.

'Daniela, listen,' he said gently with a shaky voice that could break at any moment. He squeezed my hands. 'Listen Daniela, I am sorry but I have to go. I'll be away for a few days. I'll come back as soon as I can. Please, please look after yourself. Just hang on in there.'

He kissed my forehead and was gone.

I slid down under the blanket, turned to the wall, and holding them with both my hands brought my knees to my chin.

Anne was at Cambridge. Helen was away dancing. Claire was devastated and hurting because Alan had left her for a young singer. There was no one I could call. I kept the curtains closed. I stayed in bed. I did not wash and I did not change my clothes.

# Chapter 31

The curtains are drawn. I feel as if the walls are closing in on me, pushing me further and further inside myself. Outside, a car speeds by, a dog barks and I think of Lilydog. I miss the warmth of her body next to mine, her wet tongue licking my face, how she looked up at me with her eyes searching mine, wagging her tail to tell me she was happy. I wish she was here. She would have felt my desperation and would have cuddled up to comfort me.

Marie comes in with a bowl of rice, tea and a joint. Her macrobiotic food isn't inspiring at the best of times; it looks brown and tastes brown, no spices, so bland.

'Daniela, you must eat. Try a little. You can't go on not eating. Come on, it's for your own good that I'm saying it. Come now. sit up.'

I turn my face to the wall.

She puts her offerings down by my bed and leaves.

The paint on the wall is old and faded. It is patchy with scratches that reveal former colours, making pictures. There is a man with big, kind eyes looking at me, a tree with its roots exposed, its leaves drooping, lying on its side, dying.

Outside my room the noise is escalating; people are coming and going, doorbell ringing, front door slamming.

Someone is playing the flute well. I listen. The music flows smoothly, soulfully. A guitar joins in, strumming loudly, spoiling it. There is clattering noise from the kitchen as endless cups of tea are made.

I don't know much about the people who come and go here. It is as if they have no past. They are drifters and dreamers, dropouts and lost souls on their way to nowhere.

The music stops. I hear a lot of noises coming from the living room; voices, banging, furniture moving, crockery clinking.

There is a knock on my door. I don't answer.

Marie shouts. 'We are going out. Back late.'

Silence falls.

*

I drink the tea and smoke the joint. It takes effect immediately. I lie back. I will myself away. The dark room disappears. I'm lying on soft golden sand, listening to the susurrus of waves breaking on the shore. Stars twinkle in the dark skies and the crescent moon, lying on its side is smiling. I hear the distant constant hum of the city. I feel insignificant and small in this vastness, yet a part of the universe, of nature, not more important than a grain of sand.

Into this peaceful scene my shadows walk uninvited. My grandparents, their faces unkind, unloving. Father stands next to them, angry, disapproving. Benyamin comes and look at me with a face I cannot read. He holds up a camera, the Rolleiflex. He takes a photograph of me. I know it is a souvenir.

Mother comes and sits next to me. She strokes my hair. She quietly sings a lullaby; the one about the moon looking down on a hyacinth growing in a garden, the moon asks the clouds to give it some water so that the hyacinth will thrive.

The doorbell rings. I ignore it. I close my eyes and try to return to the sandy beach.

The doorbell is ringing again. Whoever it maybe has put a finger on the doorbell and is not removing it. I have to make it stop. I go to open the door.

What meets my eyes makes me freeze; two strange looking men with a dog not on a leash are staring at me. They push by me. I close the door and follow them to the living room. The dog is a Doberman. He is looking at me as if to say, do not mess with me.

'We are looking for Jimmy,' one of them says.

I shake my head for 'No'. I expect them to leave.

'We'll wait.'

'Sit,' one says pointing to a carpet cushion. I do. I sit in the lotus position bolt upright. The men take the two armchairs opposite me. The dog positions itself, sitting up and alert next to one of the men. He stares at me. The room is a mess; dirty mugs, ashtrays filled with cigarette butts and roaches. There is a strong smell of incense and stale tobacco. I shift my position. In a flash the dog is on its feet ready for his master's command.

The master says, 'He'll be good as long as you don't make a sudden move or come near me.' He looks at the dog. The dog resumes his alert and statuesque position.

I watch this tableau with trepidation. Two strange, very thin men with pasty faces the colour of dough, with long unkempt hair sitting in shabby old armchairs, and a beautiful intense, threatening dog.

I do not look directly at the dog; I watch him from the corner of my eye. My nose starts itching, demanding a scratch. I try to ignore it. It does not stop. Keeping the dog in my peripheral vision, I start moving my arm along my body at a snail's pace, across my chest, up my neck to my nose. Relief. Carefully and slowly, I lower my arm.

We wait in silence. Time passes. Finally, the front door opens. The dog jumps to its feet and look at his master. Jimmy walks in.

I am so fearful that I cannot concentrate on what they are saying. I hear disconnected words; money, cocaine, talcum powder. I gather that they are drug dealers. Jimmy deals a little when the opportunity arises, but with people like that?

They stand up. They leave. The dog follows.

I hear the front door close. Surprisingly, I am not shaken any more, I am livid. I scream at Jimmy.

'Are you out of your mind? These men are dangerous. They barged in. They ordered me about. They petrified me. You do not cross the line with the likes of them. What did you do? Let me guess, you bought from Tom, cut it, and sold it to them?'

It is the first time that I have spoken in days. I am angry.

Jimmy starts mumbling. I ignore him. I go to my room and slam the door shut.

Sometime later, Jimmy comes in. He says he is sorry. I let it go. I ask him about the colour of their faces. He says that they are heroin addicts and that heroin changes their complexion.

'There is a letter for you in the hall,' he says before he leaves.

I go and pick up the large envelope. It's from Claire.

I put a record on the turntable. Jefferson Airplane. I put the needle on the song '*White Rabbit.*'

*One pill makes you larger, and one pill makes you small*
*And the ones that mother gives you, don't do anything at all*

*Go ask Alice, when she's ten feet tall*

I sort of float to it. my body is light, insubstantial.

*And if you go chasing rabbits, and you know you're going to fall*

*Tell 'em a hookah-smoking caterpillar has given you the call*

I sit down by the low table and hold my head in my hands. I made mistakes, I followed the wrong roads, took misleading paths, chased clouds. There was no map to guide me. I aimed too high, I had unrealistic expectations, or maybe I was just another dreamer and a drifter. Life rolls on, but I, am at a dead end.

I pick up a chillum. It is already loaded and ready to blow my head off. I put it in my mouth, light it with a match and fill my lungs with smoke, courting oblivion. It burns my throat. I have a coughing fit.

*One pill makes you happy, one pill makes you sad,*

*and some pills, if you want to, will take you to the promised end.*

I could end it all. I eye the razor blade on the mirror, sharp and shining. I avert my eyes. I open a box full of dope. There is a choice; Moroccan, black Afghan, gold Lebanese, marijuana. I choose a Thai stick. It is hallucinogenic. I start to roll a joint. I am not good at it. Looking for a card to make a filter, I see one of Anne's Z cards. The icy blond looks at me. I feel guilty. I haven't been in touch with her for a while now. I tear a strip of card for the roach. The joint is wonky but smokable.

I lie back in the armchair and inhale. The dream like effect of the Thai stick takes me over. I close my eyes. My head feels light. I swim with fluffy white clouds. A woman in a voluminous dress comes towards me, a fish with open mouth swims alongside and slowly turns into a mermaid.

The woman is now a man in a white coat. He looks like the doctor in Harley Street that I once went to see with Helen. He could get you pills, no questions asked.

I tell him that I am losing my identity. He smiles, hands me a box of pills and says:

'The world won't matter.

You will feel much better.

You won't be sad nor gay.

All your worries will go away.

And when you feel a little lost

Come and see me and I will increase the dose.'

The doctor grows wings as he floats away.

I am jolted back by the irritating noise of the record going round and round in its groove, scratching on and on. I get up. I wobble and steady myself holding on to the back of the armchair. I wait for the twinkling little pinhead stars to disappear before I go and lift the needle off of the record.

I collapse back into the chair. The mirror is in front of me. I dare not look at myself; I dread to see what it will reflect. The razor blade is inviting. Two slashes, both wrists, and it will all be over. But I know I can't do it. The pain scares me. And then there is all that red blood spewing everywhere. I don't want to arrive at the "*Promised end*" bleeding.

I open a box filled with pills; uppers and downers, speed, and acid, mescaline and magic mushrooms. I take a small bite of a mushroom. It smells mouldy and tastes earthy. I fetch a bowl from the kitchen and fill it up with downers.

I need Music. What should I play to see me out? There is no classical music. I wish I had Purcell's Dido and Aeneas. I would have played '*When I am laid in earth*'. In my head I can hear the singer's rich voice lamenting, *remember me*, it wrenches my soul. The Doors then. I put the record on.

I carry the box to the kitchen and make a cup of tea.

*This is the end, beautiful friend the end.*

'Why?' I scream in silence.

*I'll never look into your eyes again.*

'Why?' I ask loudly. 'Why?' I scream. I clutch my stomach and fold over. I go on screaming until I am hoarse.

I find a tray and put the tea, a glass of water and the pills on it. I collect Claire's envelope on my way to my bedroom.

My room feels cold. The calor gas heater barely heats the large room. I wrap a woollen blanket around me and sit on the bed. I open Claire's envelope. Inside there is a letter from Switzerland. I recognise Mina's handwriting. It is the other letter that fills me with dread. It is from Benyamin. I stare at it. With shaking hands, I take it out of the envelope. I can't read it. I can't see through the veil of tears. I drop it. I wipe my eyes. I succumb to the pain and let the tears roll down my cheeks on to my chin and drop to my lap in a constant stream.

I read the letter. He writes that he has returned to Tel-Aviv. I read the sentence again. A strange laugh rises in me, one of disbelief, sardonic. I let the letter slip from my fingers and collapse on the bed. I sob. Who am I crying for? Benyamin? Sebastian? myself? I don't understand anything anymore.

I sit up and swallow pills, I drink my tea, I wait. Nothing happens. I swallow some more. Still no effect. I start to get up. The room begins to spin. I fall back on the bed and close my eyes.

No one will miss me. If only I could just gently fade away. Sometime later, consciousness seeps back in, I am still here, with myself.

*

Lilydog's urn is on the table. I try to stand up, but I fall. I crawl and take it. I hug it to my chest. It clinks on the cameo Sebastian gave me. 'Take me with you,' I whisper to them. 'Don't leave me.' I crawl back with it and put it in my bed. I hoist myself up. I take the empty box and the glass of water. I have not swallowed enough pills.

I slowly make my way to the living room leaning on the wall to support me. The needle is screeching on the record. I take it off. I refill the box with more pills and sit in the armchair. I start swallowing them. I remember the story of The Little Match Girl, who homeless and alone sits in a doorway. Snow is falling. She lights her matches one by one, till there are no more. The little girl freezes to death. She had no choice. But I do. I take more pills. I wait.

It starts to rain. I watch the drops rolling down the dirty glass, merging as they make their way downwards.

Where is the girl that crossed the sea, crossed a border on foot and stood atop of a snowy mountain, walked the catwalk, danced on stages, where has she gone? she who saw the sunrise in Portugal and then in a mirror watched her face turn to a skeleton. At least I shall never look like that. At least I will stay beautiful in people's memory for ever.

I feel a stabbing pain. The child! I killed it. Had I told Robert that I was pregnant, we could have brought it up together. The thought of forcing his hand, of living a life I didn't want, makes me cringe.

I swallow more pills.

The rain is now coming down in torrents, lashing loudly on the window pane, running down in sheets.

A flash of memory. Water gurgling down a stream, a carpet of snow drops. Sebastian is standing next to me. He tells me that he loves the place, that it is in his blood. I tell him that he is lucky. He answers, 'Not by choice, by birth.' His roots were deep, anchored in the land. Mine are shallow. I miss him so very much. It's unbearable.

My head starts spinning. It feels heavy. I get up. I feel unsteady. I take the box of pills and the water and slowly stumble along the corridor. I lean against the wall to steady myself. I reach my bed and sit down.

Lilydog's urn is on the bed, I see her lying on the road, lifeless. I can hardly breathe. I hold my head in my hands. There is turmoil behind my closed eyes. I see Sebastian lying at the foot of the stairs in the house in Marble Arch. He is wearing his green velvet suit; his white shirt is covered in blood. I convulse. I hug myself trying to stem the pain. If I had been with him, I might have been able to save him. I was not there.

I take a handful of pills and with shaking hands swallow them.

An image comes to mind, so very clear, Rodin's sculpture, The Gates of Hell. As I exit life, there should be a ritual. I raise my glass and say out loud, *"Abandon all hope, ye who enter here."*

I swallow the rest of the pills and lie down. I feel like I am sinking into jelly, murky, dark, and thick.

I am chasing Sebastian. He is ahead of me running backwards, shouting something to me. I can't hear what he is saying. The howling wind drowns his voice. I run faster but get no closer. I can see the chasm behind him. He doesn't know it is there. He is going to fall. I open my mouth to scream, to warn him. No sound comes out. He is so near the edge. 'Sebastian. Sebastian,' I cry. He can't hear me.

\*

Someone is shaking me. I hear my name coming from far away.

'Sebastian?' I am shaking, sweating.

'Open your eyes.'

I lift my heavy eyelids slightly. The light is too bright, I turn my face to the wall.

# CHAPTER 32

I wake up in an unfamiliar bedroom. Hazy light is filtering through the curtains. My body aches, my head is fuzzy, my mind is blank. I close my eyes again to shut life away. I remember that last night Tom came, he made me throw up, drove me to this house in Virginia Waters, made me take a bath and put me to bed.

Tom comes in with a cup of tea. 'Sit up,' he tells me. I do. He opens the curtains and the room is filled with light. I flinch.

'Drink. Get dressed. We are going for a walk.' He leaves the room.

I do as he says. I drink, I get up, I wash and brush my teeth. I feel like a mechanical doll, there is no life in me. The clothes I had been wearing for days are lying in a heap on the floor. I pull out something to wear from my holdall that he had indiscriminately stuffed. I don't care that my bra does not match my panties, I don't care what I look like, I don't care about anything.

*

It's a fine, bracing autumn morning. The world glows in golds, reds, yellows and russets. We crunch the leaves under our feet.

'You have to leave,' he says gently. 'Get away from here.'

'Where will I go?' I say into the crispy cold day that makes my breath visible.

It is very quiet by the lake. It feels eerie. A sudden breeze whispers through the trees, the leaves answer with a gentle rustle as they flutter down in a shower of russet, yellow and red. In the meagre cold rays of the sun that slant through the trees, they are translucent, looking like fragments of stained glass. They come to rest on the ground in colourful pools. An earthy smell reaches my nostrils, it is not unpleasant.

There is a loud racket above us. We look up. There is a flock of geese in vee formation. They are coming from Canada, where Chris from St Moritz lives and grows cucumbers.

After a while I say, 'It is beautiful here. A little unreal.'

'Yes.' He puts his hand protectively on my shoulder.

'Is this yours?'

He chuckles, 'I rent it. In my profession, one needs to move frequently.'

We walk in silence for a while.

'I never told him that I loved him.'

'I think Sebastian knew. He loved you deeply. You do know that?'

I watch the ducks in the pond. I think of the time we swayed to the Moody Blues standing by the window in his mews house.

*Just what you want to be, you will be in the end
and I love you, Yes, I love you oh how I love you.*

\*

Early next morning, still in bed and half asleep, I hear the sound of tyres on the gravelled front. Curious I get up and look through the window. There is a blue van on the drive. Two young men jump out and go into the house. Shortly after they come out and start unloading the van. They carry many long, identical parcels in. I go back to bed. When I hear the van drive off, I go downstairs, make myself a cup of tea and walk towards the living room. Tom is playing 'Forever Autumn.' It flings me back into Sebastian's arms.

*Like the sun through the trees you came to love me*
*Like a leaf on a breeze you blew away.*

I stand by the door motionless. I close my eyes, I can feel him near me, so close that I recall his smell.

*Those fallen leaves lay undisturbed now*
*Cause you're not here*

I swallow hard and go in.

The fire is lit. The parcels are stacked neatly on the large Persian rug. Tom had already unwrapped one. Inside there is a bolt of indigo coloured silk fabric, rather beautiful.

He hasn't heard me come in.

'Good morning.'

He lifts his head and smiles.

'I thought you dealt drugs.'

'I do.'

I walk in and settle in an armchair by the fire.

'Once you finished your tea, you could help me.'

He starts unwinding the silk. There are meters and meters of it. I watch him intrigued. 'What are you doing?'

'You'll see.'

I finish my tea and go to help him. All the silk is removed, revealing a long piece of wood about a foot wide, smooth and polished.

'You can take a break now. The next bit will take a while. Make us a cuppa please. I could do with one.'

Back in the living room I find Tom carefully attacking the piece of wood with tools. I watch. To my utter amazement, he prizes off the top of it to reveal a shallow box. I begin to comprehend. The box is full of Thai sticks.

'Clever,' I say.

'Isn't it?'

He joins me by the fire and we drink our teas.

'You can always stay with me. There is room in the cottage.' He looks at me. 'I do mean it.'

'I know Tom. Thank you.'

'Now,' he says getting up. 'We'll unwrap the next one and wrap the silk onto the first box.'

We are at it for hours. All the while, my mind must have been very busy churning independently.

'Tom. I've made up my mind,' I say more to myself really. I need to give a voice to my thought, to reaffirm it.

He stops and looks at me.

'You're right. I have to get away. My free ticket takes me around the world in one direction. I shall be going to New York.'

'A bit drastic. I didn't mean for you to go far. A trip to see your friend in Switzerland perhaps.'

'How does the saying go? Here is my version. Dramatic situations call for drastic measures.'

We smile.

*

During supper, holding up his wine glass, he asks, 'What are you running away from, Daniela?' He takes a sip.

I don't give an answer because at that moment I don't have one to give. But then it comes out of nowhere. 'From myself,' I say with a wry smile.

'What are you afraid of? Life? What is it in your past that haunts you?'

'I don't know what you're talking about.'

'Yes, you do. There is sadness in your eyes, a deep-set sadness.'

I am silent for a while, and then I say a truth that had just struck me. 'Sadness is my home. It is where I feel most comfortable.'

His face, looking at me is full of concern. 'What happened to you to make you feel sad? You had that look even before Sebastian.'

'Bonjour tristesse.'

'What?'

'I just don't know how to be happy.'

He continues, disregarding my comments. 'There are things that you have never told me, but I guessed. I am no fool Daniela. Clearly you don't trust men, even the one you loved. I am a good judge of character; I have to be in my profession. I'm careful whom I choose to deal with, I need to trust them, I need to know them well in order to know how they'll behave under certain circumstances. It's not an easy affair smuggling drugs. It takes preparation, planning, and the weighing of risk. It takes judgement to do what I do.'

He pauses. We drink our wine.

'Talk to me Daniela. You carry this heavy burden with you. It affects your life. It took you a long time to trust me, even longer to trust Sebastian. So tell me.'

On hearing his name, my innards feel as if a vice is crunching them. My face contorts in pain.

'Breathe Daniela. Breathe.'

I do, and he waits for my face to relax, for the pain to lessen.

'For a man of few words, you talk a lot.' I force a smile.

'I do when I have something to say. You are seeking a meaning to life Daniela. There isn't one. Just live your life.'

'There is the problem: I cannot find my life. I thought I did.'

*

Tom drives me to the airport. Outside we hug. When we pull apart, I see that his eyes are moist. I watch him walk away.

There is plenty of time before checking in. I sit on my red suitcase wearing my old coat, the one Herr Schafferman called 'schmatte'. I watch the hustle and bustle and listen to the cacophony that fills the hall. A couple near me hugs and kisses. She walks away. He stands watching her go.

I phoned Claire, Anne and Poppy to say goodbye. 'Don't go,' they told me. 'We'll miss you.' Tom will let Helen know when she comes back to England.

In this vast hall, full of people parting, my sense of loneliness is acute. My hand rises to touch Sebastian's cameo.

I imagine myself in New York. I am standing alone with my red suitcase surrounded by sky scrapers. I look back and I see my friends standing in line, Tom, Helen, Claire, Ann and Poppy. They look sad. I feel sad too. I remember the Chinese proverb of the pearls. How did it go? "Pearls don't lie on the seashore. If you want one, you must dive for it." They are my pearls. The thought makes me smile. The next thought comes with sharp clarity. I am running away, drifting towards nowhere again.

Outside, it is grey, it drizzles, just like the day I arrived on the ship from France.

I open my bag and take out my purse. I look inside. I might have enough for a taxi.

Printed in Great Britain
by Amazon